Picture-
PERFECT
Boyfriend

Also by Becky Dean

Love & Other Great Expectations

Picture-PERFECT Boyfriend

Becky Dean

DELACORTE PRESS

GetUnderlined.com

Educators and librarians, for a variety of teaching tools, visit us at RHTeachersLibrarians.com

Library of Congress Cataloging-in-Publication Data is available upon request.
ISBN 978-0-593-56991-7 (trade pbk.) — ISBN 978-0-593-56993-1 (ebook)

The text of this book is set in 11.5-point Adobe Garamond Pro.
Interior design by Cathy Bobak

Printed in the United States of America
10 9 8 7 6 5 4 3 2 1
First Edition

To G and G

CHAPTER ONE

Hawaii was totally messing up my plans. To be fair, I rarely made plans, and when I did, they generally went badly. But this one was facing an extra challenge. Why did Maui have to be so insanely beautiful before we'd even reached the ground?

As the island grew larger beneath us, I inched the airplane's window shade up to reveal more details. Vivid turquoise-and-blue water. Brilliant green hills. Bright white line of waves.

My imagination filled with images of sights that awaited, begging me to photograph them. Towering waterfalls wreathed in rainbow mist. Ocean sunsets of tangerine and pink. Turtles and whales and tropical flowers and—

No. That was the old Kenzie. The version of myself I'd left behind eight months ago. The impractical dreamer with impossible wishes.

The new Kenzie had to pretend not to take too much notice. She could enjoy the scenery, objectively. But she didn't obsess about the best camera angle to highlight a waterfall's height, about the time of day to shoot the ocean to show the brightest shade of blue, or about the proper shutter speed to capture a leaping whale. She didn't spend the day getting sunburned while waiting for just the right shot of a turtle coming ashore, or developing prune fingers from hours of snorkeling with her GoPro, filming colorful fish.

And she definitely didn't think about the Nikon DSLR camera tucked into the back of her closet at home in its nice leather bag, alongside the tripod, assortment of lenses, and portfolio full of landscapes and animal photos.

New Kenzie cared about college applications and chemistry club and Future Healthcare Professionals of America meetings, and this week would be full of air-conditioned dinners and sitting quietly under umbrellas on the beach, and possibly days on the golf course, where the waves were a distant backdrop without sound or sea spray.

New Kenzie was utterly boring.

But also safe, family-approved, and free of criticism.

So this was my path, and I would continue on it, even though that had been growing harder lately, taking a steep climb up a rocky hill. Pushing the limits of how long I could try to be someone else. I would not let Hawaii be the thing that sent me tumbling back down.

Our descent grew choppy, wind buffeting the plane from side to side.

Beside me, Mom clutched her book to her chest. Not a romance novel or thriller or other vacation-appropriate fiction, like normal people read. Instead it was a too-long optometry text for her latest continuing education course. Based on how tightly she was squeezing it, she would have been better off holding a barf bag. Although if the book were covered in vomit, that might be an improvement.

A distraction seemed in order.

"How's the book?" I asked. "Can I borrow it when you're done?"

Her eyes got slightly less glassy. "I'm learning about a new method of detecting glaucoma. The idea is fascinating, but the writing style leaves something to be desired. I don't think this editor should be reviewing professional publications."

"Ah. Um. Well, great topic, though."

So not-great. But over the last eight months, I had to admit, my feigned interest in the family career sure had made her a lot less frowny when she looked at me. Plus, the question had achieved the desired goal of distracting her from imminent puking. Finding things to criticize about others often had that effect on her—and for once, the disapproval wasn't directed at me.

"Jacob mentioned he read an article about that," I added.

The glow in her eyes intensified. The only thing she loved more than my made-up, newfound love for optometry was my made-up, future healthcare professional boyfriend. It was good to know my imagination was able to please her, even if I rarely was.

We jostled against each other as the plane dipped lower.

"Close the shade, please. Or put on your sunglasses. The UV rays are terrible for your eyes."

I sighed and shut out the beautiful view. Maybe it was for the best, to keep me from dwelling on out-of-reach dreams.

"I hope your sister and Neal had a smoother ride."

Yes, Alana, my twenty-two-year-old sister, was dating a guy

named Neal. It was like she'd set out to find the most boring guy possible and had ended up with the only college-age guy with that name, just to prove she continued to be the perfect daughter. The one destined to achieve the ideal balance of collegiate-career success and a stable, predictable relationship that my family valued.

"I'm sure they're fine," I said. "If their plane had crashed an hour ago, the runway wouldn't be clear for ours to land."

"Mackenzie! Don't joke about that."

Ah, the We Are Not Amused voice. Hadn't heard that one recently, mainly because I'd been keeping my jokes to myself. I definitely hadn't missed the way it made me feel silly and childish, even though I thought I was funny. Old Kenzie was sneaking through again, as if the wave-swept shores below were pulling her out of the depths.

"I'm sure they're fine," I said quickly. "The odds of a commercial airline crash are, like, one in one point two million." I'd memorized that fact prior to boarding to impress someone—and to calm my always-worried mother. It was extremely gratifying to be able to use it to get myself out of trouble. "They're probably already at the resort with Gran."

Mom's grip on the book loosened. Until the plane shook, and she hugged it to her again. She inhaled slowly before glancing sideways at me. "It was too bad Jacob couldn't join us."

Yeah, well, it was hard for imaginary people to go on real vacations.

My nonexistent boyfriend, Jacob, was attending a nonexistent weeklong biology academy over spring break, fulfilling the lie that

I, too, had found a nice, dull future optometrist to date. We supposedly video chatted about chemistry and college coursework and medical breakthroughs, which would have made me run away screaming if it had been true, since those were also frequent topics at family dinners.

But it made my parents say things like *I'm proud of you* and *We're so glad you've found someone serious like your sister has.* Which were a huge improvement over what I used to hear. *When are you going to grow out of this phase?* Or *Why don't you respect the family legacy like your sister?* And my personal favorite, *Nature photography is a cute hobby but is far too risky and pointless for a real career.*

"He was sorry he couldn't come and wanted to make sure I thanked you for inviting him," I said. "But the program was important to help him get an internship this summer."

"Of course. Career comes first."

I sincerely hoped that was a *my family* thing and not an *all adults* thing, because the idea of career coming first for the rest of my life was almost enough to make me want to stay in high school forever.

My parents found work so important that I still couldn't believe we were here. But the family optometry practice started by my grandfather was doing well, and my dad's blood pressure had been high enough at his last doctor's visit that he and my mom had decided to take a week off.

Hooray, hypertension.

"We look forward to meeting him one day," Mom went on. "And if that internship doesn't work out, we'd love to have him at our office for the summer."

5

"Right. I've told him that. But he likes to stay close to home. His family is important to him, too."

"As it should be."

Family was the only thing that came close to rivaling work, although for the Reeds, the two were intertwined, like the roots of a tree. Or like an invasive species of vine strangling the tree and slowly sucking the life out of it until the tree withered, died, and toppled to the ground.

No, I wasn't proud that I'd made up a fake boyfriend to impress my family. Yes, it was rather pathetic—but since I *had* been out with real guys before, it at least comforted me to know I wasn't totally incapable of finding an actual human date.

And of course, lying was wrong.

But part of remaking myself had been proving I was serious and capable of *an adult relationship with future potential.* Something my parents had lamented was decidedly not true about those actual human boys. A fictional boyfriend who liked puzzles and science documentaries and was considering a career in optometry like my parents was just the thing.

Naturally, he went to college across the country, so my family wouldn't have a chance to meet him. Ohio State, to be specific, since it was one of the largest schools in the country and my parents had never mentioned knowing anyone from Ohio. The key to lying was making the lie hard to disprove. Like his name— Jacob Miller, handpicked from the most popular baby names list and the database of most common surnames in the US.

Really, my parents would have been impressed at the research that had gone into this lie. Especially coming from me, the child who was *impulsive, disorganized,* and *terrible at planning.* Direct quotes.

The plane bumped its way to a landing. My mom gripped the seat to keep herself from falling forward as we decelerated.

"Well," I heard my dad say from across the aisle, "if it gets worse this week, go ahead and give me a call, and we'll get that figured out."

He handed a business card to the guy in front of him.

It was possible Dad wasn't fully grasping the idea of *vacation.*

He and my brother, Tyler, stood and grabbed our bags from the overhead bins. Dad's perfectly ironed, green-and-orange Hawaiian shirt burned my eyeballs. Was he trying to blind everyone around him in some twisted effort to force them to need his services? It made me extremely glad that I'd locked my Instagram account months ago and no one else in my family used social media, so there was no chance of anyone seeing me in a family photo with such an abomination to the world of fashion.

Mom stood, and I moved to follow.

"Were you planning to leave your headphones?" she asked.

Oh. Right. I grabbed my earbud case from the seat-back pocket. And really, couldn't she have reminded me nicely?

I'd been doing so well lately. I'd only lost one school binder so far this semester, which my parents had never learned about, and forgotten lunch money twice, which, who needed to eat three times a day, anyway?

"Good news, Kenz," Tyler said as he let me into the aisle. "We've landed. You can text Strawberry Jam again."

If Jacob had been real, the nickname might have bothered

me. But that was on me for deciding that my fake boy's middle name was Andrew, giving him the initials JAM.

I ignored the teasing, as always. "He's in class. I don't want to disturb him."

"Are you sure about that?" Tyler asked, raising an eyebrow.

I actually wasn't, since I hadn't seen a clock recently and hadn't calculated the time difference. Why hadn't I thought of that?

We followed the other passengers off the plane. The airport had a casual feel, with skylights letting in bright Hawaiian sun. People in flowered shirts as hideous as Dad's exited planes, while many with lobster-worthy sunburns prepared to board them.

I was definitely not noticing the vivid fuchsia orchids forming beautiful leis, or imagining the flowers in full bloom on actual plants. Or seeing how bright white and silver the clouds were, cleaner and fluffier than back home in Sacramento.

Instead I selected a topic guaranteed to make my parents proud—by pointing to a display in the nearest airport shop.

"Hey, blue-light glasses," I said.

Dad whipped around. "Where? That's a travesty."

"Such a rip-off," Mom clucked. "Poor souls, being tricked into thinking those are needed, and at such high airport prices."

"Regular reading glasses, too." Dad shook his head. "Convincing people they can diagnose themselves instead of getting proper checkups."

"Truly tragic," said Tyler in a dramatic voice that would have sounded mocking if used in relation to an actual tragedy.

Still in the airport, and they'd already resorted to work talk and criticizing others. Two activities my parents would win gold for if they were Olympic sports. But my plan had succeeded—I'd gotten approving looks, distracted myself from thinking about photography, and ensured they didn't suspect I'd been thinking about it, all at once.

My mouth watered as we passed Hawaiian restaurants and food carts offering coconut French toast and SPAM and fresh pineapples. My parents were such unadventurous eaters, I'd be lucky to try the iconic shave ice this week.

"Ooh, SPAM." Tyler craned his neck to see a menu.

"I'm not sure about the safety of meat that lasts that long," Mom said.

"Doesn't tuna last forever?" I asked. "It has those fats that are good for your eyes."

"I don't know if SPAM is the same, but that is a good point."

That tone of voice was a more recent addition to her arsenal— one I called Surprised, Grudging Respect.

This was why I'd made the change. The new me invited so much less drama. If I'd been doing what I wanted, what the old Kenzie would have done—flitting from place to place, running into things because my face was glued to my camera, taking photos of everything in sight—they'd have been telling me to stop dawdling, to pay attention, to quit getting distracted and keep up. To apologize to the poor man with a walker I'd knocked over while watching a pretty cloud. Not that that had ever happened.

"The condo has Wi-Fi, right?" Tyler asked. "I need to keep up with my coding project."

Despite being a sophomore, two years younger than me, he was working on a fancy program for his computer class. He said it would update the optometry office's recordkeeping or book-keeping or something like that. Something I should have understood about running the business side of the practice but didn't, despite working there for months, because—boring.

"Yes, Tyler," Mom said. "I've told you many times. Everyone has Wi-Fi these days."

"Yeah, but they better have good signal strength. Not like the time we went to that conference in Boise and I could barely download the baseball scores."

"I'm sure it will be fine. But remember you're to limit screen time this week. We're supposed to be spending time together as a family."

Good luck getting him to comply with that. Not like Mom and Dad would enforce it, anyway. Not against the brilliant baby of the family, who got good grades without trying and won math awards and who never got criticized for not wanting to join the family practice, because computer programming was a parent-approved career path.

Baggage claim was located in an open-air space, allowing the humid, warm outdoors to seep in. My skin instantly felt sticky. Mom sighed and fanned her shirt, but it made me think of magical tropical nights under the stars and jungles teeming with life and hidden waterfalls.

Which I would not be photographing.

We retrieved our luggage and made our way toward the exit. A cute guy stood alone, leaning against a pillar.

He was watching us.

His light brown hair streaked with blond was pulled into

a stubby ponytail at the base of his head, leaving strands loose around his face. It was so shiny that I wanted to run my fingers through it or ask what conditioner he used. A T-shirt hugged nice arm muscles, and cargo shorts showed off tanned legs. He could have played a young Thor. When he caught me checking him out, his lips lifted.

Oh well. Not like I'd see him again.

As we moved toward him, he pocketed his phone, shoved away from the pillar, and approached. His eyes were locked on me. I slowed. My family paused.

And the cute guy's arms were around me before I could shove him away.

What? I mean, sure, he wasn't bad to look at. And I *had* been staring. But I didn't make a habit of hugging strangers in airports. I stiffened and was ready to plant my knee somewhere that would have made my junior high self-defense teacher proud, when his mouth dipped close to my ear.

"Hey, Kenzie." His voice was low and rough, his breath warm on my neck.

I yanked back. His arms kept me from moving too far, so we were inches apart as I stared into the brightest sky-blue eyes I'd ever seen, framed by long lashes. The mischievous light in them matched the quirk of his lips.

"Surprise!" shouted my family.

My gaze darted from them to the boy, bouncing around, as I tried to figure out what kind of trick this was.

They were all smiling, though the boy's expression resembled more of a smirk.

My family, at least, did not see this as me getting mauled by a random stranger.

The boy released me, stepped away, and moved to my dad with his hand outstretched. "Hello, Dr. Reed. It's nice to finally meet you in person. I'm Jacob."

CHAPTER TWO

Sorry, what now?

The boy shook my dad's hand, my mom's, my brother's.

"Look, Kenzie is speechless," the guy said. "I think the surprise was a success."

Of course it was a success, you fake, lying liar. You aren't real. Who are you?

But I couldn't say that aloud, because I was also a fake, lying liar. If I told them this wasn't my boyfriend, Jacob Miller, I would have to confess there wasn't actually a Jacob Miller. In the middle of an airport, where their disappointment and judgment would be on display for the world to see. Right before they locked me in the hotel suite for the entire week.

And if they learned I'd been lying about Jacob, eventually the other untruths from the last several months would come out, too. Namely, the lies that I didn't mind giving up photography, that I agreed with my parents' opinions about it being too risky as a career choice, that I was enjoying my science clubs and couldn't wait for college. That I was happy with this new version of me and not feeling at all trapped or miserable or like a wild tiger in a tiny cage, slowly wasting away toward a tragic end.

Hey, this guy is a fraud. Oh wait, I am, too.

I gritted my teeth and smiled. "I am definitely surprised."

Our gazes locked. His easy smile taunted me. Slight dimples in both cheeks gave him a playful appearance that was both attractive and aggravating. Somehow this stranger knew—about the fake boyfriend and about the fact that I had to play along.

He grasped my shoulders. "You look great. I can't believe I'm finally seeing you in person again. Screens don't do you justice."

"So true," I said. "I almost didn't recognize you."

He was way hotter than any boy I'd dated before, and I wasn't sure what my parents would think about the long hair. Perhaps too edgy for the guy I'd made up, though I liked it.

His dimples deepened. "After the number of times we've talked, I'll try not to be hurt by that."

Considering that number was zero . . .

"No offense." I gave him a sweet look. "It's like when you see someone in a place you don't expect, it takes you a minute, you know? Your teacher at the grocery store. Or someone who resembles a fictional character." I paused a second. "Like, from a book."

"I understand completely." His eyes twinkled. "If I met a fictional character, I'd want to hug them to make sure they were real."

"Or maybe pinch them." I smiled again and hoped my reply came across as the threat I meant it to be.

"Exactly." His half-smirk said he understood me perfectly. "Well, I'm just glad it worked out for me to come." He hugged me again and whispered into my ear, "I'll explain later."

I twitched. I wanted to drag him off immediately. What could his explanation possibly be?

"I can't believe you didn't tell me. All of you." I turned my plastered-on happy face to my family.

"We thought you would enjoy the surprise," Mom said.

"Plus, five months is too long not to see you." Fakey McFaker gave me such an adoring look, I might have believed him if I hadn't known that cute, innocent face hid a pretender.

Five months ago, I'd supposedly met my boyfriend at a weekend retreat in Atlanta for the Future Healthcare Professionals of America group. How did he know that? Fake Jacob had not been based on a real person. Tragically, I had attended the healthcare weekend, missing our school's fall festival, which I loved. I just hadn't met anyone.

When I got home, the first words I heard from Dad were about how Alana and Neal had finished their interviews with the graduate optometry program in Fullerton for the following fall. It slipped out that I had met someone, too, and of course he was interested in optometry, to help with my new image. I'd quickly created a story. Then over the last few months, I occasionally mentioned our fake online chats and pretended to receive daily texts. Naturally, he disliked social media, so no one could find him, which drove my brother crazy but impressed my parents, who thought screen time would lead to worldwide blindness and the downfall of civilization.

Two could play this guy's game of words.

"Oh, I agree," I said. "I missed you so much, I don't know how I lived without you."

"Then this surprise came just in time. I would hate to think I was the cause of any distress in your life."

The look he gave me was direct, sincere. Whoever he was, he was good.

Mr. Phony Baloney turned to my parents. "How was your flight? Thank you again for letting me come last-minute when my program was canceled. It almost makes up for missing out on the experience I would have gotten."

Again with details he couldn't know. His spring break program didn't exist. I'd made it up because it sounded like a logical reason for someone to decline a trip to Maui.

"We're glad you were able to find a last-minute flight," Mom said. "I hope your professor will be okay."

"He should be since they caught it right away. Appendectomies have a ninety-nine percent success rate. It was just bad timing."

They nodded sympathetically while I wondered if Lying Von Liarson had his appendix, so I could punch him in it.

"I hope he doesn't rush back to work too quickly. Too many people neglect their health."

Ironic, coming from Dad, when we were taking this vacation because he'd put everyone else's health above his own.

"Wise advice," Jacob said.

I snorted.

What game was this guy playing? Was he trying to con my family? Was he here to steal from us? Had my ancestors wronged his, and this was an elaborate revenge plot where he wormed his way into our confidence and destroyed our business, or murdered us in our sleep, cut us into tiny pieces, and destroyed the evidence by feeding us to the sharks?

Playing along meant I could be inviting a criminal into our lives. But I wasn't ready to lose my family's newfound acceptance until I knew it was the only option.

And now I wanted answers. I needed to get him alone so I could interrogate him and figure out why he was pretending to be my fake boyfriend and how he—a stranger—even knew I *had* a fake boyfriend. My best friend, Lucia, was the only one I'd told, and she wouldn't say a word.

Bogus Boy slipped his arm around my shoulders. His scent hit me, and I inhaled deeply before I could stop myself. Why did the insidious impostor have to smell like a delicious banana-coconut smoothie when we hadn't even been in Hawaii for half an hour?

And why was he driving me to alliteration?

"You haven't said you're glad to see me," he murmured.

I twisted to look up at him, hoping my family wasn't getting suspicious. "I'm still having trouble trusting it's you."

"Of course it's me, Kenz. Who else would it be?"

Our smiles fought a silent duel.

We must have been convincing as a reunited couple, because Tyler said, "You guys are so cute, I might puke."

The faker looked away first. Which I took as a win, until he stepped closer to my mom.

"Let me take that, Dr. Reed." He maneuvered her suitcase away from her, rolling hers and carrying his own bag as we moved on.

I shot daggers at his back with my eyeballs. Tyler fell into step beside me, and I tried to make my expression less murderous.

"He seems nice," my brother said. His lips quirked. "I was starting to think you'd made him up."

"As you can see, he's very real."

Too real. Inescapably real.

Like an octopus clinging to your face and suffocating you.

We took a shuttle to the car rental, where Dad picked up a van and loaded our luggage into the back row.

"Try to keep your hands off each other," Tyler said before wedging himself next to the bags and taking out his phone, likely hoping he could get away with using the device unseen.

That left the center row for me and Fake Jake.

Tyler's remark would have embarrassed me if this guy had been my real boyfriend. I slid to the window, while Jacob sat by the door, keeping the middle seat empty. But he stretched his arm across the back of the seat, so his fingers brushed my shoulder when the van turned. A jolt went through me, and I flinched.

He smirked.

Don't let him win.

After it happened a second time, I took his hand in mine and moved our clasped hands to the seat between us. His head twitched toward me. Surprise flashed across his face before his look turned assessing. His hand was strong and warm, and our fingers fit together perfectly, which sent another shiver through my stomach. I wanted to dig my nails into him or yank my hand away, but letting go would equal giving in.

We drove through town, palm trees and puffy white clouds

revealing we were in a tropical paradise. Vibrant green mountains loomed above, with misty clouds obscuring the tops. My imagination jumped to mystical hidden glens and bubbling creeks and lush jungles.

Then the highway led out of town into dry, brown hills, offering such a contrast that I longed to mention the reading I'd done on the island's weather patterns, the rainy side and the dry side. But I wasn't supposed to care about that anymore.

Definitely-not-Jacob shifted toward me. "You never told me how your history test went this week."

"Oh, you didn't get my text?" I asked sweetly. "It was fine."

"I'm sure you did great. You spent a lot of time studying."

"She does spend more time studying lately," said my mom. "You're a good influence on her. I'm glad she has your support."

"Oh, of course. She motivates me, too. Sending me her study schedules so I can make sure to keep up with her." He squeezed the hand he held.

I ground my teeth together. I did spend more time studying, on my own, thank you. Despite the fact that it made for a miserable senior year. Why was he trying to make me look good?

"How's Lucia?" he asked.

My eyes narrowed. "Fine."

And, unfortunately, spending the week camping with her family, no phones allowed. Her parents' policy endeared them to my parents but was exceptionally annoying, because if there had ever been a time when I needed her advice, it was now.

"She's such a nice, hardworking girl," my mom said.

"I hope to meet her one day," Fake Jacob said. "It sounds like she'll be a great vet. It's nice that you have that in common, the desire to help and care for people—or animals."

Was he stalking me? Learning about my classes and my best friend? He didn't give off creep vibes, but weren't most serial killers charming?

I tugged my hand free and turned toward the window. Whatever his game, I was done with it for now.

The ocean appeared on our left as we drove along the highway. It wasn't like I'd never seen the ocean, living two hours from the coast in Northern California. But this was magical, knowing we were completely surrounded by water, on an island full of unique animals, with treasures hidden beneath the waves, like a precious gem dropped so far from land. Ready to be appreciated by those willing to seek its views, and I couldn't wait to capture it all.

No, wait. Not that last part.

Not-Jacob's fingers brushed my shoulder again, yanking me out of daydreams. Possibly for the best. I wanted to appreciate this trip, but not letting nature suck me in would be a challenge. This boy beside me who knew too much offered a distraction, if not a welcome one.

Dad pulled off into a lookout point where cars filled a parking lot, and we climbed out.

Water stretched in front of us. A blue so deep and pure it felt like it was flooding my insides, carving out chasms and trenches, leaving a nameless ache inside. How could anyone see that view and not be moved, not stare all day and let it swallow you whole?

Sun sparkled on the surface. Two islands and the other part

of Maui were visible in the distance. People milled around, eyes or binoculars focused on the ocean. A guy with a machete sat in the bed of an old truck, hacking at coconuts.

I spotted signs about whales and other marine life, and let my sunglasses hide where my eyes were pointed as I wandered slowly, reading every word, hoping no one suspected I was imagining how to film turtles and seals and otters and every other wonderful animal described.

My parents approved of learning and didn't mind a few facts, but for me, it always became obsession, reading everything I could find on my phone, and then a desire to take five million pictures. That was when their displeasure emerged full force, along with lectures about the slim odds of success, the physical and financial risks, and how I was neglecting important things.

A voice shouted, and heads turned. People pointed. I leaned into the metal rail and followed their gazes in time to see a tail disappear into the water.

Whales.

My heart stopped. Twisted. I clutched the rail, as if squeezing hard enough might bring them back.

Three dorsal fins appeared, peeking above the surface.

A hush fell, allowing us to hear the sound of a tail slapping water. Spouts erupted, misty white spumes floating above the water.

My breath lodged in my throat, and my eyes burned. I tried not to blink. They were amazing. Majestic. Magical. Dark spots against the blue sea. A tiny rainbow formed and vanished in the mist of their spray. I wanted to hurl myself off the cliff into the sea and swim straight toward them.

People passed binoculars, readied cameras. I reached for my neck before remembering mine didn't hang on its customary strap.

A sense of emptiness hit me, like part of me was missing. I could use my phone, but maybe it was better this way. Enjoy the view. Live in the moment.

But as another tail glided gracefully into the water, at exactly the right angle for a perfect photograph if I'd had my telephoto lens, my fingers twitched and my chest tightened.

Not-Jacob leaned next to me, his arm brushing mine. I thought I sensed him studying me, but when I looked over, he was pulling a phone from his pocket. He took a short video.

"Going to post that?" I asked without taking my eyes off the sea.

"You know I don't do social media."

I lifted a shoulder. "You might have changed your mind."

"That's the kind of thing you would tell your girlfriend. You're not going to take a picture?" he asked.

"You'd get a more stable video if you steadied your arms on something."

"Cool. Thanks for the tip." He moved behind me and rested his forearms on my shoulders, holding the phone so it was right in front of my face. A text popped up on his screen, and he quickly swiped it away before I could see anything more than that it was from *Mom*.

"That's not what I meant," I said.

But my family stood nearby, and slapping him would not help sell this . . . whatever this messed-up not-a-relationship was.

I wanted to savor the beauty, not be distracted by the lingering coconut scent in my nose or the warmth of his chest, inches from my back, his shirt brushing against me in the breeze.

"Press it, would you?" His voice was low and husky, teasing.

I switched his camera from slo-mo to regular video— Really? Was he kidding? Then turned off the flash. Seriously? He had to be messing with me. Once I adjusted the angle of his screen and zoomed in, I hit record.

We waited in silence for several seconds, watching for more whales. When they appeared to the right, we shifted so the camera captured them. On his phone, they were little more than dark blurs. My telephoto lens would have been better.

Once the creatures vanished again, I stopped Not-Jacob's recording. He lingered a moment, slow to move away, before shifting and taking his delicious tropical scent with him.

It was seriously a crime that he smelled so good.

I drew a deep breath and willed my face not to flush red before I faced him. "Don't get a lot of whales in Ohio, do you? Have you ever seen one before?"

"Not in Ohio, I haven't."

Well, that wasn't helpful. I'd been hoping for a hint about where he really lived. Judging by the gleam in his eye, I could tell he saw through me.

"Anywhere else?" I pressed. "Vacation, maybe? Or somewhere you used to live?"

"You know I've never lived near the beach."

Fake Jacob had lived several places before college, all north and east and far away from California. I'd figured that saying he moved often would make it harder for anyone to look into him, if my family had decided to try. But this guy wasn't going to let anything slip. He should try Hollywood and that young Thor gig, because he sure was committed to his role.

The whales were moving on, and the viewers around us pushed away from the railing and returned to cars.

"Well, that's something," my mom said.

"I'm glad we got to see them already. We can check it off the list." Dad sounded far too cheerful while he was reducing amazing creatures to one of his ever-present checklists.

My shoulders tensed, and I drifted away from my family toward the end of the parking lot, trying to recapture the joy of that first glimpse of a whale. Why did this guy and my family have to complicate everything?

Totally-Not-Jacob followed. The wind had pulled more strands of hair from his ponytail, and they blew around his face. He tucked them behind his ears, both hands and both ears at the same time. The gesture was not cute. *He* was not cute. He was twisted and evil.

We were far enough from the others that I could talk freely. I whirled on him.

"Who are you?" I hissed. "What are you doing here?"

He shoved his hands into his pockets. "I'm Jacob Miller."

"Jacob Miller is fake."

He leaned on the railing. "My driver's license says otherwise."

"You know what I mean."

"Don't believe me?" He took a crumpled boarding pass from his pocket. "Right there."

I snatched the paper. The name was right. He'd flown to Maui from LAX, which didn't tell me much, since that was a major airport and he could have flown to LA from anywhere.

"Did you steal this from someone?"

"Nope, it's all mine."

I narrowed my eyes. "You said you'd explain later. It's later. Whatever game you're playing . . ."

"Is this any way to welcome your long-distance boyfriend?"

"You are not my boyfriend." My voice rose too loud. I quieted before continuing. "Whoever you are, you are a big, fat liar."

"Says the girl with a fake boyfriend."

Fair point. My teeth ground together.

His dimples danced. "I thought you liked surprises."

"I do. When your friends wake you up on your birthday with strawberry pancakes, or when your sister does your laundry without you asking, or when you're photographing a flower and a butterfly lands on it. Not when a stranger tries to con your family."

He shifted his head toward them, tucked his hair back again. "Do they seem conned? They like me. Your mom was super nice when I told her I wanted to come."

"How did you get her number? How are you . . . Argh."

"Relax." He placed his hands on my shoulders. "You don't want to get high blood pressure like your dad."

A cute boy was touching me, and all I was thinking about was whether I could push him over the cliff edge and make it look like an accident.

"You might fool the others, but I know the truth. And I know psychology. This is . . . mental warfare. Or something."

His smile widened.

"How'd you learn so much about us? Bug my house? Hack my computer? How many crimes have you committed?"

"I'm hurt. I will have you know that I have broken exactly zero laws. Not even a speeding ticket."

"Written laws, maybe. But there are laws of—of common decency. And you have definitely crossed that line."

He laughed, loudly, and I did not admire his dimples. Not for long, anyway.

"Look," I said earnestly. "If you want to come back to the hotel with my family, I need enough to know you aren't a serial killer. I obviously don't want to tell them the truth. I know that, and you know that. But you're a stranger, and every true-crime podcast warns about stuff like this."

His expression grew more serious. "Let's just say I . . . learned of your situation and I needed to come to Maui, so it offered me an opportunity. One that helps both of us."

"You don't even know me. Did you hack my computer? Threaten Lucia? How in the world would you know about my *situation*?"

"No and no. And I can't tell you that, except to say we have a mutual friend."

"Lucia wouldn't do this, and I haven't told anyone else. Who was it?"

"I can't say."

I glanced at my family. "I could turn you in right now."

"But you won't, because then your family would learn the truth, about me and about a lot of other things."

My nostrils flared as I drew a deep breath.

Tyler wandered closer, and I fell silent, trying to erase my scowl. My family had to believe I was happy to see this guy, thrilled at the surprise, excited to spend a week together in person after months apart.

"Dad says we're leaving," Tyler called. "Please save the reunion kiss for somewhere private."

Heat rose to my face, and my fist clenched.

Jacob grabbed my hand. "I have a good reason for being here, and I need this. Obviously you do, too. Can we agree to help each other?"

"Fine. But this isn't over," I hissed.

For my family's benefit, I smiled—my face was going to freeze in this fake cheerful position. Or my cheek muscles were going to cramp and I was going to need some sort of face masseuse to fix them.

Then I made our clasped hands look romantic and not like a hostage situation and led Faker to the car.

Whoever he was, I would figure it out.

CHAPTER THREE

The rest of the drive offered glimpses of gorgeous beaches, leaning trees, and rich blue water. It was peaceful and beautiful, and even the three-hour time difference and several hours of flying didn't dim my enthusiasm. But I couldn't stop thinking about Jacob-whoever-he-was, a shadow looming over the glimpse of paradise. And this alleged *mutual friend.* It had to be true, because how else would he know all about me and my family? Which I supposed was enough to continue the charade for now.

We passed through one town and headed to Ka'anapali, where our resort was. The grounds were perfect, with sprawling pools connected by lazy rivers that meandered throughout, complete with hidden nooks and waterfalls. Palm trees and grass-roofed huts dotted the whole area, and the lawns were so green, they looked fake.

In a cavernous open-air lobby full of ferns and rich mahogany wood, employees told us aloha and draped us with leis, which immediately set Tyler to sneezing. We deposited our bags with a porter before going to our suite, where Gran had checked in with Alana and Neal.

Did they know about the surprise?

When we knocked, Gran opened the door.

"Aloha!" Her gaze went straight to Jacob. "You must be Jacob." She was hugging him before either of us could react.

Apparently they did know.

"Gran, don't smother him."

Or if you do, do a complete job of it.

She wore her usual bright red lipstick. Her chin-length hair, which had been pure white for as long as I could remember, was sleek and straight. A neon-pink-and-blue tie-dyed cover-up hung off one shoulder, revealing an orange swimsuit underneath. Her round, full-rim glasses were the same bright orange, showing that a love of bright colors must be genetic.

"It's all right," Jacob said as he stepped back and patted her shoulder. "Great to meet you, Gran. Can I call you 'Gran'? I feel like I know you already."

"Of course you can."

"Great." He gave her the full-wattage dimpled smile.

Gran sized him up, then winked at me.

My face got hot. No. She was not allowed to like him. That was not okay.

"Come in, come in." Gran moved so we could enter a large living room.

My sister and Neal sat on one of the many couches.

Alana stood. How were her makeup and gentle waves so perfect in this humidity? I'd hoped my recently shortened hair would be more manageable, shoulder length waves instead of long and wild, but the humidity had attacked it full force. I'd resisted the urge to wear my cartoon whale shirt that said *Whale, hello there,* but did she still look at me and see a kid?

"How was the surprise, Kenz?" she asked.

"Surprising," I said. "Hey, Neal. What was the lens's excuse when he got arrested?"

His eyes lit up. "I don't know, what?"

"I was framed."

His laugh snorted out. He might have had an unfortunate name and been rather dull, a stereotypical academic with pale skin and a neat, short haircut, but he was nice. And incredibly easy to win over. I smiled at him.

"You need this shirt instead of me." He tugged his T-shirt, which said *I Tell Cornea Jokes.*

"Good one," I said.

But my laugh faded. I liked that he was confident enough to wear his dorky shirts, since I'd mostly stopped wearing mine with animal sayings, like the whale, in public.

Great. Neal was braver and more honest about himself than I was.

"How was your trip?" Mom asked Alana.

"Fine, until we got into the car with Gran."

Gran waved a hand to dismiss the comment. "It was a lovely drive."

"Yeah, because you were looking at everything but the road."

"There's so much to see," she went on, as if my sister hadn't spoken.

"Obviously not the road signs." Alana leaned on the kitchen bar. "Or the other cars. And that convertible was not meant for three people and luggage. Neal had to hold one of Gran's suitcases on his lap the whole way."

"It was the one with my swimsuits. It wasn't that heavy." Gran pulled a pitcher of lemonade from the fridge she and Alana had stocked.

"You brought a whole suitcase for swimsuits?" Mom asked.

Gran ignored her. "Who's thirsty?"

"Convertible?" Dad asked. "We agreed on two vans."

"*You* agreed. I upgraded. This is my first vacation in ages because my cheap husband, God rest his soul, refused to take a break."

"Mom!" My dad frowned.

I smothered a giggle. I sure had missed Gran.

Gran took out cups and poured. "You know I loved your father, dear, but that man had the money to travel. He just wouldn't stop working long enough to do it, no matter how many times I asked. Wives want vacations. Young men"—she pointed at Neal, Tyler, and Jacob—"take note."

Neal glanced at Alana, not at all embarrassed. Had they talked about marriage? They were college seniors, but marriage felt so *adult*. Tyler rolled his eyes, and Jacob smirked at me.

What did he think about my family? Maybe our quirkiness would scare him off, deter him from his nefarious mission, whatever it was. Cause him to run away screaming and not come back.

Then I wouldn't get answers about who he was, though . . .

"I don't know if that's always accurate, Gran," Alana said.

"It was accurate in my house, and that's what matters." She

shoved a cup of lemonade at me and one at Jacob, who grinned and thanked her, earning him a pat on the cheek.

He winked at me. "She likes me."

"It's hard to like someone you don't know, isn't it?" I smirked and lifted the cup to hide my mouth.

"I find first impressions are rather accurate."

"Oh, me too. If someone annoys me right away, it's hard to overcome that."

"Lucky for me I make a great one, then." He winked. "Enough to win you over the moment we first laid eyes on each other."

"I'll definitely never forget that moment."

"See, I told you I make a great first impression."

Even though I wanted to scowl, a smile threatened to break through. This was the most *me* I'd felt in months. But that wasn't good. Real Jacob was evil, and Fake Jacob was supposed to reflect the new, responsible, boring me, not the old, sarcastic one. So I smothered my happiness by taking a long swig of lemonade, and coughed. How much sugar had Gran put in that? Good thing we weren't a family of dentists.

A knock on the door announced the arrival of our luggage, which we distributed to our rooms. I wanted to tell the employee to put Jacob's bag in my room so I could search it, but Jacob was watching.

The condo had four bedrooms—a master suite for my parents; a room for Gran; one for me and my sister; and one for my brother, Neal, and Jacob, where a rollaway bed had been added to two beds, proving they'd known to expect Jacob. The linens were bright white, and large photos of tropical scenes adorned the walls. I fought the desire to inspect them all.

Would my pictures have been good enough to hang in resorts, if I'd kept going? They hadn't been good enough for the local travel photo contest. The one I'd been so certain I would win that I'd used it as a bargaining tool with my parents—if I won, I'd prove it was a viable career choice and they'd let me pursue it. If I lost, I'd agree to give it up.

I'd been so confident, so proud of the picture. Had worked so hard to get the right one. But apparently I didn't know as much as I thought, because that gamble had utterly failed.

I shook my head to clear the flood of memories and the sense of loss. It didn't matter. I was done with that. And things were fine. Better to focus on the Jacob issue.

The room situation might prove problematic. Hopefully, Tyler would be so wrapped up in his computer project that he wouldn't ask too many questions. And hopefully Neal wouldn't want to talk optometry, because whoever this Jacob was, even someone bad at math could calculate the odds as *extremely low* that he truly was a biology major at Ohio State.

The condo had a large living area with tile floors, and a fancy kitchen with granite counters, shiny new appliances, and a coffee maker that resembled a tiny spaceship. One whole wall opened to a patio that I'd read was called a lanai, with more chairs, a large dining table, and a grill.

Alana gave everyone a key, which I vowed to myself I wouldn't lose. At least, not within the first two days. When she handed one to Jacob, I wanted to snatch it away. He winked at me as if he could read my thoughts. I narrowed my eyes briefly, which only made him grin.

I couldn't wait to step foot on the beach, but I needed to keep an eye on Jacob. Plus, my dad had dinner planned, and we had to keep to the schedule.

Schedules did to me what seafood did to Mom—made me feel itchy and short of breath. Unfortunately, since that wasn't an official diagnosis, no one cared.

I wandered to the lanai to check out the view. The resort grounds spread beneath us, and I could see portions of the pool. Beyond that was a row of hedges and then the turquoise ocean. The scent of flowers and grass and grilling meat, probably from a poolside grill, mingled on the breeze. From the pool, voices echoed, and the crashing of waves reached my ears. I inhaled deeply and closed my eyes, allowing my mind to soak in the details and be at peace.

The door cracked behind me, shattering the mood.

"Kenzie, dinner," said Tyler.

I sighed. "Why don't we eat out here?"

I motioned to the table that was large enough for all of us. On the grounds, I'd also noticed cute tables next to koi ponds and under awnings beside waterfalls and on the brilliant lawn with just a hedge separating you from the ocean.

"Seriously?" he asked. "Gross. It's so humid."

That's what the breeze was for.

I trudged inside. What was the point of that huge lanai if we were going to stay inside?

I caught Jacob staring longingly at the door as I closed it. His gaze met mine and his lips tucked in, a sympathetic expression, like he understood my disappointment and agreed.

Dad was opening room service platters to reveal pot stickers, crab cakes, fish tacos, a salad with several odd toppings, roasted chicken, steak with green sauce, pulled pork, mashed potatoes, bright purple fries, and colorful vegetables. My mouth watered.

"Aw, no SPAM?" Tyler took steak and potatoes until Mom said, "Vegetables, too," and he added two carrot sticks.

"This is . . . an interesting selection," Mom said.

"It was advertised as a family platter." Dad frowned at the fries.

"At least there are a few acceptable dishes."

I couldn't contain a slight snort. A few? Every single item looked delicious.

Alana and Neal ignored the appetizers, while Mom went heavy on the salad and avoided anything fish related.

I helped myself to a sample of everything, and so did Jacob. Our fingers brushed as we reached for the purple fries everyone else was ignoring. A zing went through me. His eyes leaped to mine, and he smiled slightly. I returned it before remembering who he was and that I shouldn't be friendly with my nemesis, even if he also wanted to be outdoors and was the only other one besides Gran trying the actually interesting food.

Mom put a scoop of vegetables next to her salad. "So, Jacob, Kenzie hasn't told us much about you. You're studying at Ohio State, right?"

"That's right. Biology."

"And you're considering a career in optometry?"

"Either that or podiatry."

I narrowed my eyes. Now he was going off book? I didn't know how he knew the lies I'd told in the first place, but making up his own was worse.

"Interesting," Dad said. "In this field, usually someone knows if it's their calling."

My grip on my fork tightened. Was Jacob going to ruin everything?

"I get it," Jacob said. "But I had a moment like that for both fields, and I'm having trouble picking. My dad got LASIK when I was nine, which sounded fascinating. I wanted to watch, begged them to let me sit in on the procedure."

"And did they?" Mom was looking skeptical. This was not good.

"Oh, of course not," he said, and Mom relaxed. "Instead I watched every video I could find on YouTube. It was so interesting. But then two years later, my grandmother broke her foot, and I went with her to the podiatrist. They had this huge model of a foot, with all the bones and tendons and everything. So complex. Like the human eye."

They were nodding like this was some sage insight, while I debated stomping on his foot to see if he knew which bone was which when they were broken.

"Anyway," he said. "I decided to study biology and spend time researching programs in both fields, do an internship in at least one, but both if I can. I have two years to decide, but I know either one would be great." He shifted his gaze to me. "Kenzie's interest in optometry might sway me in that direction. She's always trying to convince me it's the best field."

It was a wonderful speech that impressed my parents, and I was certain every word of it was a total and complete lie.

But my parents were beaming at me.

I smiled at him. "Obviously I want you to be happy and *be yourself.*"

He held my gaze. "It's something you're so good at. I really admire that about you."

I clenched my fork tighter.

"And in your free time?" Alana asked as she scraped coleslaw off the fish tacos, unaware of the hidden barbs and the daggers Jacob and I were throwing at each other with our eyes.

I shoveled a pot sticker into my mouth, coated in sweet sauce I couldn't identify but definitely liked. My family was already testing my patience. Why come to Hawaii if they didn't plan to experience it?

"Outside of class, I don't have much free time," Jacob said. "I like science shows. My bad habit is puzzle games on my phone, though I try not to be on it too much, except to talk to Kenzie."

Mom was ready to adopt him or marry me off. How did he know these things?

"Have you seen that show about the oddities of the human body?" Neal asked.

"Oh yes, that's a good one. What was your favorite episode?"

"The earwax, I think. Who knew it was actually sweat?"

A slight twitch in Jacob's jaw was his only reaction to the utter randomness. He hid it with an earnest reply. "Right? So weird."

Well played, Jacob. I doubted he even knew what that show was, and I was now trying not to gag.

"You don't like sports or computer games?" Tyler asked. "I thought all college guys do."

Jacob shrugged. "I don't have a lot of time for video games, and I'm not on any sports teams."

But had he ever been? He seemed athletic. He definitely excelled at the sport of vague answers.

"What about you?" Jacob asked my brother. "You play football? Baseball?"

"Baseball. Do you watch? Who do people cheer for in Ohio?"

"Oh, Cleveland mostly, but it's not my thing."

I took a bite to hide a scoff. *Nice save, obviously-non-Ohio-dweller.* Tyler made a humming noise.

"We're so glad your family let you come this week," my mom said. "We look forward to getting to know you better."

"My sister was jealous. I can't thank you enough for inviting me. Would you like more salad?" He reached for the bowl and served my mom.

Did he really have a sister? Or did he mean the imaginary younger one I'd given Fake Jacob to make his family sound real?

He was driving me insane, and he seemed to know it. And be enjoying it, if his permanent, tiny smirk was any indication.

"Family is important," he went on, "which means meeting Kenzie's family is, too."

He reached out a hand from his place across the table, palm up. Oh, he was good. I'd give him that. I placed my hand in his, and he squeezed briefly and let go. I flexed my fingers and tucked my hands safely into my lap.

Conversation shifted, and I watched him. Every bite. He ignored my stare, but his lips kept twitching as he tried to conceal a smile around mouthfuls of food.

I wanted to grill him, too, but not in front of the others. My questions would build on the ones I'd asked at the lookout point and would be much harder than the ones my family asked.

After we ate and cleaned up, the entire family went to the lanai to watch the sunset. I stood at the rail, and Jacob moved to stand beside me, his shoulder touching mine. I couldn't deny it felt nice, even if it was for show.

This was supposed to be romantic. Low clouds hugged the island on the horizon, turning pink and purple and orange as the sun sank toward silvery water. Palm trees became dark silhouettes against a twilight sky. Jacob faded as I imagined wandering the grounds and photographing the trees, the sky.

Then he leaned close, so his arm pressed against mine fully. "I sure am glad to be here," he murmured into my ear, sending goose bumps down my neck.

"Oh, I anticipate many interesting moments this week."

"As do I."

We shifted to stare at each other, his eyes navy in the fading light. A spark in them made a flame flicker inside me, longing to rise to meet his challenge. I held his gaze. He seemed to be studying me, trying to figure me out. What was he looking for? And what did he see?

He broke eye contact first, and when we went inside, I tried to corner him in the hallway.

"Want to sit on the lanai and talk?" I asked, trying to sound like I meant "catch up," not "cross-examine," in case the others overheard.

"I'm so tired. Jet lag. I'm three extra hours behind you, remember?"

I narrowed my eyes. "Are you?"

"Aren't I?" He raised his eyebrows. "We'll have all day tomorrow to hang out, yeah?"

He side-hugged me, winked, and vanished into his room faster than a whale submerging beneath the waves, leaving me glaring at the closed door.

CHAPTER FOUR

Thanks to the time difference, I was wide awake at five a.m. Since early mornings were the only part of the day not scheduled this week and I liked predawn hours, when the world was quiet and the light was soft and gray, I changed into running clothes and decided to go outside.

I stared at the door to the guys' room. Barging in to wake up Jacob, dragging him with me, and forcing him to talk was definitely not something my parents would like. Answers would have to wait for a more decent hour.

Rustling sounds greeted me in the dining area, and my heart leaped into my throat. Neal sat at the table, reading a book.

I pressed a hand to my chest. Way to scare me. And seriously, working at this hour?

"Morning," I said. "I'm going for a walk."

He probably didn't care, but in case I was carried away by a rogue wave or a shark, I figured someone should know where I was.

But he looked up and met my gaze. "Do you do that often? Get up early to exercise? Alana loves her morning yoga. She's always trying to convince me to join her."

I actually used *going running* as an excuse to spend time by myself outdoors, now that I didn't visit parks or gardens to take pictures.

I shrugged. "It's more jet lag."

"Me too."

"What are you working on?"

"Oh, it's not work." He held up the book so I could see the cover—a young adult fantasy novel.

Huh. Who would have thought?

"Cool. I liked that one. The second book in the series is even better."

His eyes brightened. "Good. I have that one in my bag."

My hand was on the front door when Alana's voice called, "Hey, wait for me."

Of course the one person I wanted time alone with wasn't one of the early birds. I wasn't sure which was worse: Jacob joining me and continuing to pretend he was a character I'd invented, or him staying behind with my family without me there to supervise.

I sighed and opened the door for Alana, who wore workout leggings and a tank top. The air was already warm and sticky. It was too early for the pool to be open. Some of the waterfalls were turned off, and the world was silent other than a chorus of noisy birds. Plumeria trees dotted with white flowers gave the air a fresh scent. A carpet of fallen blooms covered the grass beneath them, and I stopped to pick up a perfect one that must have just fallen, crisp and white, with the faintest yellow in the center. The hibiscus flowers remained closed, waiting for the sun. Workers cleaned the pool and raked the grass. The pale gray sky offered great lighting for photos.

"Were you going to run?" Alana asked.

"Um."

Running on the beach in the sand, in this humidity, sounded dreadful. Neal's corny cornea shirt had inspired me to wear one of mine. It reflected my general workout philosophy, showing a picture of a sloth, with the words, *Sloth running team—we'll get there when we get there.*

"Maybe just a walk?"

"You can join me for yoga," Alana said.

"No, that's okay."

I took off my shoes on the spongy grass, and we found a path to the beach. I sped up to dig my toes into the cool sand. Gentle waves lapped the shore with soft swishes.

Alana stopped in the dry sand to stretch, bending in half in a way I didn't think the human body was meant to move.

I left her saluting the sun, which hadn't risen above the mountains behind the resort, or being a warrior, or whatever it was called, and moved to the silvery water. It was cool but not frigid, and I let it swirl around my ankles, carrying my worries out to sea.

The ocean spread before me, deep blue at this hour, humid air scented with salt. Wispy silver clouds flecked the sky, and I heard nothing but the sound of waves.

Two joggers passed, but it was mostly quiet. I wanted to hunt for interesting pictures—the waves, the patterns they left in the sand, the palm trees, or birds pecking along the shore. Instead I walked through the shallow water, squishing sand between my toes and breathing in the peace.

Thoughts of Jacob intruded. I couldn't escape him. Staying out here too long was risky. Who knew what he'd get up to, what he'd say, while I was gone.

When I wandered toward Alana, I found her sitting, watching the ocean. I sat beside her, ignoring the urge to rush back to the room. I would not let that impostor ruin my enjoyment of Hawaii.

Once we were seated side by side, I didn't know what to say. Alana had moved away for college when I'd been starting high school, and the four-year age difference meant we'd never been close. Now I saw her less frequently, though she sent a weekly text every Sunday evening. They always felt less like she wanted to chat and more like she was checking off her big-sister duty. Confirm Kenzie is alive, and cross that off the list for one more week.

"How have you been?" she asked. "You have to decide on a college soon, don't you?"

"Yep."

"Any idea where you'll choose?"

"Nope."

"Mom said you applied to several schools. Are you considering Ohio State?"

I sifted a handful of sand through my fingers. "Too cold."

Also, I'd been planning to break up with made-up Jacob over the summer, ensuring I never had to go visit.

"Good," she said. "Don't move across the country for a boy. I mean, if you liked the school, okay. But not for him."

No danger of that happening.

"We'd love to have you in LA. I could help you learn the city, introduce you to my optometry school professors. Obviously, I'll keep saving my notes."

I grunted.

"Or if you went to Davis, you could keep working part-time with Mom and Dad. Even commute."

Yes, that was the grand adventure I dreamed of after high school. Nothing changing except the location and level of difficulty of my classes. Same bedroom, same expectations, same conversation topics I had to pretend to care about.

We were silent.

When Alana spoke again, her voice was more thoughtful. "You've changed this year. I have to admit, I wasn't sure it would stick."

What was that supposed to mean?

"I'm proud to see how you've grown. And I'm excited we're both going to follow Mom and Dad. Working with you one day will be fun. My baby sister isn't a baby anymore."

My jaw tightened. I didn't know if she'd always seen me that way simply because I was younger or because of our extreme personality differences. We might be in our eighties in a nursing home, and she'd still be calling me *baby sister*.

She finished with, "I'm glad you finally settled down."

Like I was some middle-aged dude going through a life crisis? Or a party bro whose parents thought he needed to find a spouse and get a job?

Breathe in with the crashing wave. Breathe out with the crashing wave.

"I'll help however I can," she went on. "You know, when you consider a school, you should look for programs that have good optometry admission test pass rates and highly rated science programs. I can put together a spreadsheet for you."

Thanks for murdering my peaceful beach vibes, Sis. Her color-coded spreadsheets haunted my nightmares. The one she'd made to track her college applications would have impressed NASA. They also suspiciously resembled our schedule for this week. Alana was proudly carrying on Dad's legacy in more ways than one.

"Make sure you get a roommate who's serious about academics. It's a major pain when you have to deal with someone with different priorities. And like high school, it's important to find activities you enjoy but that also look good on your resume."

So basically, college was going to mirror the last four years, when she'd provided her old class notes, her homemade SAT study guides, her analysis of every teacher at the high school. As if I couldn't get through it without her wisdom and without doing things exactly like she had. I had to admit, over the last several months, after I'd decided to pretend to care about chemistry and calculus, her materials had come in handy. And they had succeeded—at least in making me more like her.

I stood and brushed sand off my legs. "We should get back."

Halfway across the grounds, she said, "Jacob's nice. Do you think it will last?"

"I'm in high school. Who knows?"

"You two have a lot in common. Sharing life goals and passions is important."

"Right."

"I'm looking forward to getting to know him this week. And getting to know the new you."

Fan-freaking-tastic.

I had to do something. I couldn't let Jacob keep taking advantage of my family, who were being so nice to him. I would come clean, admit I'd made him up. Maybe I could do it without revealing everything else. If I claimed I'd been feeling left out because Alana and Neal were so serious, my family might understand why I'd invented a boyfriend. I could tell them this Jacob guy was a fake, say he caught me off guard at the airport.

And then they'd ask way too many questions.

Ugh. This was going to be a disaster.

We returned with plenty of time to shower and keep to the schedule, which had us driving north up the coast to the Nakalele Blowhole. When I entered the condo, Jacob was eating a banana and helping Gran set out fruit, cereal, and toast on the kitchen island. His attention went to my shirt, and he smiled.

Oh yeah. The sloths.

His expression seemed to hold genuine amusement, not mockery. That was not enough for me to let him off the hook.

"How was the beach?" he asked.

"Great," I said.

Then I scanned the room. My parents sat at the table with Neal. Tyler was on the couch. Everyone was here. Perfect.

I cleared my throat. "Look—"

"I made your favorite." Jacob cut me off with a slight smirk. "Peanut butter, banana, and chocolate smoothie."

"Isn't that sweet?" Gran said.

No. No, it was not. Not when I was about to reveal him as a fraud.

"When we first met and I heard you order it, I had my doubts," he said. "But after I tried it, and I confirmed your research about how it's a good blend of protein and fiber, I realized I should never doubt your word."

His gaze met mine, challenging. Like he knew I'd planned to out him and was determined to make it as difficult as possible. While also making me look good.

"Did you tell him about the time you forgot to put the lid on the blender and it got all over the kitchen?" Tyler asked. "That was hilarious."

"Hey," I said.

It had actually happened twice, but the second time, I'd been home alone and had cleaned it before anyone noticed. In my defense, I'd spotted hummingbirds in the honeysuckle outside the window, begging to be photographed. Though it was after I'd given up photography, I'd gotten caught up watching them.

Thanks, Tyler. Hopefully they'd remember that I wasn't that person anymore. Even if that second time had been last month . . .

"I just want to make sure Jacob knows what he's getting into," Tyler said.

"Oh, I know." Jacob smiled as he extended the glass. "Would anyone else like one?"

I snatched the cup and sat down next to Mom with a huff. Okay, revealing the truth was out of the question. They'd never believe me, not unless I told them everything.

Jacob finished helping Gran and delivered plates to everyone, insisting they not move.

Suck-up.

If I couldn't expose him and get him banished from the island, at least I could figure out who he was. I sipped my smoothie and plotted. I needed to find out more about him, somehow.

After breakfast, we trooped to the cars. Gran aimed for a bright yellow convertible.

Since we wouldn't all fit into the van, Gran twirled her keys.

"I'll take Kenzie and Jacob," she said. "I want to get to know him."

"Good luck," Alana muttered to me.

I needed it more than she knew.

CHAPTER FIVE

We missed the red Jeep by two inches. Gran didn't even notice.

Her bright yellow convertible meandered in and out of the correct lane as she craned her head to watch the ocean on our left. I debated grabbing the wheel, but she'd made it to her mid-seventies without an accident, so maybe it was better to sit back, enjoy the ride, and ignore the multitude of traffic violations.

The speakers blared a playlist of songs I didn't know, and she sang along, stopping only to say "Oh look" and "Amazing" and "Wow" over and over again.

It *was* amazing. The highway didn't run right along the coast, so Gran had taken a road through town, lined with trees, flowering bushes, and ocean views. The morning sun was warm but not hot, and flowers occasionally scented the air before we whipped past them.

My phone rang. Dad.

"Kenzie, please tell your grandmother to get back on the highway," he said when I answered. The wind muffled his words. "That route is too slow."

"Gran, Dad says to take the highway."

She sighed. "My son knows how to suck the joy out of everything."

Jacob snorted.

I didn't disagree, but it felt disloyal to laugh and side against my dad with this stranger.

We rejoined the main road, though the slower one might have been safer, given Gran's driving tendencies. If we crashed, it wouldn't be at high speed. Also, it gave other cars more time to see us coming and move out of our way.

We passed through a nice area of fancy resorts and green, green lawns, then spotted a golf course. Golfing was scheduled for later this week. Because spending half a day in paradise walking around in the grass sounded like a great use of time. Admittedly, the glimpses of a beautiful turquoise bay were stunning. Small boats dotted the water. A sign advertised kayak and snorkeling tours; I might have missed it if Gran hadn't almost run it over.

"We should come back this week," Jacob said. He'd been remarkably quiet, although his phone had chimed multiple times before he muted it. I had been trying to pretend the back seat was empty.

Absolutely was on the tip of my tongue. Instead I said, "I don't think that's on the agenda."

He leaned forward between my seat and Gran's. "Yeah, but you're not an agenda kind of person."

I twisted to see him. "You know me so well?"

"Better than you think."

"Better than you should."

His eyes sparkled. "Unlike you. You know every single detail about me. More than I know about myself."

"That's sweet," Gran said.

I scowled. The wind had pulled strands of his hair free, and they swirled around his face. He tucked them back, again with both hands, both ears at the same time, and his dimples sparkled as brightly as his eyes, sending a fluttering sensation through my stomach.

"Tell me about how you met." Gran spoke loudly over the music and the wind.

"Ah yes," I said. "It feels like only yesterday."

Jacob grinned.

"You said it was at a school thing?" Gran asked.

"Future Healthcare Professionals of America weekend," Jacob said easily. "I took one look at her and knew she was going to bring so much joy to my life." The smile on his face said he might actually believe that.

I grunted as Taylor Swift came on. I was going to enjoy the view and the wind in my hair and stop engaging with him. I cranked up the volume and sang along with Gran.

The road soon led away from inhabited areas. The good news was, there were fewer cars. The bad news was, the road twisted through brush-covered hills. Signs warned of falling rocks, turn-outs offered places to stop and see the ache-inducing blue of the ocean, and Gran drove like both lanes were meant solely for her.

Jacob showed no concern over our numerous near-death experiences. The guy I'd made up would have responded like Alana—listing every traffic violation Gran was committing.

Instead the real guy appeared to share my approach—feelings of mild worry we'd decided to ignore.

He leaned forward again, studying his phone. I tried to peek at whose texts he was ignoring, but the screen showed a map.

"It's coming up soon," he said.

"Thanks, dear. He's helpful," she added to me.

"Mm-hmm." Whether you wanted him to be or not.

Ahead a dirt area contained several parked cars. My family stood against the van. Alana and Mom waved, and Gran pulled in.

"What took you so long?" Dad asked. "We've been waiting. We're twenty minutes behind schedule."

"Oh, hang your schedule. This is vacation. If I want to take my time and enjoy the views, I will. Ooh, banana bread." Gran trotted toward a rickety table with a handwritten sign.

If only I had the courage to say things like that. Being old came with the perk that you could get away with it. Or maybe having a personality like Gran's. How did she ever raise someone like my dad?

"I was impressed by the schedule," Jacob said. "It's very thorough. I especially like the color-coding."

I snorted and tried to cover it with a fake cough.

"You okay?" Alana asked, eying the convertible like it was responsible for Gran's bad driving and might attack her even without Gran behind the wheel.

"Sure. It was an adventure."

A slightly terrifying one, but I wasn't throwing Gran under the bus.

Gran returned with two small foil pans wrapped in plastic, full of golden brown bread. She tucked one into her bag. "Now we're ready."

Mom eyed the food with the suspicion I reserved for schedules. "Are you sure that's safe?"

Gran popped a piece of bread into her mouth before offering a chunk to me. I gladly accepted. It was sweet and moist, with a crunchy crust but soft in the middle.

"Do you think they have a food permit?" Mom's gaze drifted to the table.

"All right, people, let's move." My dad sounded more like a drill sergeant than a doctor.

The beginning of the path was dirt, heading through patches of green grass, with the blue sea in the distance. But it soon grew rocky, and for once I was glad the schedule had told us what to wear and I'd listened to its blue-box command and put on closed-toed shoes.

Another hand-painted sign sat on the ground. This one held a warning. Mom stopped in front of it as the rest of us kept going.

"Mom, it's okay," Alana said. "We'll be careful."

"Of course we will," Gran said. "More banana bread, anyone?" She broke off pieces and handed them to Jacob and Tyler.

"Thanks, Gran. It's delicious."

I narrowed my eyes at Jacob. He responded by taking my hand to help me over an uneven pile of rocks. I wanted to pull away. But Alana and Neal were holding hands, and Dad was helping Gran, and if I refused, it would remind them of the old Kenzie, charging into danger alone. Not appreciating the sweet gesture of a boyfriend I'd missed for months.

"Thanks," I said. "Whatever would I do without you?"

"Good thing you don't have to find out." His sincere expression with those impossibly blue eyes nearly made me blush. Nearly.

We skidded down another patch of loose rocks. Jacob's grip was steady. I would have been fine without him—I'd been hiking plenty of times on my own—but his hand was comforting.

Interestingly shaped rock formations dotted the landscape. I knew they were volcanic, but the terrain resembled an alien planet. The sprawling vista stretched to the water in the distance, where waves hit rocks with a muted roar. My gaze kept snagging on angles that would make good photographs, with rocks framing the sea. I paused to admire one view, and Jacob's hand kept me from tripping.

Nope, no lingering.

"For someone who doesn't have much free time, you sure are good at this," I said. "You never mentioned you liked hiking."

"Neither did you."

"I guess there are lots of things we haven't talked about."

Alana and Neal paused beside us.

"It's good you two have this week to get to know each other better," Alana said. "Long distance is fine, but there's no substitute for time together in person."

"We can't reveal all our secrets, though," Jacob said. "It's good to keep some mystery."

"I like mysteries." I met his gaze. "I enjoy the challenge of solving them."

"I look forward to seeing you try."

We smiled, but our jaws were set in a challenge that only the two of us knew existed. Sparks fizzed inside me, and this time, I was the one to move first.

We reached a flatter area, still rocky, forming a shelf above the sea.

My mom and Neal, in a bucket hat to shield his fair-skinned face, stopped many yards away.

A small spurt shot up from the rock, spreading foamy water across the stone around the hole and leaving a fine, white mist in the air. The water drained down the hole, and another smaller blast surged upward.

And then there it was. A huge geyser of water erupted from the rock, a pillar of white. Rainbows gleamed in the mist. The sound of bursting water filled the air. After the water came back to earth, tiny waterfalls dripped on the rock cliff near the hole.

It was magical. So powerful, an explosion of water from solid rock, sudden and grand. I knew the science of it, but that didn't make it any less impressive.

A gust of wind blew a sheet of mist toward us, leaving me damp. My hair was surely growing wild. Good thing I didn't care what Jacob thought.

The blowhole repeated every few minutes, some spurts small but some enormous, accompanied by a booming that vibrated my feet. Waves continued to pound the rocks beyond.

A shirtless guy was making his way right up to the blowhole.

The next eruption totally obscured him until he emerged, drenched and laughing.

My mom frowned. "They really should have a rail, since some people can't control themselves."

Yes, putting up fences was a great way to enhance the natural beauty of a place.

"This is a lawsuit waiting to happen," Dad said.

"Still, I suppose it is rather grand," Mom conceded. "From a distance."

Tuning out my parents, I stepped closer to the blowhole. Jacob caught my hand.

"Now, now, Kenzie. Control yourself." He said it quietly enough for only me to hear, with an undertone of sarcasm. And yet the words were ones I'd heard many times, usually in my mom's voice. "What would your family think?"

He was right. They'd think I was regressing, that wandering up to the exploding water hole of death was something I would have done a year ago but that they thought I'd grown out of. Fine. I could watch from a distance, no lawsuits imminent.

I did not intend to thank him for stopping me. Surely he wasn't doing it to be helpful. Just to taunt me.

I started to circle the hole, keeping far enough away to satisfy Mom, but searching for new angles. Would the best photo show the water spout against rock? Or from down low with the ocean and sky as background? Maybe up above, looking down, to capture the scale? A slow-motion video would be amazing.

I wanted to capture it at its full height, with that blooming cloud of water filling the air. Close enough to show the true volume of water, to elicit awe. To make people marvel at the wonders of the world.

But since I didn't do that anymore, those questions didn't matter.

"How does it work, anyway?" Tyler asked. "Is there a giant—"

There were many ways he could have ended that question, and at least two-thirds of them were inappropriate, so I said, "The ocean wears away the rock beneath, usually in a sea cave, until it forms a shelf. Then, when there's a hole at the top of the cave, when the waves come in, the water is forced upward through the hole. It's best at high tide, and the height of the eruption depends on the wave. They're most common in lava rock."

"You're such a nerd," Tyler said.

Everyone in our family was a nerd. I had just directed my nerd-dom in a different direction, one that my family didn't appreciate as worthy of effort.

"Very impressive, Kenz," said Jacob.

I squinted at him, not sure if he was mocking or trying to compliment me. "It's basic science. Not that complicated."

"Where's Gran?" Alana asked.

We looked around. She had wandered closer, near to where the brave/stupid/lawsuit-pending guy had gotten soaked.

"Mother, please come back," my dad called.

A small wave surged through the hole. She stopped to watch.

"I'll help her," said Jacob.

He picked his way along the wet rock, confident and sure-footed.

"Watch out for the hole," I called.

He flashed a smile over his shoulder that acknowledged he'd heard the sarcasm in my voice. The grin nearly knocked me over, as sure as the blowhole would.

"Your boyfriend is so brave," Tyler said. "But then, he'd have to be to date you."

"You can comment when you're actually dating someone."

The irony of my response was not lost on me.

Jacob neared Gran and called to her. She was digging in her bag and turned to face him.

"Oh no." Her loaf of bread fell out of her bag and tumbled across the rock, and the retreating surge of water carried it away.

The blowhole erupted. Spray coated them. And at the top of the eruption, a small, dark object soared, riding on the water.

The hole had vomited up Gran's banana bread.

It sailed through the air and landed several feet away in a puddle of seawater.

Gran laughed, and I did, too.

"I got it." Jacob hurried to grab it, and they rejoined us, Gran clutching his arm.

He was not cute when he did that, his dimples on full display, gamely helping the grandmother of a girl he didn't know stage a rescue mission for baked goods, not minding getting soaking wet. He was an impostor. I couldn't let myself forget that. An impostor whose secrets I would uncover.

An impostor whose toned chest looked way too good in that wet shirt.

Gran unwrapped the adventurous loaf. "Thank heaven for

plastic wrap. It's fine." She popped a piece into her mouth and gave one to Jacob.

Jacob opened his arms to me. "Do I get a hug for being so heroic? I rescued not only your grandmother but the banana bread, too."

He was soaking wet, so I had a good excuse to shove him away to hide the fact that I wanted to ogle him. "I only hug dry heroes."

He grinned. "Take a picture of me?" he asked. "For my family. You can text it to me."

"Or you could give me your phone, and then you'd have it." And I could steal a peek at those text messages.

"Nah, the camera on yours is much better." He smirked, totally seeing right through me.

Gritting my teeth, I reluctantly pulled out my phone. It wasn't like I hadn't taken any pictures in the last several months. With Lucia, at the holidays. This wasn't a total backslide into the ways of old Kenzie. I could do this.

He positioned himself with the blowhole in the background.

"Move to your left," I said. "No, *your* left. Yeah, there."

I waited for the right moment, when the water was erupting and the spray caught the light in a sparkling rainbow. I snapped a couple of pictures, which I couldn't text him since I didn't have his number. Then I tried not to admire the image on my screen, either the gorgeous scenery and impressive blowhole—the way I'd caught the light and the colors—or the cute guy.

"I can take one of the two of you." Alana reached for my phone.

Jacob extended his arm, and I clenched my jaw as I joined

him and let him put his arm around me. His hand twitched against my ribs.

"Try to look happy," he said close to my ear.

Did he briefly press his nose to my hair, or was I imagining it? I smiled for the camera.

"You're imagining pushing me down the hole, aren't you?" he asked.

"Oh, of course not. This is my happy, innocent smile." I kept it in place and slid my arm around his waist. He was damp but warm and left my clothes slightly wet.

As Alana handed my phone back, she said, "Remember when you were little and you used to take all those pictures?"

"You mentioned the photography." Jacob focused on me. "Tell me more. What do you like taking pictures of? Besides my handsome face."

"Oh, trust me, there's nothing worth shooting quite like your face." I paused. "With the camera, you know. Photographer humor."

He snorted. "Really, though, tell me about it."

I shrugged, aware of my family listening. I didn't want them to know how tense it made me to hear them talk about my passion as if it had been a passing childhood whim, rather than a career I desperately wanted to pursue, even if I told myself I was fine without it.

Emotions threatened to seep in, ones I had tried to bury, twisting my stomach and squeezing my chest. The crushing disappointment of not winning and all that had meant for my future. But also my parents' reaction. A brief *Sorry* leading directly into *Didn't we tell you it was hard?* They'd seemed relieved, like they were glad I'd learned a valuable lesson, and that had hurt more than losing, the knowledge that my family didn't even try to see how much photography and the contest meant to me.

"I don't know, landscapes, animals. Nature. Stuff like that." I tried to sound unbothered, like months of pain weren't threatening to burst out of me like water out of that blowhole.

"She used to run off with her camera, and we wouldn't see her for hours," Mom said.

Tyler snorted. "Yeah, it took forever to go anywhere because she'd stop every five feet."

"Or we couldn't find her, and she'd be hiding under a bush waiting for a bird, or feeding the squirrels while lying in wait, or wandering off because she saw a pretty tree," Alana added.

"It was cute," my dad said. "You were an adorable kid."

An invisible fist squeezed my throat. My lifelong ambition was *cute* to them.

I swallowed hard and kept a pleasant smile.

"You were late for school once, weren't you?" Tyler asked. "Picture day. When you finally arrived, you were covered in dirt."

I'd seen a deer and had lost track of time stalking it. And I'd been late more than once, but no one needed to know about the day with the fascinating funnel cloud I'd had to photograph and then research, or the other time when an adorable family of ducks had made me miss a Spanish quiz.

"Are you using that camera I gave you?" Gran asked. "Did you bring it this week?"

That question was the worst, a stab through the heart. My Nikon from her, a few years ago, had been my favorite gift ever. Above the life-sized stuffed dolphin and my first personal bike, rather than a hand-me-down from Alana, with a sparkly unicorn horn on the handlebars and a matching helmet.

"I've been so busy, I don't get to use it as much these days. School and everything." I couldn't meet her eyes, didn't want to see her disappointment. "It took up half my suitcase, so I had to leave it at home."

In the spot where it had been for eight months, out of sight but constantly in my mind, no matter how hard I tried to ignore its siren call. Putting it away had been like ripping out part of my heart, and numbing myself was the only way to move on.

I swallowed hard and stared at the blowhole, watching another eruption.

"Time to go," Dad called.

Of course it was. No time to simply sit and marvel at the wonders of nature or soak in the magic of this place.

"All hail the spreadsheet overlords," I muttered, and Jacob snorted.

During the last eight months, I would have kept the comment to myself, but their dismissal of my interests had stirred up my snarky side.

My clothes and hair were damp from the mist as we climbed up. Jacob offered me a hand on an area of loose stones, and when his gaze met mine, his eyes were sharp, like he was seeing too much.

I met the look defiantly, chin raised, daring him to speak.

His face softened, and his eyes became gentler. "All right, Kenz?"

I didn't know how to answer. Did he mean with the climb? Or with the personal attack my family had unknowingly launched?

When I didn't reply, the sympathy I might have imagined on his face faded. "How'd the picture turn out? You can take as many of me as you want this week. I'm very photogenic, and I know you want to shoot me."

"You have no idea," I said.

Then I yanked my hand free and finished on my own.

CHAPTER SIX

The schedule commanded us to spend the afternoon at the beach. Because nothing was more relaxing than a piece of paper requiring you to enjoy the sun and the sea. Still, I was happy to spend all week there, so an entire afternoon dedicated to enforced beach fun was fine with me.

The paper was highlighted in pink, for sunscreen required— I assumed to match the color our faces would be if we ignored the wisdom of the all-knowing spreadsheet.

"That's safe sunscreen, right?" I asked Alana as we got ready in our room.

"What?"

"You're supposed to use the kind that won't hurt the reefs."

"It is. I bought it here."

"Okay, good."

"That's very responsible of you."

She didn't have to sound so surprised. I might frequently lose my keys, or leave my completed homework on my desk at home, or forget to shut off the oven—one fire alarm, and you never live it down. But one thing my family had never bothered to notice was, when it came to the things I cared about, I knew what I was doing.

And the outdoors was one thing I cared about. Plus, since I was the only person in this family not allergic to fresh air and nature, I knew way more about it than anyone else.

She slathered the thick sunscreen onto her face. "You and Jacob seem awkward. It must be weird to be together in person after being used to long distance."

If we'd been the kind of sisters who were close, I might have confessed right then. Gotten her advice. Enlisted her help in figuring out who Jacob was. But we were not those people, and she would immediately tell everyone and judge me and undo my last several months of effort.

"It's definitely weird," I said.

When we joined the others, you'd have thought they were going on a monthlong expedition instead of taking a five-minute walk across the resort grounds.

Mom and Alana wore giant straw hats, with baseball caps for Tyler and Dad. Neal had a long-sleeved swim shirt to block UV rays, and his face was paler than usual when coated with a thick layer of sunscreen. Not that I could see much of his face beneath a wide-brim bucket hat. I barely kept myself from asking if he was part vampire.

They carried several large bags stuffed with who knew what, a stack of beach towels, and reusable water bottles—those had been my requirement. Gran held a bulging grocery bag, but I couldn't see its contents.

Jacob was the only one like me, carrying nothing more than a small backpack. He wore a gray T-shirt with the Ohio State University logo.

"Do I have to come?" Tyler asked.

I spun to stare at him. What kind of person had no interest in a Hawaiian beach?

"Yes, Tyler," my mom said. "This is family time."

Her voice held a sigh but none of the exasperation it would have if I'd been the one asking.

He groaned. "But there's so much sun. And sand."

I shoved his arm. "That's the point."

"Your schoolwork is important," Mom said. "But if you had worked ahead, like we told you to, you wouldn't have to worry this week."

"I'm not worried. I just like it."

Her face softened, but she said, "The point is to spend time together as a family."

He grunted and grabbed a towel.

My brother was weird.

"Nice shirt," he said to Jacob. "You must really like your school."

"I do. Lots of Buckeye spirit."

"Oh yeah?" Tyler asked. "What's your favorite part? Football is big there, right?"

"Yeah, plus the band with the whole dotting the *i* thing. The campus also has several museums, and an arboretum, plus an amazing medical center."

I huffed. Google had told me those exact details when I'd searched for a place for my imaginary boyfriend to attend. Jacob wasn't as clever as he thought he was.

The others were leaving, and as we followed, an idea struck.

This would be the perfect chance to do some digging. Search for Jacob's wallet, see if I could find his driver's license, an address. An Ohio State ID that I was certain he didn't have. Maybe check his phone, though I probably couldn't unlock it.

Ooh. Was he a heavy sleeper? If he had face or fingerprint lock, I might be able to manage that in the middle of the night, ninja style.

I slid the sunglasses from my head and hid them in a pocket of my swimsuit cover-up, then waited until we were getting off the elevator on the ground floor.

"I forgot my sunglasses," I said. "I'll run to the room real fast. You guys go on. I'll meet you."

"Oh, Kenzie." My mom sighed the words in her You Have Greatly Let Me Down tone. As if me having to take five minutes and go upstairs was more inconvenient than Tyler trying to avoid a family afternoon at the beach altogether.

Number of days since last disappointment? Scratch out the number, back to zero.

But it was worth it if I found answers.

"Didn't you just have them?" asked Alana in a tone that frighteningly mimicked Mom's.

"We can wait," Dad said.

"No, don't worry about it. The beach is right there. I'll find you. Gran's suit stands out."

Today it was lemon yellow and matched her green-and-yellow-swirl glasses frames.

I reentered the elevator and pushed the button. As the doors started to close, someone slipped inside.

Jacob.

I swallowed a growl.

"I couldn't let you go alone," he said.

"That's so kind of you. Thought I might get lost?"

"Thought you might forget which room was yours and, I don't know, possibly end up in the wrong one." He stared at me and twitched his eyebrows.

How did he do that?

"What did you say you forgot again?" he asked.

"My sunglasses."

"Something wrong with the ones you had on your head?"

"I don't know what you're talking about."

I brushed past him out the elevator and checked my pockets for my room key card. Nothing except the incriminating sunglasses. No. I did not lose my key on the first day. I dug through my mini backpack. Phone. Water. Sunscreen.

"Need a hand?"

"No."

Wait. I'd put it in the tiny interior zippered pouch. There. I exhaled, yanked the card out, and opened the door. That would have been ironic, pretending to forget one thing and losing something more important.

Jacob followed me all the way to the hallway leading to the bedrooms and waited while I went into mine. He was good, I'd give him that.

And we were alone. The perfect time to interrogate him and force him to answer my questions. Except there was a chance someone else might return. I could play along for a few more minutes before I pounced.

I pretended to rummage around in my nightstand, then

pulled the sunglasses from my pocket and rejoined him, waved them in his face. "I'm ready now."

"Great. Glad you got everything you came back for," he said.

We stood in the hall, our gazes locked. His held amusement. I was the first to move and march past him.

The route to the beach meandered through the grounds, along the enormous, sprawling pool, where people lounged in chairs. Multiple waterfalls and fountains meant I could close my eyes and imagine I was in a jungle. Palm trees offered patches of respite from the bright sun, and so many flowers bloomed.

Now I had a new goal. I couldn't snoop through his things, but I could demand answers.

Spotting the perfect place, I dragged him down a path leading to a nook behind a waterfall. The sound of the water would muffle our words, like in a spy movie. The wall of water blurred everything outside, leaving our rocky cave a private pocket.

"Okay, Lying McLiarface. Time to talk."

His eyes flickered, and I could tell he was considering another snarky brush-off.

"I want answers. Now."

He studied me, and his face went serious in the blue light filtering in through the waterfall. I tried not to notice how its vivid shade matched his eyes.

"Fine," he said. "I can't tell you all the details—"

I crossed my arms. "Can't or won't?"

"Do you want *any* of them?"

"Yes. Sorry."

Wait. Why was I the one apologizing? I scowled.

He leaned against the wall. "I told you my name is Jacob Miller. I go by Jake."

"Who is this mutual friend you mentioned?"

"I still can't tell you that."

"What exactly *can* you do? It's not too late for me to turn you in."

"Yes it is, because you've already played along. And the truth seems to be something you're afraid of."

My pulse spiked, sending blood roaring in my ears. "Afraid? How dare—"

He stared at me, chin raised. I hated that he was right, about more than I wanted to admit. And that he saw me as a liar. I didn't like lying, but he knew nothing about my life, for real, and why lying had been necessary. Besides, he was one to talk.

If I kept pushing, he would stop talking altogether. Could easily shove me into the pool and escape, and I would have zero answers. Time to try a new angle.

"Where are you from? And don't say Ohio." I gestured to his shirt. "You're way too tan for that."

He smirked. "Good to know you've been checking out my tan."

Heat rushed to my face. "I am going to drown you."

"You're rather prone to violent tendencies."

"You have no idea. I have a very active imagination."

His dimples formed. "What have you imagined about me?"

Definitely not touching his hair. Or those dimples. Or that this dark nook was a perfect spot for kissing. "Just the violence."

He laughed, a rich, unrestrained sound. "If you say so."

A loud splash sounded outside, followed by children playing. Their carefree, sunny world seemed far removed from this damp cave, scented with chlorine, dark and private.

"All that stuff you told my family about wanting to be an optometrist? You totally made that up, didn't you?"

"Not *all* of it."

It was my turn to raise my eyebrows.

"My dad did have LASIK. And I did think it sounded cool, until I learned they didn't use lightsabers, like I imagined."

I snorted. "And the podiatry?"

"My grandmother really took me. And that model of a foot . . . I may have knocked it over and scattered the pieces all over the lobby. Got home and found a toe bone in my pocket, so major apologies to whoever tried to put that sucker back together."

It sounded so much like something I would do that my laugh escaped before I could force myself to scowl again.

"You're taking advantage of my family."

"I'm not freeloading. Your parents and I settled on an amount, less than I would have paid if I'd had to rent a room myself. Hotels and Airbnbs aren't cheap here. Not to mention hiring Ubers since I'm too young to rent a car. Plus, it's making your family happy. They love me."

They loved the fake version of him, the one telling them everything they wanted to hear. I didn't know which annoyed me more, that he was lying, or that he was better at it than I was.

"You're lying to them," I said.

"So are you. For a lot longer and about more things than I am. I don't like lying. *I* don't make a habit of it."

My jaw tightened.

"But I have a good reason for being here, and I need this," he said. "Can we agree to be terrible people for a week? Help each other? Enjoy Hawaii, go our separate ways, and then you can break up with me and create all the future fictional boyfriends you want. Your family will never have to know."

"The breakup *had* been my plan anyway . . ."

"See? It will be fine."

"How do I know you aren't up to anything . . . dastardly?"

"I promise it's nothing illegal, immoral, dastardly, reprehensible, or otherwise nefarious."

"You know lots of big words. Are you in college?"

He studied me. Chewed his lip. Started to talk, then stopped, before saying, "It will be safer not to get personal. So in your mind, I'm exactly the Jacob Miller you made up. For all you know, I do live in Ohio and I do want to work in healthcare."

I refused to admit that I was more than a little curious about who Jake was. He had a good point. "How did you learn all those details, anyway?"

"That's part of what I can't tell you."

I rolled my eyes. "Convenient."

"Why'd you make up a boyfriend, anyway? Couldn't get a real one?"

"I could, and I have." If he wasn't going to explain himself, I certainly didn't have to defend my choices. I wasn't offering him any more fuel for his mocking.

"If you say so."

I grunted. "Whatever. We'll do this. But we need a plan for when they ask questions."

"I thought it was going rather well so far."

"What about when they get more personal or want details?"

"Like, we should have a code sign? You can tell me when I'm free to make something up or when I should let you take over because you told them a lie about that topic?"

I narrowed my eyes. "This isn't a game."

"I didn't say it was. I told you, I hate lying. But I'll put up with it if it gets me what I want."

"Oh, great, thanks for putting up with me." I glared at him, then sighed.

"There," he said. "That's perfect."

"What is?"

"The way you scrunch your nose." He tapped it, and I swatted his hand. "It's adorable. That will be our sign. If you do that, it means I have a green light to do my own thing."

"Don't mess it up. No ridiculous lies. And try to stay in character as Jacob."

"I can do that."

"The way you rushed toward a blowhole today minutes after telling me to be careful?"

"I was saving your grandmother. And her magical flying banana bread."

I couldn't help but snort at the memory of the snack sailing through the air in the arms of a blowhole eruption, and we both laughed. I suspected we were the only ones who had found that hilarious.

His laugh faded to a smile. "You *are* going to have to pretend to like me. You can still plot my painful death. Just do it while you're holding my hand and making heart eyes at me."

My teeth ground together. Then I schooled my face into a happy expression, reached out, and slipped my fingers through his. I fought a shiver, once more ignoring the perfect fit.

In a sweet voice, I said, "Have I told you yet how glad I am that you're here this week, babe?"

His eyes twinkled. "I don't think Jacob is a *babe* type of guy. Too sentimental. Stick with my name."

"Oh, I'll stick you with something." I kept the *heart eyes* and squeezed his hand, hard.

He threw his head back and laughed again. "That look right there. Perfect."

I yanked my hand away. "We need some ground rules. Holding hands is fine. You can put your arm around me if you have to. But no kissing."

"You don't like kissing? Or you've never done it?"

"I've done it, and I like it. But not with you."

"You might like it with me. You've never tried it."

His gaze dipped to my lips briefly, raising the temperature of our little cave, before he smirked. If he'd been a stranger who wasn't messing with me, I definitely would have thought he was worth kissing, which only made me want to shove him into the pool.

I folded my arms. "Your loss, not mine, I'm sure."

"All right," he said. "No kissing. Simple displays of affection only, and you'll throat punch me if I try anything more." He reached out again, and I stared at his extended hand. "We should go. We've been gone too long, and your family might suspect we're up to something. Like kissing."

"Heaven forbid," I said dryly.

"You've made that abundantly clear."

I strode out without taking his hand, but as we headed down the path toward the beach, I didn't fight it when he tried again.

I minded less than I should have. His hand was firm and strong. I hadn't held hands with a guy in months. I'd casually dated guys before the reinvention of Kenzie. That had been part of what had convinced my parents I wasn't serious—no relationship had lasted more than a couple of dates, and they'd never approved of the guys, for various reasons. Like a teenager was supposed to find lasting commitment rather than hanging out and having fun.

My talk with Jacob—Jake—had left me with more questions. He did seem like a decent guy. He was funny and quick, which I appreciated. He got my humor. Even though I shouldn't have, I believed him when he said he wasn't up to anything bad.

But what did he want? And how was he here? It was going to drive me crazy until I figured it out.

Which I would, no matter how many promises I made to play along. I'd needed a few answers from him today. But I would be getting more of them soon.

CHAPTER SEVEN

The plumeria trees and hibiscus plants were in full bloom now, illuminated by bright sun. I slowed as we passed a bush whose red flowers glowed like jewels. That would have been a great picture.

A tug on my arm reminded me that I held Jake's hand, and he stopped beside me.

"Hibiscus," he said. "In the mallow family. They attract bees and butterflies."

I stared at him.

"Jacob Miller is a man of many talents," he said. "I prefer the birds of paradise. More unique."

He led me past a nearby bush of blue-and-orange flowers I'd always loved, sharp and pointy and resembling a bird with orange feathers atop its head. I'd spotted them in a nursery once and had spent two hours taking pictures, to the employees' amusement. Pretty sure I missed a dentist appointment that afternoon . . .

"I like them, too," I said quietly, avoiding his suddenly serious gaze on me.

He couldn't have known that. This wasn't him trying to

put on a show or impress me. Was this a real thing we had in common?

No. It didn't matter. One week of faking a relationship, a couple more weeks of lying to my family, a breakup, and we were done. He was right—it was safer if he was Fake Jacob Miller, no one else.

We continued to the beach, where my family was easy to find under rented umbrellas. Neal and Alana lounged on chairs under one, still in shirts and hats. Neal was reading his fantasy novel, while Alana held a biography of Eleanor Roosevelt.

Tyler lounged near Gran, who lay in the sun eating a bag of red licorice sticks. Mom and Dad shared another umbrella, and she was scanning her surroundings. When she saw us, she relaxed into her chair. Had she seriously been worried I'd get lost or mugged?

Apparently satisfied knowing we were safe, she reached into her bag and took out the giant, boring optometry book.

"'Glaucoma,'" Jake read from the cover. "That looks interesting."

Mom's eyes lit up. "It is. I'd be happy to discuss it with you later."

"Can't wait," Jake said, and I hid an eye-roll. He grabbed two chairs and rejoined me. "Sun or shade?"

Ever the attentive boyfriend.

"Sun. Thanks for asking."

"I just want to make you happy." He winked, then slid the sunglasses from the top of his head over his eyes.

"Jacob, those sunglasses look flimsy," my dad said. "Are you sure they offer full UV protection?"

"Of course, Dr. Reed. I wouldn't wear anything that didn't."

"Good, good."

Jake settled in his chair and lowered his glasses enough to wink at me again over the top.

Jacob. Not Jake. I couldn't let myself get familiar or casual or whatever. He was the guy I'd made up, like he'd said.

But how did he know to be that guy?

When he pulled his shirt off, my mouth went dry and my eyes refused to comply when I tried to drag them away. Further proof the boy did not know it was winter in Ohio. His toned chest was as tanned as his arms and legs. Surely there was a biological explanation for that. He could be naturally tan, no matter that he wouldn't have been outdoors in the sun for the last six months. Surely it wouldn't make everyone suspicious.

I felt self-conscious removing my cover-up, which was ridiculous. I didn't care if Jake found me attractive. I yanked it off to reveal my halter top and high-waisted bottoms, and plopped down with a huff.

I couldn't see his eyes behind his sunglasses, but Jake paused, his face pointed my way, before he shook his head and shifted.

The sand was hot on my feet now, soft, and whitecaps flecked the water. A breeze blew a fine layer of sand into my skin.

"You were gone for a while." Tyler raised his eyebrows at us.

"Couldn't find my sunglasses. And we were catching up on some things."

"I'm sure you were. I bet you had lots to *talk* about."

Was it warm out here? Stupid tropical sun. Now they thought we'd been making out. I refused to look at Jake and focused on the ocean instead.

The regular crashing of the waves, the warm sun, and the

wind lulled me. I closed my eyes, my muscles relaxing, peace enveloping my mind.

"Want to play catch?" Jake's voice jerked me out of my ocean trance.

I peered at him, but he was talking to my brother and holding a Nerf football.

Tyler shrugged and stood. They moved to the shallow water and tossed the ball back and forth. Thankful for my sunglasses to hide the direction of my gaze, I allowed myself a moment to admire Jake. Just because he was a dodgy liar didn't mean I couldn't enjoy the view.

When I forced myself to turn away, I spotted his backpack, sitting there in the sand next to his chair. And he and Tyler had moved to near the water, which meant he might have left his phone here instead of in his pocket, in case he got wet.

I scooted my chair a few inches closer. Peeked to make sure he was distracted.

My heart raced as I eased the zipper open.

Inside I found headphones, sunscreen, his key card. No wallet, unfortunately.

There. An interior pocket held his phone.

After checking again to ensure he wasn't looking my way, I eased the phone out. Notifications said he had six missed calls from Dad and twelve unread texts from Mom. The most recent said, *Where are you? Call us now.*

What was that about? Did his parents not know he was here? Were we harboring a runaway or a fugitive? I thought he was over eighteen, so we couldn't be charged with kidnapping.

Gran settled beside me in the chair Jake had left. I jumped and shoved the phone back into his bag, remembering to return it to the pocket, then grabbed his sunscreen like it was no big deal.

"Jacob's a nice boy," Gran said. "I'm glad he and Tyler are getting along."

Yeah. Jake was easy to like. Which made this all so much more complicated. I slathered sunscreen on my arms even though I didn't need more, before putting it back and zipping up Jake's backpack.

Gran couldn't have been behind this, could she? She'd instantly liked him. But we didn't see her often since she'd moved to a retirement community in La Jolla after my grandpa had passed away. She wouldn't have had a way to know I'd lied. Would she?

I was a terrible spy.

A gust of wind blew over me, tugging at my hair and flinging sand across my bare skin.

"Oh," said Neal.

A piece of fabric had sailed into him from somewhere down the beach. He tugged it off himself and held it up.

It was one of those large cover-up shirts with a drawing of a person—but not the usual curvy, bikini-clad woman. This one had a super-buff flexing dude, wearing a man-thong covered in flames, beneath six-pack abs that could have grated cheese if they'd been real.

And Neal was holding it against his chest so it perfectly matched up with his body.

I couldn't contain a sniff of laughter. Gran laughed, too.

Alana's face went red—not from the sun—and she yanked it down.

Mom frowned. "Who does that belong to? Why can't people hold on to their things?"

Um, maybe because of a thing called trade winds.

An old man hurried up, short and scrawny, who had surely never resembled the dude on that shirt a day in his life. He retrieved it with an unashamed chuckle, pulled it on, and marched off. I took one glimpse of the backside of his shirt—more flaming thong and buff man-butt—and looked away. I needed eye bleach now.

Still chuckling, Gran lay down in the sun.

I was ready to try the water. I trudged through hot, dry sand until my feet sighed in relief at the squishy wet stuff. Jake joined me, waves surging around our ankles.

A row of surfboards sat in the sand nearby. People were forming a circle around them.

"I've always wanted to try that," I said.

"Let's do it."

"Really? Can we join?"

Jake jogged toward the instructor, a guy in his twenties with light brown skin, wearing a baseball cap and board shorts. "Hey, man, is this open to anyone?"

"Sure, I have plenty of boards."

"See?" Jake said as he rejoined me.

I stared at the boards.

"Scared?" Jake asked, and I couldn't tell if he was curious or taunting.

A little, but not for the reason he likely meant.

"You know you want to," he said.

Those surfboards did look fun . . . And having someone encourage my curiosity and spontaneity was a nice change.

I returned to where the others mostly huddled under umbrellas. "Can we try a surfing lesson? Jacob was saying he's always wanted to learn."

"That's right." He gave no indication that my lie annoyed him. "It looks so exciting, but there's no opportunity in Ohio. The waves are low enough here that it's safe for beginners."

Considering he'd rushed to help Gran next to a giant death geyser, I doubted *safe* was a general concern of his, but my parents' faces softened.

"I wouldn't mind trying," Alana said.

"I don't know," Mom said.

"The waves are low. And kids are out there." My sister gestured to the group, which included a family with two children.

Thank you, Alana. Letting her make my case would definitely increase the odds of our parents saying yes.

"How long will it take?" my dad asked.

"There's plenty of time on the schedule, Dad," said my sister. "Anyone else want to come?"

"Sounds like too much work." Tyler turned to Jake. "You're into surfing?"

Jake shrugged. "I thought I should try it."

Were football and surfing too much? Was Tyler getting suspicious?

Neal declined, and Gran was snoozing now, so Jake, Alana, and I joined the group.

The instructor had boards lined up in the damp sand just

beyond where the waves were breaking. He showed us how to lie on our stomachs and pretend to paddle with our arms. Then we practiced jumping to our feet over and over, with him coming around to correct the placement of our feet, the bend of our knees.

Jacob did it perfectly. I narrowed my eyes at him. One shoulder twitched upward as his mouth twisted into a half smile.

He had totally done this before.

I didn't know whether I wanted to laugh or shove him over. Not that I could have, with his perfect balance.

Once the instructor was satisfied with our sand-surfing abilities, he had us take the boards into the water.

The first wave that crashed up my legs was cool and shocking, but once I was wet, the water felt great. I pushed the board in front of me through the shallow water, then paused to watch the waves as they rocked my body and tried to tug the board away.

The way they slowly built and then crashed down, curling perfectly over themselves, was fascinating. I'd always loved photographs taken from inside a wave, where the photographer was inside the curve, water on one side and the beginning of the foam on the other, often with sunlight glinting through water and a view out the open side, of the sun or a beach.

Was this how they did it? Lie on a board with a waterproof camera, waiting for waves to build? It would need a fast shutter speed, with how quickly the waves broke. Probably a small aperture to get a small depth of field. And lots of attempts to get the timing right. Maybe someone to hold you in place?

"Kenzie?"

Alana's voice calling.

Right. I wasn't here to take pictures. The rest of the surf students were deeper, except Jake, who'd been waiting as I zoned out. His expression and his shoulders were relaxed.

Embarrassed, I joined him.

"What were you thinking about?" He stared at me with no mocking, only curiosity.

Don't mind me, just imagining more impossible things.

"Just admiring the waves."

I lay on the board and paddled as the teacher had shown us. Up and down, over the swells, in a rhythmic motion. The warm sun and cool water were intoxicating. We stopped beyond where the waves were breaking, and bobbed gently. I could float there all day, lie back and stare at the clouds, the water, the mountains. But I did want to try actual surfing.

The instructor told us how to watch the swells building and when to paddle to stay in front of one.

"Who wants to go first?"

I eyed Jake, who was staring at the horizon. Of course he didn't volunteer. He probably knew exactly what he was doing but was trying not to show it in front of my sister, who wouldn't expect a science nerd from Ohio to be an expert on a surfboard.

"I'll go."

I didn't know why I said it. I should have been challenging him, not bailing him out, even if we were kind of on the same team now. I ignored the brilliance of Jake's admiring smile as the instructor moved closer, giving me final directions.

I missed the first wave, barely, having not paddled fast enough to get in front of it. The second time, the instructor gave me a shove, and then the water was carrying me forward.

I tried to remember the stance and jumped to my feet. I stayed up for a few seconds before the board shifted and I toppled over backward into the water. The strap around my ankle kept the board from floating away. I came up sputtering but thrilled. It hadn't lasted long, but I had surfed!

I rejoined the others as another guy went.

Jake gave me a high five. "Great job for your first time."

His smile was happy and proud, and the compliment sounded genuine. Also like something someone would say if they knew how to surf.

"Your turn," I told Alana.

She went next, wobbling when she stood up and immediately crashing. I was slightly pleased that I had done better, before deciding that was petty.

It was also the old me, who'd made everything into a contest. My family never understood me wanting to ride my bike faster or swing higher or chug milk faster than my siblings. They believed your most important competitor was yourself—do your best, improve on your personal effort, don't worry about others. But I'd always thought competition added to the fun. I'd tried to hide that part of me along with so many other things.

Which ended up being a good thing. It was exhausting being competitive in a family where you were always being compared, even if no one admitted it, and inevitably falling short.

While Alana was close to shore, I paddled closer to Jake, who was chilling on his board like he lived there. "You've done this before, haven't you?"

"No idea what you mean."

"Oh, I can't wait. You're either going to be the star pupil and have to pretend it's beginner's luck, or you're going to fall on purpose."

He tucked his hair behind his ears. "You know me so well. Which will it be?"

"Uh-uh. I'm not guessing, because then you'll do the opposite."

He grinned. "Want to make it interesting? I bet you can't last ten full seconds next time."

How could I run from that? I knew better than to make it a flat-out contest, since he obviously knew what he was doing. But that didn't mean I couldn't rise to the challenge.

"Challenge accepted. In return, I bet you can't fall convincingly three times in a row."

"You're on."

Alana rejoined us.

"That was close," I said, to make up for my momentary pettiness of wanting to best her. "You'll get it next time."

She studied me, curious, confused. Likely used to me wanting to win and rubbing it in if I was better at something, especially since she was four years older. "Thanks."

On my next turn, I didn't count the seconds, but I stayed up for a while before losing my balance as the wave died out. I wasn't super steady, but I crouched low and kept my arms out.

When I paddled back out, I raised my eyebrows, and Jake nodded to say, *Well done.*

He failed to catch two waves, like he was trying to outdo me. Each time he repositioned himself, his lips twitched and he purposely avoided looking at me, which was wise, because I would have laughed.

When he finally got the timing right and rode the board toward shore, he balanced so easily, I was half convinced he was going to do tricks, appearing tan and athletic and totally in control. Then his board shot into the air and he sailed backward, and landed with a splash.

I had to bite my lip not to laugh. It was such an intentionally over-the-top crash. He came up grinning, hair plastered to his face.

"You okay?" I called.

"Great." Even from a distance, his dimples were killer.

My insides hummed with electricity. For a moment, I forgot the lies, the faking. There was just his smile and the thrill inside me at the whole situation—Maui and surfing and a cute boy.

"I'd hate for you to hurt yourself," I said as he got closer.

"Because you want to be the one to hurt me?"

Alana was gone, so I said, "I did say you had to fall *convincingly.*"

"Once again, I have no idea what you mean. It's a difficult sport."

"Hmm. Right."

We spent the next hour issuing challenges when Alana wasn't close. She did well, her yoga apparently giving her good balance.

I managed to ride several waves, getting more stable each time. It was fun, working in tandem with nature. Plus the time between runs, relaxing on the board.

After two more equally dramatic falls to satisfy my challenge, Jake stayed upright on the rest of his rides, and added more flair to the last one.

I won bets for a ten-second ride, catching three waves in a row, and riding all the way to shore, but I couldn't manage touching the nose of the board with my hand without crashing. I grudgingly gave him credit for the falls, and he won "most waves caught" and "the longest ride of the whole group."

He was permanently Jake in my head now. It could not be undone. Jacob was bland and serious and responsible. He'd rather stay in and read than go outside. Years of advanced schooling waited in his future, followed by an indoor job. Jake was full of life, confident, sarcastic, bold, funny. At home in the water. Mysterious . . . Oh, bother.

As we paddled toward shore, it was the lightest I'd felt in ages. The physical challenge, the extra bonus of betting, the fresh air and water and sunshine. I wanted the afternoon to last forever.

"You're really good, aren't you?" I asked him quietly.

"Why, thank you."

I flicked water at him. "It was a question, not a compliment."

"Must be natural skill. And a good teacher."

"Right. Beginner's luck, I'm sure." I made sure no one was nearby. "Could you have done more?"

"Wouldn't you like to know?"

He splashed me in return, stood in the shallow water, and winked as he tucked his board under his arm like he'd done it a million times. He shook hands with the instructor and gave the board back, then took the rubber band from his hair and shook his hair out. It was darker when wet, and though full of salt like mine, I wanted to touch it.

I swallowed hard.

"Got to say, Kenz, you did pretty good." Alana came up beside me and bumped me with her elbow, her gaze on him.

She did not mean the surfing.

Yeah. If only.

No. I was not allowed to wish this were real. To admire his smile or his competitive spirit or his hair or his surfing skill. I was definitely not allowed to think he was hot. We might have a truce, but he was keeping major secrets, and I would uncover them. His dimples would not distract me.

As he tied up his wet hair once more, I made myself look away.

CHAPTER EIGHT

It was a miracle. We were dining outdoors. We had dinner reservations at one of the resort restaurants, and though the seating area was partially covered, it had no walls, allowing a tropical breeze to waft through. A nearby waterfall poured into a koi pond, and I picked the seat closest, with a view of the water where I could hear it trickling. Jake sat beside me.

He was wearing shorts and a white button-down with the sleeves rolled up. I'd seen him emerge from his room with the top two buttons undone, but he'd fastened them quickly when he'd seen the other guys in conservative polo shirts.

It was for the best. That triangle of tanned chest would have distracted me all night. A few seconds of it had short-circuited my brain.

The way he'd scanned me, taking in my short sundress and slightly wild hair, tracing my face with his eyes, I was hoping the distraction was mutual. It only seemed fair.

Mom and Alana also wore sundresses, while Gran was in a fancy beaded dress that sparkled, along with red lipstick. She looked fabulous. Her dress wasn't overly low-cut, but it revealed her upper chest, which was nearly as red as her lips, though splotchy.

"Are you okay?" my mom asked. "What happened there?"

"Oh, I forgot sunscreen and fell asleep holding a handful of Twizzlers," Gran said cheerfully.

Once she'd spoken, I saw it—the long skinny outline of four licorice sticks where her skin remained pale, surrounded by sunburn.

I wanted to laugh, but Mom was frowning at Gran's lack of caution, not that Gran cared. She shot me a wink.

"Aren't you overdressed, Mom?" my dad asked her.

"Nonsense. You should always dress for the job you want."

"Nightclub singer?" he asked.

"Wealthy heiress?" Alana offered.

"Fabulous woman on vacation who intends to enjoy it." She brushed past them and parked herself in a seat like a queen. "Enough about my outfit. Let's eat."

"Would they let me eat here if I dressed as Wonder Woman?" I muttered so only Jake could hear. "Because that's totally the job I want."

"The sword might be a problem. Also, don't you think Wonder Woman is aiming high for entry-level superhero work? Maybe start with the Green Lantern, get some experience first?"

"Why so much disrespect for the Lantern? I could totally be Wonder Woman."

"My mistake, sorry." He smiled.

My joke would have earned me rolled eyes from everyone else. But his appreciating my humor and making me laugh in return did not eliminate my suspicion of him.

The waiter greeted us with an aloha. After asking for three

confirmations that her food wouldn't touch anything that had come in contact with creatures from the sea, Mom ordered salad with chicken, mango on the side. I supposed it was better than her asking them to hold the scary tropical fruit altogether.

I opted for the fish of the day—can't go wrong with something that's just been caught—though I was also eying the steak, which Jake ordered.

Dad's attention fixed on the table next to us. "Excuse me, sir? Are you having trouble reading the menu?"

The guy lowered the page from where he'd had it inches from his face, and blinked at Dad.

"I'm an optometrist." Dad was standing and moving toward the other table without waiting for an answer. "I would love to help. Do you wear glasses?"

Dad pulled up a spare chair and sat.

Great. He was going to give the guy an exam right here next to the koi pond. Tyler and I exchanged a grimace and sank in our chairs.

"What do you think it is, Kenzie?" Mom asked. "Myopia? Cataracts? Presbyopia?"

Instead of answering, I finished shoving a bite of fried calamari appetizer into my mouth. I knew those words. In theory. But I'd been watching the way the ripples from the waterfall made the water lilies dance on the surface. And debating about what the staff would do if someone climbed into the pond for a better photo angle.

Theoretically, of course.

"Kenzie is always saying it's dangerous to make assumptions without getting all the information," Jake said.

Mom smiled at him, then at me. "You're right. It is. Very wise."

The approval in her eyes fed the monster inside that had led me to this place.

Jake leaned closer and murmured, "You're welcome," in my ear as the waiter distributed plates.

My mom called my dad back.

He settled into his seat. "Can you believe that guy has never been to an optometrist? He thought everything was fine and his declining vision was a result of getting old. Hadn't thought to do anything about it. I told him how to find a good optometrist in Portland."

My mom shook her head. "It's hard to believe some people are so casual about their health."

Her eyes darted to Gran's candy tan lines, but Gran was finishing off a scallop and either didn't notice or was ignoring her.

This led to a discussion of how many patients they saw who hadn't been to the doctor in years or didn't show up for appointments or frequently lost their glasses and needed replacements or generally failed to live up to my parents' idea of perfection.

I feel you, you vast multitude of fellow imperfect humans.

The mahi mahi was delicious, crusted in bread crumbs and hot and flaky, but I couldn't stop eying Jake's plate.

"Here, have a bite." He extended his fork with a piece of medium-rare filet.

"Oh, no. That's okay."

"You've been staring at my piece of meat like it's a piece of meat, if you know what I mean."

I snorted.

It was totally not a joke Fake Jacob would have made. Had anyone else heard? Were they wondering why this guy sounded nothing like the one I'd been talking about for months? Not to mention the tan and the surfing skills.

I gave in and accepted the bite, our eyes meeting and holding. "Oh man. That's amazing."

"You know you have to pay me back now, right?"

I raised my eyebrows. "I can think of many things I'd like to pay you back for."

He smirked and nodded to my plate.

"Ohhh. That."

I shared, too, maintaining the eye contact, both of us half smiling as I raised a fork to his mouth. His gaze held a slight warning like he suspected I might shove it down his throat.

"You like seafood, Jacob?"

Mom's question broke the spell, and I let him eat the bite normally before returning my attention to my plate.

When he'd swallowed, he said, "I do. Kenzie said you're allergic. Food allergies are difficult. My sister's is tree nuts, and she has to be careful, especially with desserts."

"Oh yes, that can be serious. Tell us about her. Are you two close?"

"As close as any siblings who are a few years apart, I suppose. She's a good kid."

"And your family? Do you take vacations together?"

I scrunched my nose, fairly certain I hadn't gotten into that.

"Small, local stuff, mostly," Jake said. "Nothing as nice as this. I can't thank you enough."

He truly was a master of deflection.

A worm of doubt wriggled in my stomach. My family was being so nice, trying to get to know him, and every reply was fiction.

"What do your parents do, again? Kenzie said one was a teacher?"

"My mom. She teaches high school math, and my dad practices family law."

He'd perfectly known my lies, professions that wouldn't let anyone easily search for his imaginary parents online, and that required enough higher education and a community focus to make my parents respect them.

"Those are excellent careers," my mom said.

Nailed it.

"It's weird having your mom for a teacher, but she's good at it," Jake said. "And both of them like to help people. Like you." He nodded at my parents.

He was doing well as Jacob. Properly dull and boring, locking his real self into a box and dimming the light I'd seen glimpses of. Little remained of the vibrant thrill seeker, funny and charming. I already missed that version of him, from surfing lessons and the blowhole and our verbal sparring.

Jake had become Jacob somewhere between the beach and the dinner table.

It was a good reminder that I needed to do the same.

"So, how'd you like surfing, Kenzie?" Neal saved Jake from further interrogation.

I'd loved it. The waves and the sun, the salt on my lips, the feeling of freedom, the quiet moments between catching waves, when I could close my eyes and imagine it was just me and the ocean. But to my family, I couldn't gush about it or ask to rent a board tomorrow or talk about how I wanted to go out with a camera. That's what I would have done before. If Jake could be boring, so could I.

"It was fun," I said. "It was an interesting challenge."

Jake studied me, his expression now flat, no more teasing.

I cocked my head. "What about you? Was it all you'd hoped?"

"I also enjoyed it. The teacher was competent and made everyone feel safe." It was like he was trying to outdo me for how boring we could make surfing in Hawaii sound. "Kenzie did a great job. You did, too, Alana."

"Thanks," my sister said. "So, you're a freshman in college, right? I've been telling Kenzie about what to expect. The transition academically but also possibly moving away from home. Any advice based on your first year?"

Was he in college? If so, where, and what was he studying? He could have been a senior like me. It was hard to tell exactly. Fake Jacob lived in a dorm.

Jake hesitated just a second. "I'm sure the same things you've told her. How important it is to make a schedule. Getting plenty of sleep. Not getting distracted from your goals."

My parents nodded as if he'd imparted rare wisdom.

The peeks I'd seen into the real Jake made me strongly suspect that was not the advice he would give, or at least not the advice he lived by, but it was exactly what my parents wanted to hear.

"What drew you to Kenzie?" my sister asked.

"The first time we spoke, I liked that she was clever and funny."

The sincerity in his voice made me wish it were true, which was ridiculous.

"What about you, Kenz?" Tyler asked. "What did you think when you first saw him?"

I swallowed a snort. "Oh, I was speechless. After that, everything happened so fast. Like I just had no control over it."

We looked at each other, and his dimples had emerged again in their half state, as he suppressed a full smile but couldn't quite hide them. Those things should be classified as a deadly weapon because they were slowly killing me.

"What about you?" he asked Neal. "Kenzie says you two met in college and are starting optometry school in the fall?"

Alana and Neal told us about meeting during their first week of college, talked about exams and interviews and applications, and I could finally breathe. Jake had done okay, nothing too suspicious, though he hadn't answered much, but I was relieved to have the focus on others.

After dinner, I was glad I was wearing a loose dress, because I was stuffed. We trudged upstairs to the rooms.

"Why are you trying to make me look good?" I asked him as we lagged behind.

"Isn't that what Jacob would do? Compliment his responsible, hardworking, honest girlfriend?"

I narrowed my eyes at his emphasis on *honest*. "Just . . . tone it down."

His eyebrows rose in challenge. "You don't want to date a guy who compliments you? Admires you?"

Of course I did, but I wanted one who knew me and complimented the real version of me, rather than inventing lies to make my parents happy.

Which, okay, yes, that was exactly what I'd been doing lately.

"Movie time," Dad announced as we entered the suite.

Would they let me go for a walk on the beach instead? The sun had set, and the sky was dark, but maybe if Jake came, they'd think it was safe. But then they'd think it was a romantic escape. And in our absence, Tyler might make jokes about what we were doing. Even if Jake was supposed to be my boyfriend, I didn't want that.

The others clustered around the screen and pulled up the movie menu, debating options.

"They'd probably veto *Jaws*," I said.

"Cliché," Jake said. "I was thinking *Sharknado*."

"Which one?"

"It makes me happy that you know there's more than one. A marathon, definitely. All of them."

"That might be more excitement than my family can handle. *Cast Away*?"

"*Baywatch*?"

"I do like the Rock, although I'm sure that's not why you suggested it." I elbowed him.

"It's exactly why. Who doesn't love the Rock?"

The problem with this game we were playing was, I couldn't tell if he was joking. I actually did like slightly cheesy but fun action movies, where you knew the good guys would win and nothing too terrible ever happened. And even if the Rock was old enough to be my dad, it didn't hurt when there were muscles to admire. But was Jake saying things because he thought Jacob would say them? Or because the real Jake truly liked them? Or to mess with me?

Ugh. It didn't matter. This was fake. All of it.

"Or maybe *Liar Liar,*" I said.

His lips quirked. "What about my personal favorite, *Catch Me If You Can.*"

He winked and moved away.

Despite the dig, I was smiling. This wasn't real. *Remember that.*

"I'll get drinks for everyone." I moved to the fridge.

Jake followed me to the kitchen, face more serious now, and asked in a low voice, "Why were you being so fake at dinner?"

"Shhh." My gaze darted to the living room, then his word—the one I'd just been reminding myself about in relation to him—registered. "*You're* being fake."

"That's my job for the week. And it's not my family."

"Exactly," I snapped quietly. "So keep your opinions to yourself."

Gran approached, and we fell silent as we assembled cups of lemonade and carried them to the living room.

He had no right to call me out. What he called being fake was a survival mechanism, a necessary strategy. Surely he'd heard my parents over the last two days, judging and offering comment on everything and everyone.

I'd been the target of those barbs too many times to count. I might be fake, but I was happier.

No, not fake. I was fine. Other than the boyfriend lie, things were fine. Why was I letting him get into my head?

My family had settled on a historical drama without our input, with Sherlock playing some World War II genius. Because nothing said *fun evening at the beach* like complicated math and Nazis.

"Haven't you seen this one, Jacob?" I asked.

"Yes, but it's so good, I'd love to watch it again."

His voice was so earnest, his face so sincere.

When I looked at him, he met my gaze directly, as if challenging me to call him out.

"Excellent," my dad said.

My parents shared the love seat. Alana and Neal curled up on one side of the L-shaped sofa, with Gran at the other end.

Tyler sat in the oversized armchair but jumped to his feet when we approached. "Here, you guys take this one. I might go work on my project."

"Really, Tyler?" my mom asked.

"We were gone all day. I didn't have much time."

She sighed. "Okay."

That was it? He always got off so easy.

He looked pointedly at the armchair and wagged his eyebrows at me, as if wondering how cozy I'd get in front of Mom and Dad, before vanishing down the hall.

I should have been happy with the arrangement. A chance to snuggle with my boyfriend in a dark room.

Jake's face was unreadable as we wedged ourselves in. The chair was just big enough for two, except I had to sit sideways, partly in Jake's lap. Our legs on the ottoman were pressed against each other.

"Is this on the approved PDA list?" he murmured, his lips brushing my ear.

Sarcastic replies fled from my brain. My mind went blank.

He emitted that banana-coconut scent, and warmth, like the sun was still soaking his skin. His arm had come around my shoulders, and his fingertips brushed my bare arm, making goose bumps skitter across my skin.

My heart was trying to pound its way out of my chest, and I hoped he couldn't feel it.

He was tense at first and kept shifting, but eventually relaxed into a position that felt too much like an embrace.

Did the real Jake have a girlfriend? I should have asked earlier. Snuggling with someone else's boyfriend was not acceptable, even if this wasn't real.

Focus on the movie. Fake. Lying. Impostor.

No matter how nice this was, I would not allow myself to enjoy it.

But my pulse didn't get the message.

CHAPTER NINE

The next day, the plan was to spend two hours of fun time at the resort pool and then go to the nearby town of Lahaina—the schedule's color codes were pink and green, telling us to bring sunscreen and a jacket.

I was awake early again, the perfect time to sit on the lanai and read more about the ecology of Hawaii before my parents were around to tell me to stay off my phone.

But when I left my room, Tyler and Jake stood on the lanai, talking.

I watched for a second. Then an idea hit. This was a perfect chance. I headed back down the hall just as Neal was exiting their bedroom. Bingo.

"Hey, Neal. Jacob was just looking for you. He had a question about an article he read about progressive lenses."

Neal's face lit up. "I'd be happy to talk to him."

I let him pass and waited until he rounded the corner. Then I darted through the door he'd left cracked. My heart pounded like the time I snuck into our neighbors' backyard to photograph their sunflowers.

Entering the guys' room wasn't totally foreign—I had a brother, though I generally avoided his bedroom at all costs. His room at home smelled like old socks, and I was afraid of tripping on his fancy computer cords and breaking something. This room smelled fine, thanks to hotel housekeeping.

The bag Jake had carried at the airport rested at the foot of the cot.

I hovered in the middle of the room, staring at it.

This was wrong. But so was pretending to be someone you weren't, blindsiding a girl at the airport, and refusing to answer her questions.

There was going to be underwear in there. I shouldn't do this. What were his boxers going to tell me, anyway?

A pair of shorts hung off the edge of his bed. What were the odds that I might find something useful in his pockets? I tiptoed forward and eased them up like they might bite me.

"What are you doing?" Jake's voice came from the doorway.

I spun and hurled the shorts at him. My heart had leaped through my throat and was racing for the door. Much like I wanted to.

"What are *you* doing?"

He held up the shorts. "This is my room."

"Right. And Tyler's. He said I could borrow something."

Jake crossed his arms and leaned against the doorframe, blocking my exit. "That's his bed there." Jake nodded to the unmade one on the right, with my brother's fancy headphones and tablet, and a sweat-stained baseball cap with our high school mascot on it. "I can see the confusion, though, since Neal and I also love Warriors baseball."

I gulped.

Jake pushed away and moved to my side. "Kenzie, Kenzie, Kenzie." His low voice hummed near my ear. "I'm so disappointed. You didn't think I'd catch on when Neal told me you sent him? Give me some credit."

Yeah, I really should have thought that through better.

"I have no idea what you're talking about." I grabbed the hat. "I'm just here to borrow a hat."

It felt grimy and smelled like a locker room. Holding my breath, I jammed it onto my head. Or, tried to. The humidity was making my hair large again, and I had to wiggle the hat so it stayed down. My hair was surely sticking out. And now I needed to wash it and my hands before I caught something. Seriously, did Tyler store this thing in a dumpster?

I swept out of the room, hat on my head, ignoring Jake's smug expression. My stomach was in knots. How did spies do their jobs without having frequent heart attacks?

Tyler was lounging on the couch. "Is that my hat?"

"Just go with it," I said.

"You look funny."

I huffed and tossed it at him.

"Jacob was looking for you. Something about making sure you didn't lose your sunglasses again? You guys are weird."

What did that mean? Was he not buying our relationship?

Jake rejoined us, his lips still tucked into an amused smile, which widened when he saw I was no longer wearing the hat. Why hadn't I just said I was retrieving it for Tyler? Ugh.

Trying to play it cool, I headed to the kitchen to fill my water bottle. Jake leaned on the bar, watching.

"Ready for two hours at the pool?" I asked, my voice too bright. "Apparently, it's exactly the right amount of time, no more and no less. Ninety minutes wouldn't give you the full experience, and two and a half hours might turn you into a sea monster."

"The spreadsheet is my master," he said in an excellent *Toy Story* alien impression.

"I think I'd prefer the claw," I said.

The pool was gorgeous, though. Flowers all around, shadows of trees flickering over turquoise water, waterfalls. I stood under one and let the water wash over me, eagerly dreaming of it being a real one soon. The others mostly sat in the shade or took quick dips before returning to books, but Jake stayed nearby. Surprisingly, he didn't speak, and I enjoyed the time in silence where it looked like we were hanging out, but he was giving me my space.

I occasionally found him watching me, his expression guarded. Was he upset about the room break-in? Or thinking something else entirely?

I briefly considered what else I could do to make him talk, but I could resume that when I wasn't so relaxed. Besides, I needed the alone time to recharge and prepare for the rest of the day, when I wouldn't be able to escape my family.

After the prescribed two hours, we changed into nicer clothes and made lunch. Jake played waiter again, assembling sandwiches and filling cups and fetching chips and apples. My parents ate it up—Jake's service and his ham sandwiches.

It was sweet, but sweet like Gran's lemonade, in that I liked it but it almost made me want to puke.

Our first stop in town was a huge old banyan tree that took up an entire city block. The main central trunk appeared to be made of multiple trunks that had grown together. The limbs stretched out to form a huge canopy, like appendages of some great beast. Hundreds of small, straggly strands dripped from the branches.

"Those are actually roots," Jake said.

"Yeah, I read about it. They grow down and eventually turn into trunks." I liked the idea that those tiny things held so much potential.

"Did you know it's a single tree that covers two-thirds of an acre? It's the largest in the US."

"Almost a hundred and fifty years—"

I stopped as my parents approached. They didn't need to hear me geeking out over a tree.

"What were you saying, Kenz? Something about the age of the tree? You're full of so much knowledge." Jake took my hand and swung our arms, a challenge in his eyes.

I squeezed as hard as I could.

Once my parents had wandered on, I glared at him. "You knew the plants at the resort yesterday, too."

"Like I said, I'm a man of many talents. One who isn't afraid to show it." His sharp gaze met mine.

My science knowledge might have impressed my parents. It proved I'd read up on the place. But that wasn't the kind of thing I was supposed to do for fun anymore. Maybe if I wanted to know about trees for the purpose of using their sap to find new cancer drugs or come up with a plan to stop global warming. But not because I wanted to take pictures of them.

I ignored his barb, freed my hand, and meandered toward the tree. Beneath, it was like another world. It was slightly creepy, with the roots and branches. Twisted, but fascinating. I felt like I might get swallowed whole, wrapped up and absorbed into the trunk and never seen again.

How *would* I take a picture of it? To capture the whole thing, I'd have to move back. Use a wide-angle lens. But it offered interesting close-up opportunities, too. It would be better without the people. Although, I couldn't fault them for hugging the massive trunk. They'd show friends at home just how big it was, and it might inspire others to think about how many fascinating things there were on this planet. Which is what I wanted to do with my pictures.

Jake tugged my hand, bringing me back. He angled his head to show that my family was moving away.

Stop obsessing over trees, Kenz.

How long had I been standing there? It was very possible everyone else had held an entire conversation I'd missed. That had been known to happen. But Jake had waited quietly and wasn't mocking me.

"What were you thinking about?" he asked.

"Nothing."

"No, really. I'm curious. The tree is interesting, isn't it? And I can tell you were thinking. You had a look on your face, like your mind was elsewhere."

"Yes, good old Kenzie. Her mind is always somewhere else." I reached up to touch a dangling root.

Something flickered in his eyes before he shifted his gaze to the tree. "I like thinking about how old it is. Usually you think of mountains or oceans being permanent, but growing things can be, too."

The thoughtful tone of his voice made it easier to share my thoughts. "I wish it could talk. Tell us what the island was like when it was first planted, before tourists took over."

"It's not a native species. Not as dangerous as some invasive species, but still."

"If it isn't harming the environment, though, it's cool that so many people get to see it and learn about it who otherwise wouldn't."

He returned his attention to me, our eyes meeting. A slash of sunlight pierced through the tree branches to illuminate half his face. "I guess it is."

In silence, we studied each other, more blatantly than we had yet, and his expression held openness and, I thought, interest.

We joined my family outside the Baldwin Home Museum, an old white house with dark green railings. The others stopped to read a sign about its history before we entered.

Inside, it was . . . a house. I was sure it was interesting if you liked history. Alana inspected everything, from the china on the table, to the furniture, to a wooden bucket with a hole in the top and a lid that I realized was a toilet.

I shuffled Tyler past it before he made a joke.

Shelves held black-and-white photos of people who might have been Baldwins. Those were dangerous to look at, because my mind wanted to wander down rabbit trails. Like, there were so many things they wouldn't have been able to capture back then, with how long cameras took. All those instants, those fleeting moments, waves and wildlife, that didn't sit still. Photographers had only been able to capture mountains and trees and things that didn't move, but so much of nature was in constant motion. You couldn't ask a bird not to fly away or a whale to pause midleap.

And, there I went again. Jake's voice yanked me to the present.

He and Alana were discussing ventilation and how the people would have cooled the house in the summer. I would have bet my AC that he had no real interest in the topic.

As we continued, I was the only one who could tell he was faking, reading signs aloud, bending over shelves with my sister, pausing in front of every lamp and chair.

That was what I got for making up a boring boyfriend. I couldn't help but wish for the real Jake, who would escape with me to study trees.

And yet, in a way, it was sweet. Even if he didn't care, Alana was enjoying herself.

We moved on into an area of town with shops and restaurants lining both sides of the street. Mom and Dad pulled ahead while Gran paused to peer into every window. Tyler trailed behind, typing on his phone, about to trip himself. And he thought *I'd* been bad with my camera.

In case my brother was watching, I took Jake's hand, since that's what a normal girlfriend would do while exploring Maui. Jake didn't flinch, which was good. I didn't want Tyler to think we were weird.

A brightly colored window display caught my eye. It was an art gallery, packed with gorgeous photos. Beachscapes, sunsets, leaping whales, turtles, so many amazing images. I could have spent all day studying them, trying to figure out how the pictures had been taken, admiring the lighting or the detail or the mood they captured.

This was a huge step above hotel art. I definitely wasn't good enough to have my photos in a place like this. Still. Just because I would never see that dream realized didn't mean I couldn't admire others' work.

My family had moved on, except Tyler and Jake. Tyler was shuffling toward me, while Jake stood by my side.

"They have a contest," Tyler said, and then he returned his attention to his phone and meandered past us.

A sign in the window advertised a photography contest, sponsored by the gallery, local businesses, and a group called the Maui Nature Foundation. The theme was Inspiration in the Natural World, with the requirement to submit any nature photograph from the island and a deadline of the day we were scheduled to leave. There was a small cash prize, plus the winning photograph would be used in the foundation's ads. The judge was a local travel photographer, Rob Nichols.

I swallowed hard. For a moment, my heart had leaped like a breaching whale. So many possibilities came to mind. The blowhole. The flowers. The banyan tree. The waves. And those were just what I'd seen in the first two days.

But I'd been there, done that, wasn't about to try again. My heart couldn't take the hope of entering or the pain of failing.

"Let's go in." Jake's hand on my back was steering me through the door he held before I knew what was happening.

Inside, thoughts of the contest fled, and I melted. The walls were covered. Turquoise water and magenta sunsets and apricot sunrises. Trees and beaches and waves and turtles, and I was swimming, flying, soaring, drowning.

Someone squeezed my arm. I blinked, and a man came into focus. Around forty years old, tanned, with sharp eyes that seemed to take in hundreds of details at once.

"Can I help you?" he asked in a way that implied it was not the first or even the fourth time he'd asked, though a smile flitted about his lips.

"I was just admiring the photos." *Admiring* was far too weak a word. "They're amazing."

"Thank you."

I focused on him. "Did you take them all?"

"I did."

"So the shop is yours?"

"It is. I'm Rob."

Oh. Made sense, the contest judge.

"When I'm in town, I manage this place," he said. "I travel a lot, obviously." He waved a hand.

"How did you . . ." I didn't even know what to ask.

"Get started?" He didn't seem bothered by my lack of vocabulary.

I nodded.

"I always liked taking pictures. I grew up here, so there are plenty of great scenes. When I traveled, I'd take pictures, too. I enjoyed it, so I took classes, sold photographs to magazines. Then opened an online gallery, and finally I decided to open a physical one to spend more time on the island with my family."

His words lit my imagination on fire. I saw myself exploring every inch of this island, but other places, too. Majestic landscapes and dramatic vistas. I'd take stunning images like these, that showed people the beauty of the world and brought far-off places to them. Filled them with wonder. Inspired them, either to travel themselves or to protect the gorgeous places and animals.

Hot tears pricked my eyes.

"Can you tell us about the contest?" Jake asked.

"Sure. I'm working with a local nonprofit. Entry fees go to their environmental conservation work, and it gives them publicity. I offered my services because I believe in their mission and like to encourage aspiring photographers. Is that you?"

He aimed the question at me.

My mouth was frozen, incapable of forming words.

"Yes," Jake said. "It is her."

I tried to glare at him, but the expression held no heat.

I wanted to beg Rob to teach me everything. To hire me. To take me on an adventure somewhere no one else had seen, and compare cameras and dissect every photo in this room.

But my gaze darted to Jake. Jacob. The fake boyfriend to fit the fake me, who had done the practical thing and given all this up.

"We should go," I said, my throat tight. "But your work is amazing. Really. Thanks."

"I hope you'll consider entering the contest."

As he spoke, I was already hurrying out the door, forcing myself to ignore the pictures, the contest flyer, the longing and the pain and the hope. My family was waiting.

CHAPTER TEN

Gran insisted we stop at the top-rated place for the Hawaiian specialty of shave ice. It was a perfect distraction from the photo gallery. I'd power walked until we caught up with the others, leaving Jake no chance to speak.

Not that he would. Not that he cared.

And not that I needed a distraction. I'd admired the work of a skilled artist and moved on. Nothing more. The colorful, fantastic images were definitely not lingering in my mind.

We joined a line to order at the outdoor counter of a wooden shack. The menu said each cup could hold three flavors. Gran ordered a large, then spent forever studying the list.

"How will I know what I like best if I don't try them all? I changed my mind. Make that three smalls," she said. "Mahalo."

"Just for you?" I asked.

"Of course."

The menu listed the nine most popular flavors, so she asked for those.

"I'll have to come back to try the rest."

I scanned the rest of the menu. "That's, like, thirty more flavors."

"Life is too short not to enjoy dessert, Kenzie. Do what makes you happy. Chase your dreams. Right now my dream is lots of sugary ice."

Jake leaned against me and offered Gran a fist bump, which she returned. "I love a woman who knows what she wants and goes after it." He paused. "Like Kenzie, working hard to chase her dreams. It's one of the things I admire about you."

His direct gaze held a challenge that sent an uncomfortable jolt through my stomach.

Whatever. He had no right to judge me. I forced a smile, my jaw tight. "That's so nice of you. I admire that you're always so open about your opinions."

Our eyes locked, and lightning coursed through the connection.

"Mom, are you sure that much sugar is wise?" my dad asked as Gran moved aside to let the rest of us order, breaking Jake's and my stare. "It can't possibly be good for you."

"I didn't come on vacation to be wise. I came to enjoy myself. And sugar makes me happy."

I loved how simple it was in her mind. See it, want it, go for it. If only my life were so simple.

We watched a machine spit ice into cups like a burst of snow. Workers took syrup bottles and poured generous amounts on top of the giant snowballs. The shades were vivid, and where they overlapped, they made new colors, so each cup held a miniature piece of art. They would make a pretty photograph, even if it wasn't nature and it wouldn't help for that contest I was not still thinking about, *stop thinking about it.*

I helped Gran carry her three cups, along with my blend of kiwi, passion fruit, and mango, which sounded properly tropical. Mom and Dad were splitting a vanilla, and Alana and Neal decided to share strawberry. I tried not to roll my eyes. Tyler held the largest cup they offered.

Jake snapped a picture of me holding mine, and I blinked at him. What was he doing? He shrugged and smiled, a tiny half one.

"It was cute, the way you were staring at it."

His attention made my insides squirm as I used the tiny wooden spoon to take a bite. The ice was smooth and soft, not chunky or icy like typical snow cones, and the sweetness melted in my mouth. Who would have thought a tropical island had perfected sugary, powdery snow treats?

Gran snuck bites of mine in addition to hers. When I finished, syrup remained in the bottom, and I tipped the cup and drank it.

"What's the verdict, Gran?" I asked.

"Too soon to tell. Passion fruit is the front-runner. Or what was that green one you had?"

"Kiwi."

"That, too. We'll come back."

Gran's tongue was bright red. Mine was probably a strange color, too. I extended it and wiggled it around to try to see.

"Wow," Tyler said. "I can't believe you got a boyfriend, doing things like that."

Jake stuck his out, too, blue around the edges, and aimed it at Tyler. Tyler rolled his eyes, and Jake, Gran, and I laughed.

"Time for some shopping," Mom said.

"Do we have to?" Tyler asked.

"Why don't you ladies go ahead, and the guys will . . . do something else," Dad suggested. "Another museum, maybe."

"That sounds sexist," I said.

I had no desire to shop my mom and Alana's way—with a checklist, same way they did everything else. A predetermined list of souvenirs and gifts for the neighbor watching our house, the employees at the office, Alana's roommate. They wouldn't quit until they had purchased every single one, like a search-and-destroy mission.

"What if Neal loves shopping and wants to go?" I asked.

He looked at me. "I actually don't."

"Or Jacob?"

"I don't, either," he said. "I'd love to visit another museum. You know how much I like them."

"Oh yes," I said. "Almost as much as you love schedules."

"Oh," Alana said sadly. "I love museums, too."

"Don't worry." Neal took her hand. "If it's good, we can go again."

She nodded.

I rolled my eyes. "Fine. You guys go learn lots of fascinating things, and you can give us a full report later."

I was pretty sure Jake was the only one who caught my sarcasm.

I let Mom, Gran, and Alana drag me from store to store along the main street. My eyes soon crossed from the unending parade of shirts, hats, magnets, shell necklaces, snow globes—really, in Hawaii?—and other standard tourist fare.

I picked up and put back random items that caught my eye, like tiny ukuleles and shark-tooth necklaces I hoped weren't real. We passed more art galleries, with photographs but also a variety of paintings and sculptures, blown glass, and beautiful wood carvings.

I couldn't stop my mind from wandering to those gorgeous photos and that flyer. Was it Maui's way of offering me a second chance at my dream? Or my own weakness tempting me to something I had left behind and didn't need to return to?

Imagine my parents' reaction if I announced I was entering another contest. It would transport us to the days before I'd told them I would pursue optometry, when they'd constantly pointed out the things I was doing wrong. My grades weren't good enough, the guys I dated were slackers, I spent too much time on frivolous pursuits.

I sighed and shook a globe to make it snow on a tiny palm-tree-lined beach.

When we were in the fourth, or sixth, or maybe fifteenth shop, I glanced out the window. It was gorgeous out, with a few clouds, and I'd seen the ocean through breaks in the buildings. What a shame to waste a nice day in shops when nature was right there.

Wait.

A person was darting down a side street. One who suspiciously resembled Jake. He peered over his shoulder and power walked around a corner and out of sight.

What was he up to?

I rushed to the door. Took two steps onto the sidewalk. And skidded to a stop.

I was holding a dashboard hula dancer. I hurried back inside, checking to see if anyone had spotted my accidental near-shoplifting. I plunked her onto the shelf before I ended up in Hawaiian jail.

What would jail be like here, anyway? A lava rock cave with no windows, deep inside the volcano? Or a cage beneath the waves, with sharks circling? That might be better than eighteen more stores.

Mom was browsing shell coasters, and I'd lost sight of Alana and Gran.

"I'm going to go back to that first shop," I said. "Get something for Lucia. I'll catch up with you guys."

Before she could argue, I hurried away, this time without committing any misdemeanors.

That was an old Kenzie move, impulsive and unpredictable. The leaving quickly, not the shoplifting. My running off wouldn't totally shock her.

I went in the direction I'd seen Jake go, scanning every person I passed for a sign of my dad or brother or Neal. I didn't see them, but I did spot Jake's green shirt ahead.

Staying a block behind, I followed.

He was striding toward the banyan tree. A secret meeting? Or maybe he just really liked trees.

But then he veered toward the water. A low stone wall separated the sidewalk from a parking lot.

Boat masts rose up like a forest. Palm trees lined the way, and umbrellas and tents shaded tables that were selling goods or offering snorkeling, whale watching, or fishing tours. We'd be coming in another hour or two for our sunset cruise, so what was Jake doing? He bypassed the booths and headed along the walkway bordering the harbor.

I hesitated, trying to make sure I stayed hidden, in case he turned around, but his attention remained fixed on the boats. Many spots were empty, but he paused at some slips, inspecting the boats. Talked briefly to people before moving on. Stopped to type on his phone.

Was he looking for something? Admiring the yachts? Planning to stow away? Maybe two days with my family had driven him to set sail for Tahiti. Or this was tied to his mysterious reason for being here.

I trailed him to the end of the harbor, where a stone jetty jutted out and then veered parallel to shore, forming the protected rectangle of the harbor. The sea side offered fewer hiding places, so I remained on land, ducking behind a tree and watching as he walked down the other side. I paralleled his course from my side. He occasionally went out of sight when he passed behind a boat.

My phone buzzed in my pocket, startling me.

A text from Alana read, *Where are you? Mom's worried.*

I'd been gone too long. After sparing one last glance at Jake, I hurried away.

He was definitely up to something.

CHAPTER ELEVEN

When I rejoined the others, Mom raised her eyebrows. "Where's the gift you went back for?"

Ah. Good point. I wasn't holding a bag. But I could salvage this situation. "When I saw it again, I realized it was overpriced compared to the other stores we'd visited. I'll keep looking, now that I know what a good value is."

Some of the disapproval left her face.

Math, for the win.

Our cruise left at five, so after I gave in and bought kukui nut leis and shell bracelets for myself and Lucia, and some chocolate-covered macadamia nuts, we dropped our packages in the car and rejoined the others near the harbor.

Where Jake had already been. What excuse had he given my dad to get away?

I wanted to ask him about it, but I needed to wait for the right moment. When it would have the most impact and he wouldn't be able to escape. Like, after tying him to a deck chair or dangling him over the side of the boat by the anchor rope as hungry sharks circled below.

After we boarded our ship, my parents stopped in the interior lower deck with rows of benches. I continued on, climbing to the top, where tables filled half the open space. There was a bar at one end and a microphone at the other.

Jake joined me without us discussing it, seeking sunshine and fresh air. It probably looked good to my family, like we were on the same page. More of the real Jake showing through, the guy who—like me—would rather be outside, seeing everything.

The guy who was hiding something.

We took spots at the rail as the boat pulled away.

Jake was a captive audience on the boat, but other passengers were close enough that I knew I should hold off on questioning him. Here, I'd receive a brush-off or a lie.

We cruised slowly out of the harbor. Jake watched the other boats in their spots. But when we left the harbor behind for open sea, a slight frown left his face and he refocused his attention on where we were. What was he thinking about?

"Did you have a good time with my dad and everyone?" I asked. "Did you find another museum?"

"Yep. So much more history. Alana missed out. You might not have enjoyed the old whaling photos very much."

I shuddered. "What did you think?"

"Jacob Miller loves museums. The more historical the better, especially if there are huge signs with tiny text and lots of historical facts."

"And Jake Miller?"

"Uh-uh." He shook a finger in my face. "We agreed, no information about him."

"Oh please. Like I haven't figured out more than you know."

"Oh really? Enlighten me." His dimples shone.

"He likes to surf, likes the outdoors. He's adventurous, a doer. Adaptable. Can be charming when he wants to be."

"Careful," he said. "You wouldn't want to get confused about who you're dating. That doesn't sound like your ideal, made-up boyfriend."

Jacob wasn't ideal for *me,* just for my family, but I wasn't about to admit that. "I have no doubt you'll help remind me. You're also not a bad actor. My family has no clue."

"That's good, right? That's what we want." His voice was tight now.

It was, and yet complimenting his lying skills felt wrong.

We studied each other.

Someone approached, and I jumped, surprised to see Neal. The sun was still up, and I'd thought he might burst into flames if it came into contact with his skin.

He bit his lip and blinked at me. "Can I talk to you? And, Jacob, would you mind distracting Alana?"

Jake and I glanced at each other.

"Sure." Jake vanished down the stairs.

Neal shifted into the shade of the boat's cabin and twisted his hands. "So, I have something to tell you and then a favor to ask."

I leaned against the rail. "Shoot."

"I already talked to your parents, but I wanted you to know, too. I'm going to propose tonight."

"Propose . . . marriage? To Alana? Shut the front door. Really?"

I threw my arms around him. Wow. I mean, they were only

twenty-two and wouldn't even graduate from college for a couple of months. But they had been dating for three and a half years, so I guess it wasn't totally surprising.

He chuckled and patted my back. I pulled away. He was not a hugger. That was the first time I'd done that.

"Sorry," I said.

"I'm glad you're happy."

"Of course I am. Alana loves you. You love her. You make her happy. And what a setting."

In front of the entire family and all these strangers didn't sound like an ideal proposal to me. Alana wasn't exactly an extrovert, either. But a sunset cruise in Hawaii sure was romantic, and she was big on family, the way my parents wanted, so she'd probably like it. Plus, Neal was winning major points with my parents, who would be thrilled to be involved.

"I wanted it to be memorable."

"It definitely will be. So what's the favor? I won't tell her. Obviously."

He smiled. "Would you take pictures for us? I want to do it right at sunset."

"Oh. Um. Yeah, of course."

"You take really good pictures, and I want them to be worthy of framing."

"I don't know if I'm that good. But I'm happy to help."

No one could fault this. My parents couldn't judge me for helping my sister in this way. And I could totally handle it. Face the temptation. Take a few photos tonight and emerge unscathed and not feed my past addiction.

"What are you talking about?" His face was earnest. "Your pictures are amazing. I know you'll do great."

At least one person thought so, and wanted me to continue, even if it was only for a night.

"Thanks, I guess. I'm happy for you. Have you guys talked about, you know, marriage?"

Wow, that was a weird word in relation to my sister.

"Yeah, she picked out the ring."

Of course she did.

"And we've talked about what it will be like when we move for grad school. We want to officially start that chapter of our lives together. She just doesn't know I have it planned for tonight."

"She's going to be thrilled. And I'm happy to help."

He squeezed my arm. "Thank you. I'd better go back before she gets suspicious."

I watched him descend into the cabin.

Definitely weird. My sister had met Neal the first week of their freshman year of college, which was supposedly the year Jacob was in. Now when I "broke up" with Jake, I was going to seem less serious, although my parents could hardly expect a high school relationship to last.

I shook my head. This was about Neal and Alana, not my fake life. I'd do my part. My phone would be fine. It had a dual camera with automatic adjustments for contrast and saturation, and took professional-quality photos. I didn't need the camera. So why was I missing it again?

We cruised away from shore, the harbor and town shrinking behind us. Bright white boat masts glowed against a row of trees, with the central island mountains rising behind them, hugged by brilliant clouds that cast interesting shadows over the hillsides.

I stood alone, pretending I didn't want to photograph the view, and when no one returned, I went inside to find my family.

Mom was lying on a bench, sleeping with her head in Dad's lap.

When I raised my eyebrows at Dad, he said, "She took the wrong Dramamine. It was supposed to be the non-drowsy kind. I'll let her sleep until dinner."

"Even if there are whales?"

The boat was supposed to go in search of them before we sat down to eat.

"I'll stay. You guys go on."

The rest of us went to a side deck. Wind blew off the water. The boat had picked up speed once we'd left the harbor, and was cutting across gentle swells. Several other boats were out as well, and I could see one of the neighboring islands.

My mind drifted from Mom's embarrassing napping habits to the proposal. Not the ask-her-to-marry-him part. The part where I would be taking pictures of a glorious Hawaiian sunset over the ocean.

With, you know, my sister and Neal in them. Because they were what mattered about tonight.

"What's up?" Jake leaned against my arm.

I jumped. Looked at him. And around. We were the only two left. Gran had moved to the front of the boat. Tyler had probably climbed to the top in search of cell service, while Neal and Alana hid from the evil sun like it was the Eye of Sauron.

"Just thinking."

We stood in silence, watching the waves, the ripples, the colors of blue. The wind tugged at our hair, and he did the tuck-it-behind-both-his-ears-at-the-same-time thing. I briefly imagined him doing it to my hair, too, or me doing it to his, before shaking my head.

Several minutes later, someone shouted. The boat slowed. And in the water nearby, a whale surfaced.

The boat got closer than we'd been from the lookout point, and being in the water near them was even more magical. Two gray backs formed arcs above the water. One poked up a head first and splashed down sideways. Spray erupted as another surfaced. The boat cut its engines, and we drifted nearby.

My gaze was locked on them. Awe bloomed inside me. They were so big and so graceful.

One splashed a flipper like it was waving at us, slapping at the surface, and I laughed.

I couldn't believe I was really here.

In the distance, four more puffs of spray appeared. The boat made a wide circle of the first two whales and cruised toward the larger group, which were leaping and splashing.

I gave in and took pictures. My parents were inside. I didn't see Tyler, Alana, or Neal, and Gran stood several yards away. It wouldn't hurt anything.

I barely blinked for several minutes as I watched, wanting to brand this memory into my brain forever. One by one, their tails showed, meaning they were diving deep. The animals moved on, and the boat did, too.

I leaned out to try to catch a final glimpse, until we had sailed far past them. I sighed.

"What do you love about them?" Jake asked.

"Everyone loves whales."

"I'm not asking everyone. I'm asking you." He rested against the railing, facing me, and his interest sounded genuine.

I shrugged, and stared at the ocean when I replied. "They have interesting migration patterns, and the sounds, how they communicate, is so cool. They're larger than dinosaurs, and incredibly intelligent. But it's mainly the size, the majesty, and how they're so graceful. They're huge and yet not really dangerous. And they live in a totally different world than we do. It's so . . . mysterious."

I'd shifted to face him directly, and he watched me, listening intently, as I grew more and more enthusiastic.

"Don't you like them?" I asked.

"Sure," he said. "You're right—who doesn't? But I'm not as passionate as you. I like what you said, though, about the other world. They have families and all that, and yet everything about their life is so different."

I'd geeked out, and he wasn't rolling his eyes and telling me it was dumb or looking like he'd rather be somewhere else. In fact, his gaze, while probing and direct, was more pleased than usual, warm and aware. A slight smile tilted one corner of his mouth. Not a mocking one, but a happy one.

"You know a lot about them. Why do you hide that?" His question was genuine, not judging.

One aspect of biology I did like—wildlife biology. If you

wanted to take pictures of animals, it helped to know their habits and their habitats, their behavior, what they ate and where they moved. Unfortunately, my family didn't see that as a useful application of science, not when the end result was me wanting to photograph them.

That thought plunged me instantly into a cold sea, a reminder that I'd let myself get carried away. And that wasn't what I did anymore, wasn't who I was now.

I turned away, ending the moment. "You wouldn't understand."

CHAPTER TWELVE

For dinner, we filled two tables on the top deck side by side. Neal kept sneaking peeks at Alana and smothering a smile. It was cute. But also weird.

Servers gave us the option of steak or fish. Jake, Gran, and I were the only ones who chose fresh seafood. Maybe better for Neal. He didn't want fish breath when he proposed.

My mom's eyes were half-closed, and she had her chin propped on her fist. But she blinked up at our server, a young bald guy.

"Your head is very shiny," she said. "You should wear a hat."

I closed my eyes and imagined I was living permanently with the whales, safe and hidden in the depths of the sea.

The server cleared his throat. "Right. Well. Can I get you anything else?"

Mom's head had gone to Dad's shoulder, and her eyes were closed again. The server made a fast escape.

Gran went to the bar and returned with a brightly colored beverage with fruit stuck on top. She drained it quickly, and when she stood again, my dad said, "Don't you think you should slow down? I know you aren't driving the boat, but that can't be good for you."

Gran waved a hand. "They're nonalcoholic. The alcohol interferes with the flavor of the sugar."

Alana chuckled into her non-virgin mai tai, and Dad shook his head.

When our food arrived, it came with steak knives for the others.

"These are too pointy," my mom announced. "It cannot possibly be safe to have such sharp objects on a boat that's rocking. And why *is* it rocking so much? They should fix that."

"I'll send your memo to the ocean," I muttered. "I'm sure it would be happy to accommodate you."

Jake sniffed. "Dr. Reed, would you like some butter for your rolls? Can I pass you the salt or pepper?"

She focused on him long enough for the server to escape again. *Well played, Jake.*

The fish was amazing, crusted in macadamia nuts, and came with rice, mango salsa, mashed purple sweet potatoes, salad, sweet rolls, and chocolate cake.

No wonder Jake was lying about who he was. I would pretend to be pretty much anyone to get a cruise and a meal like this. Which brought back the memory of him sneaking around the harbor, and with it, the suspicion. He had a reason for being here beyond a nice vacation, and I needed to return to figuring out what it was.

After the dessert plates were cleared, the sun was getting low, the light golden. Gray-and-white clouds said we had a little time until full sunset. Mom was more awake, possibly thanks to the food, and had rediscovered the filter between her brain and her mouth.

We listened to the guy at the end of the deck singing and playing a ukulele, and during a break in the music, Neal stood.

"Alana, I have a very important question for you."

It was happening! My heart beat faster, and I grabbed Jake's hand without thinking and squeezed. He blinked. Why had I done that?

Oh, right. My phone. I pulled it out and slowly, carefully got out of my seat and edged sideways so the view behind them was ocean and sky and not other diners.

Dad elbowed my mom, who sat up straight.

Alana blinked up at Neal. "What is it?"

Neal got on one knee next to her chair and withdrew a box from his pocket.

My sister's eyes widened as a smile spread across her face.

Someone nearby said, "Aw."

I snapped picture after picture.

Mom was fully awake now, eyes shining with tears. Gran bounced in her seat. Even Tyler was paying attention.

Neal opened the box. "I don't want to move on to the next part of my life without knowing you'll be in the rest of it forever. I love you. Will you marry me?"

"Yes, yes! Of course. I love you." She threw her arms around him and kissed him.

I took more photos, a sweet warmth spreading through me, tempered by a slight ache inside. I loved that they had found each other and were so perfect together. I was happy for them. And yet . . . would I ever have someone look at me that way? Know me and want me in their life just as I was?

Neal pulled away, took the ring from the box, and slid it onto Alana's finger. They kissed again, and everyone around us cheered.

My family swarmed them, hugging, but I stayed back long enough to take more candid photos of the family before joining in.

The sky was now shifting to gentle pinks and oranges in preparation for a glorious sunset. People drifted to various spots on deck, some dancing on the cleared area. Others were going below.

I took charge, making Neal and Alana pose so I could photograph them, the ring—which was a perfect-for-her classic round diamond in a silver band—and them at the rail in front of the sunset.

"Remember not to look at the sun directly," my dad said. "Even if it is setting."

I ignored him. And might possibly have snuck in more pictures of the view as the colors brightened to tangerine and fuchsia, reflected on the surface of the silvery water. A few jagged clouds and some puffy ones decorated the sky, deep purple lit with gold. The glowing ball I was definitely not looking directly at sank into the sea, swallowed into the depths for one more night.

The others drifted away, and the scene darkened until the clouds were pewter, the sky barely pink. Something about the ocean and the sky here filled me. Like the huge, vast expanses condensed and morphed into a Kenzie-sized ball that ignited me from the inside out.

"Can I see the pictures you took?" Jake's question reminded me of his presence, long after the others had moved on.

Had he been there the whole time?

My grip on my phone tightened. I hadn't shown anyone a photo since the one I'd sent to the contest. It was fine. New Kenzie didn't measure her worth through photos, and I'd have to show Alana anyway. I could do this.

"I guess. No peeking at my other apps." I handed him my phone, opened to the pictures to help him avoid the temptation of reading the *Help me* texts I'd been sending Lucia, though she wouldn't see them.

He scrolled, pausing occasionally to zoom in or tilt the screen.

"Kenzie, these are amazing." His voice was low, intimate. It was the first time he'd said my name where it sounded genuine, not teasing or mocking or fake flirting. The rough sound of it sent a pleasant shiver through my midsection.

I shrugged. I hadn't gone through them, but I knew several would turn out well. Neal and Alana would be happy.

"It's a Hawaiian sunset. It's not hard to get a good picture."

Jake held up the phone to show one of Neal and Alana smiling at each other with the sunset behind them gilding their heads in rosy light. Then another of her ring up close, sparkling, with a blurry ocean vista behind Alana's hand. Then one where a sailboat had crossed our path. The silhouette of its triangular sail was perfectly framed in the golden path of the sun reflecting on water.

"Seriously," he said. "I'm impressed. I don't know a lot about photography, but I'd hang this one on my wall. Not everyone could take pictures like these, regardless of the nice scenery."

I took my phone from him. I didn't need his compliments, no matter how much I liked them. I was a fine photographer. But nothing special.

"I bet people would pay you for pictures like this," he said. "Proposals or weddings or whatever."

My parents might see that as a more stable career, though less acceptable than optometry. It was a good one, capturing people's important life moments. But though I was happy to take pictures for my sister, weddings and people weren't what I dreamed of, what I longed for.

That sunset, on the other hand . . .

I shoved the phone into my pocket.

"It's okay to acknowledge that you're good at something." Now Jake's voice held a sterner tone.

"I'm decent. It doesn't matter, though."

"Of course it matters, if it's something you love. Which, by the way, you're allowed to like something even if people around you don't."

I swallowed a scoff. Why paint a target on myself?

"We should dance," I said.

My parents and Alana and Neal were on the dance floor as twilight descended and the sky went deep purple. They would wonder why Jake and I weren't dancing, too, in such a perfect setting. And I didn't need to be interrogated about hiding who I was by the person literally pretending to be someone else.

I let Jake lead me onto the dance floor, slide his hands to my waist. I rested mine on his shoulders, keeping my gaze focused beyond him. My spine was stiff. He didn't have the right to comment on how I lived my life.

"Relax," he said quietly. "You're supposed to be enjoying this, not looking like you're preparing to jump overboard. Or shove me over instead."

He was right. I could debate both those options, as long as my face didn't reveal that I was considering them.

I tried to loosen my muscles. Shifted closer and moved my hands to the back of his neck, where I could run them along his tied-up hair. Which was as soft as I'd imagined when I played with his stubby ponytail. I forced my fingers to lie flat instead.

"Why do you smell so good?"

The question was out before I could stop it, and I made sure to lean in close enough that I couldn't see him smirk.

"Hair product."

That was all he said, and his voice sounded tight. His fingertips ghosted up and down my spine.

We passed Tyler dancing with Gran, and my brother raised his eyebrows. "You guys look like you've never danced before."

"Not much dancing at healthcare weekends," Jake said.

But my brother had a point. I had to make this look natural. As Jake steered us away from them, I shifted a little closer, relaxed my shoulders. How close did I need to be for this to look real? Probably into the danger zone.

"Don't worry," Jake murmured. "It's just dancing. I'm not going to kiss you."

Right. The PDA rules. Which had completely fled my mind.

Jake's arms were warm and solid around me. Our thighs brushed, and I almost jumped at the charge that shot through me. We swayed, breathing the same air. I didn't know which part of the evening was more dangerous—how much I had enjoyed taking pictures or how much I was enjoying this.

"Is Jacob a good dancer?" he asked. "No, wait. He's not the kind to dance, is he?" His voice was soft and gentle in my ear, like we were having a real discussion.

Once again, his nearness scrambled my brain. I had to concentrate, find a reply so he didn't notice.

"Maybe he's secretly a ballroom champ and was embarrassed to tell me." My voice, on the other hand, sounded far too breathless. "Can you tango? That would add depth to his character."

"Hmm, I don't know. It doesn't fit with the narrative you've developed. Too far-fetched. I might be able to sell a basic waltz."

He spun me and twirled me out. When he brought me back in, he pulled me close, his eyes locked on mine. The air whooshed out of my lungs.

Yeah, a tango was definitely a bad idea. I didn't think my pounding heart could take it.

Jake definitely had skills Jacob would not have.

The breeze was slightly cool, but Jake emanated enough warmth that I barely felt it. Stars twinkled overhead. The music's soft island vibes added to the magic.

This was far more romantic than the last school dance, when my wannabe break-dancer date crashed into the refreshment table and spilled Mountain Dew on half the girls' volleyball team.

Mom looked relaxed with her head on Dad's shoulder as they danced. I spotted Alana dancing with Tyler, and Neal with Gran, but none of them tried to cut in on us.

I was embarrassed to meet their eyes, like I was doing something I shouldn't have been.

Eventually we sat as the boat cruised toward shore under a dark sky. Jake put his arm around me, tracing slow circles on my shoulder like it was subconscious. Lights sparkled in the harbor, yellow on black and dancing on the water.

It was hard to remember that none of this was real.

After docking and disembarking, we were halfway to the main road when Jake stopped. "I left my jacket on the boat. Would you mind if I went back to get it? I know how to find the car. I'll run and meet you there."

Oh, nice try. I recognized that tactic, since I had used it the day before—when I was up to something sneaky.

"I'll go with you," I said, and gave him the heart-eyes expression he'd made me practice.

Whatever he was up to, I was going to keep an eye on him.

CHAPTER THIRTEEN

"**Y**ou don't have to come," Jake said when my family had continued on and we were alone in the dark parking lot next to the harbor.

Of course they had been nice and understanding about *him* forgetting something, when all I got was annoyance. It wasn't even something Jacob would do. *He* was responsible.

He was also imaginary, so . . .

"I want to be there for you." I continued using my fake loving voice. "It's such a beautiful evening for a walk along the water with my boyfriend."

It was. The air was warm enough, with a gentle sea breeze. Water slapped against hulls as ships bobbed nearby. A sprinkling of stars twinkled overhead.

Jake grunted.

"Look," I said, this time in a frank tone. "I know you're up to something. I followed you here earlier. So you can either keep pretending, lie to me, or tell me what's going on."

"I'm rather fond of option one."

"We aren't already doing enough pretending for you?"

A muscle twitched in his jaw. He shuffled away slowly, not like he was escaping, more like he needed to move. I stayed with him.

"Why did you follow me?" he asked.

"I happened to see you out a window, and you were totally sneaking."

He angled his head toward me. "So you did some sneaking of your own?"

"Exactly. We can have a contest to see which of us is sneakier."

"Well, since I caught you sneaking into my room this morning, I think we're even."

"I don't know what you're talking about. I was borrowing a hat. So that leaves this afternoon, which, let me think." I rubbed my chin. "Yep, puts you ahead. Also, can we stop saying the word *sneaking*? It no longer sounds like a real word."

He tucked his hair behind his ears and tipped his head back to stare at the sky. "Fine. I'm looking for a boat called the *West Wind*. That's all you're getting."

Not what I'd expected. "Drugs stored on board? Illegal fish smuggling scheme? Pirate treasure?"

"Is illegal fish smuggling a thing? Is there money in that?"

I glared at him.

"Do you want to help or not?" he asked. "There were lots of empty slips earlier, so I wanted to check them again now and see if any boats have returned for the night."

"Fine. Let's go."

I had so many questions, but that was the first semi-real thing he'd told me, and it was a ridiculous thing for him to be lying about, so we fell into step as we circled the harbor. The boats were everything from large ships like we'd cruised on, to smaller yachts, to catamarans and smaller fishing vessels.

I scanned the names on the hulls as we walked. When boats were too close together or in the dark, Jake would lean out or shine his phone light on them. There were some clever names—*Retirement Plan, On the Rocks, The Rodfather.* But none were called the *West Wind.* Many slips remained empty.

"Did you check those earlier, or were they empty then, too?" I asked.

He looked at his phone. "I have a list. There are several that have been empty all day."

"Are you sure it's here?"

"No." His shoulders slumped.

"So . . . we're looking for a boat that might not exist?"

"It exists. It's not a haunted ghost ship that's risen from the depths."

"That would be fun, though."

He sniffed a slight laugh. "No questions tonight, okay? Besides, we need to go. Your family is waiting."

"Sorry," I said, even though this was proof he was hiding something and had some ulterior motive. Besides, he was right—we had no time.

"What about your jacket?"

"You mean this one?"

We were passing a grassy area with large rocks, and he grabbed an item that had been tucked against a rock.

"You get definite sneaky points for that," I said.

"I thought we were done using that word?"

He seemed dejected, so as we walked quickly toward the car, I took his hand well before we were close enough to need to for my family's sake.

He squeezed it and avoided my gaze, his head down rather than looking at our surroundings, except to rise long enough to stare at the banyan tree, which was now lit with strands of twinkling lights that turned the whole block into a forest fairyland. The dangling roots glowed, and the light was warm and soft.

The sight stirred that feeling inside me, the one where my heart and my lungs felt too big for my chest, like I was full and bursting and didn't want to be anywhere except this exact place in this exact moment.

We paused to marvel in silence. I pulled my hand free and took out my phone. I'd be quick. I moved back and snapped pictures, one with Jake silhouetted against the lights, the branches stretched above him like an embrace.

Then we hurried to the car.

I was no closer to getting answers about who he was or why he was here, but I sensed this night, his partial truth, had meant . . . something.

Alana and Neal loved the photos. When we got back, I Air-Dropped the best ones to them, from the candid proposal shots to the posed ones afterward. Then I offered to edit everything when we got home and give them a flash drive. The words were out of my mouth before I could think.

"I couldn't ask you to do that," Alana said. "You're busy enough with school and college prep. I don't want to take away from your studies."

Please, take away from my studies. "You didn't ask. I offered. It's your engagement. Of course I want to help."

Like my math homework was more interesting. I was already trying not to dream about opening my photo editing account for the first time in months. I'd offered without fully thinking through how much temptation this was going to provide.

"Okay, then. These are good. I'm impressed, Kenz. It looks like we had a professional photo shoot. Thanks for documenting our night." She held up her hand and studied her ring, a dreamy expression crossing her face.

"It's nothing." I'd already visited that topic with Jake, and I didn't need to dwell on my supposed photography skills. Or lack thereof.

The two of us retreated to our room.

I kicked my shoes off into the middle of the floor. "I'm so happy for you. Neal's a good guy. Although, it's weird to think about my sister being married. You're so old."

"Shut up," she said with a laugh.

"No, it's true. I'm going to get you dentures and a Life Alert bracelet for your wedding gift. Are you going to pick out china patterns and towels and stuff? Oh, if you register for, like, garden gnomes or a churro maker, can I help?"

"I guess we'll register. We have four years of school, so we won't get a big place. I doubt we'll have a yard. We'll mostly ask for the basics."

Jake would have laughed at my question and made a churro joke. I should buy Alana a sense of humor for her bridal shower. I perched on the end of my bed. "When will you get married, do you think?"

"We don't want anything huge, so we're thinking August before optometry school in the fall." She removed her shoes and set them neatly next to the wall.

"Is that long enough to plan?"

Of course it was. I was talking to the junior queen of planning, who had learned from our parents, the masters. She probably already had three color-coded spreadsheets and a binder.

"We're both organized and know what we want, so I think we'll manage." She retrieved my shoes from where they'd fallen and moved them out of the way. "You'll be my maid of honor, right?"

"Seriously?"

"Of course. My friends from school and Neal's sister will be bridesmaids, but you're my only sister."

"I'd be honored. Ha. Maid of *honor*."

She shook her head at my bad joke. "Hopefully Jacob will be able to get away. I know he's looking at internships this summer, and I don't know when school starts for him."

"As soon as you have a date, I'll let him know."

The lighthearted mood took a plunge off a cliff. I swallowed hard, unease in my stomach. Jake and I would be "broken up" by then, and he wouldn't be attending anything with us.

I needed to come clean. We were having a huge sisterly bonding moment, and I was plotting what lies to tell her. Guilt wormed inside me.

But tonight was her night. I couldn't disrupt it with my confession, make her confused and possibly upset or mad at me. Would she tell Neal, who had said I'd be his new sister? Or our parents, who were so excited?

No, I couldn't do it now. I'd figure out the details later. I'd announce the breakup I'd been planning, far enough before the wedding that my family wasn't feeling sorry for me for being single *at* the wedding.

For now, I'd celebrate.

And stop thinking about Jake and his mystery boat.

"So, do you have any idea what kind of dress you want? Or that you want for me? I look great in blue. Just saying."

She laughed, and I pushed the guilt down deep. We stayed up way too late searching for dresses on our phones. I would save the worries for another day.

CHAPTER FOURTEEN

I regretted staying up so late when the alarm went off for an early tee time the next morning. As if I hadn't been dreading golf day enough.

I liked walks outdoors. Meandering ones, through wild places. Doing it on perfectly manicured lawns while swinging metal sticks at tiny objects ruined everything.

If I were any good, I might enjoy it more. My lessons had started with my grandfather. Those had been fun. After my parents joined his optometry practice, he allowed himself one day off a week. Then, once he "retired," he only worked three days a week, and he spent time with his grandkids. My dad was an only child, so that just meant me, Alana, and Tyler. Gramps taught me the basics and insisted that we didn't have to keep score, even though I did in my head. And then we ate ice cream.

Over waffle cones towering with mint chip—he and Gran must have partially fallen in love over a shared addiction to dessert—he told me stories about his childhood, where golf had been out of reach for people like him. He talked about optometry school, what it was like to start his practice and run a business. I'd always admired him and enjoyed his corny jokes. He would have liked the one I'd saved for Neal.

After Gramps passed away, Dad took over occasional golf outings. Those were more serious affairs, full of analyzing distances and angles and reading reports on each hole. I spent the time wishing I had a camera to explore the rough areas. Especially considering that's where my balls usually ended up.

As if in protest of today, I defied the colored commands of the schedule and wore a bathing suit under my shorts and tank top. I also threw a pair of flip-flops into my small backpack with the sunscreen and sunglasses. Maybe I'd find a nice water trap to swim in. Or I'd hit my ball into the ocean accidentally and take a dip while I pretended to look for it.

"Have you ever golfed before, Jacob?" Dad asked over breakfast, and I'd been thinking of him as Jake so often that the name sounded weird.

When Jake glanced at me, I wrinkled my nose.

"No, sir, can't say that I have."

"I learned from my father, who taught the kids. We'll be happy to show you the ropes. And no pressure. It's more about spending the day together than how well you do."

Jake's eye twitched, and I recalled his competitive streak at the surfing lesson. I suspected he agreed with me that even if you didn't like the game, keeping score was kind of the point. At least I'd learned on a small par-three course. Jake was starting with the big leagues, a fancy beachside course used for major competitions. In all its eighteen-hole, several-hour glory.

This was going to be a long day.

Somehow Tyler had gotten out of this excursion to work on his computer project, claiming he needed a break from the sun. Too bad I hadn't planned an escape route. Not that it would have worked for me. Tyler always got off easier than I ever did.

As we trooped downstairs, Jake leaned close. "Is this going to be as dreadful as I expect?"

"Probably more," I said.

"Hmm." He had a calculating glint in his eye.

In the parking lot, he wandered toward the convertible. Seven of us could have fit in the van, though it would have been tight.

Gran met Jake's gaze, and her eyes sparkled. "I'll take the kids again."

She motioned me toward them, and I followed before Dad's frown could become an argument.

"We have a tee time," he said. "Please take the freeway, Mom."

She waved a hand without turning.

The ride was the same distracted death journey as before. Jake was on his phone in the back.

"Gran, are you wearing a swimsuit?" I asked. "For golfing?"

"You did, dear."

"Wishful thinking," I said.

Jake leaned forward. "There it is."

Gran slowed, and I spotted the sign for kayak and snorkel tours that she'd almost leveled during our first drive.

I looked from her to Jake as she turned onto a small road.

"Did you two plan this? You could have warned me."

Her red lips curved. "Jacob or I would have, if you hadn't put the swimsuit on."

"You two are terrible." But I was laughing. Suddenly things were looking up.

Jake wore a smug expression.

After we pulled into a shaded parking lot next to a beach, Gran called my dad and put the phone on speaker.

"We took a bit of a detour, Richard. Golf was your father's thing, not mine. I'm taking the kids kayaking."

"Mother, we have reservations."

"You have four people. That will make one party. I'll cancel the second booking. I'm kidnapping Kenzie and Jacob today. We'll be fine."

"Are you—"

"See you later!" She hung up on him midquestion.

I laughed. I seriously loved her. "You are so bad."

"I am," she agreed. "Now, who wants to go snorkeling?"

Jake and I raised our hands.

"Excellent."

We slathered up with reef-safe sunscreen, changed from tennis shoes to flip-flops, and walked to the sand, which was still cool. The beach was empty except for a row of kayaks, a pile of snorkel gear, and a few people standing around—a family with three boys ranging from toddler to maybe fifth grade, an older couple, and a couple in their twenties.

The guide gave everyone basic instructions on how to hold and maneuver the paddles, which I tuned out since I'd been kayaking before. I watched the waves until the word *turtles* jolted me. He was explaining that we'd kayak around the point and into a protected bay, where we'd jump out of the kayaks to snorkel.

And he reminded us to keep our distance if we saw turtles.

This was so much better than golf.

Gran joined the guide in one kayak, while Jake and I grabbed another, shoved off, and jumped aboard. It was a standard plastic sit-on-top kind, and our bags and snorkel gear rested in the bottom.

The morning was quiet, the sun not yet above the mountains, the water a dark blue. A deep sense of peace laced the air.

We paddled in silence as the others launched. The familiar figure-eight motion relaxed me, but I had a captive audience, and it was time to take advantage of it.

"So. Let's talk about last night."

"You mean your sister's engagement?"

"Yep, and then that whole thing afterward where you lied to my parents so you could look for a boat."

"How's Alana today? She must be happy. I guess you knew in advance about the proposal."

Was it my imagination, or did he sound hurt?

"Neal told me after we boarded, asked me to take pictures. When he sent you to distract Alana."

Was it my imagination, or did *I* sound apologetic? Ridiculous. I didn't owe Jake anything. And he surely didn't expect it. Right?

"Alana is thrilled. We looked at dresses half the night. You're invited, by the way."

"To wear a dress? No, thanks."

"You couldn't pull one off anyway. I meant to the wedding. They're thinking August."

"I'll have to check my calendar."

I found myself a little sad to think he wouldn't be there. I'd known him for three days. And I still didn't trust him. But I did like him, more than I should have. Nothing could happen, though. I wasn't sure if he even liked me. There were moments when we connected that I thought he might. Times when his gaze on me was warm and tangible, or physical contact went beyond what was strictly necessary. But other times he seemed to be judging everything about me and not liking what he saw.

Focus. Get answers. How had I let him distract me?

"Back to the other part of last night, Mr. Question Dodger. The skulking-around part."

"So we're officially done with the word *sneaking*? Is *skulking* better? What about *creeping*? Or is *lurking* similar?"

"Enough with the thesaurus. What were you doing?"

We paddled several strokes in silence before he spoke. "I'm looking for a boat that's supposed to be in Maui. It's not for anything illegal or in any way questionable. It's personal, and difficult to talk about, and I can't tell you more."

Can't. There was that word again. And curse him, for knowing that his admitting it was difficult for him would lessen my desire to push.

Next to us, another kayak pulled up. It contained one of the older kids from the family, the dad, and the smallest boy sitting in the middle in his life vest. He stared at us, and I smiled.

He responded by chucking something at me.

I flinched, and the object sailed past me.

"Aidan!" the dad yelled. "Sorry, sorry!"

They continued past us, veering erratically.

The item had landed in the water nearby. It was a tiny shoe.

Jake paddled us closer, and I leaned over and scooped it up. The other kayak had cruised away, so I stuck the shoe into the bottom of ours, and we continued on.

The water was calm, the green hills shadowy, and the clouds wispy.

I hummed. "I love the water. The cruise was amazing last night, but I prefer this. It's peaceful. I feel more alone with nature when there's no engine."

Jake was silent for several strokes of the paddle. "I love the water, too."

His words were quiet, barely loud enough for me to hear. I wanted to turn around and look at him but didn't want to stop him from revealing something real.

"What do you like about it?" he asked.

I stared at the horizon. "It used to be one of the places I could escape to. Where I knew no one would find me or track me down or interrupt or criticize me."

"Like a place where you could be yourself."

"Yeah." I sighed the word. "Do you live near the water?"

"We agreed it was safer not to talk about that." He didn't sound like he meant the words.

I didn't answer, waiting.

"I live in San Diego." His reply was soft. "And I'm on the water almost every weekend."

San Diego. That fit. The tan, the tropical scent, the surfing skills, the beach attitude. I savored the tiny bit of information, a little more to make him his own person. But it was one piece. Many were missing, and I wasn't sure what the whole puzzle looked like.

"You're not bad at this," he said.

"I've been on a few lakes and rivers, but it's been a while."

"Did you ever go with your camera?"

My heart stuttered. "Not my nice one, but a GoPro."

"Did you bring it this week?"

I shook my head. That one was a neighbor to my DSLR, in my closet.

Another kayak glided straight toward us, and we reversed to get out of the way. It was the dad and kids again. The smallest boy yanked off his hat and flung it into the air. The wind carried it straight into our boat. I picked it up to throw it back, but they'd moved on.

"Sorry," the dad called again.

"Apologize to the turtles for raising a litterer," I muttered.

"That would be entertaining," Jake said.

We cruised on.

"I needed this today," I said. "Nature. Being alone with my thoughts, getting away from the schedule and the people."

"I'm not people?"

"I guess for today you're not."

And I actually didn't mind his presence. Usually I preferred alone-alone time, not even with Lucia. But I liked having him here.

I cleared my throat, uncomfortable at that thought. "My family isn't big on the outdoors unless it's carefully managed. As I'm sure you've noticed. It's nice of you to put up with them."

"They're nice," he said. "Especially Gran."

"When did you two plan this?"

"It was barely a plan. The beginning of one. Just an idea, really."

I snorted.

Could she have been in cahoots with him somehow? Maybe that's how he knew so much about my family?

I shifted to locate her. She sat in the front of her kayak, occasionally dipping her paddle into the water, but mostly craning her head to take in the scenery while the guide did all the work. I chuckled softly.

"What's your family like?" I asked. "Or is that too much?"

After a long pause, he said, "I do have a younger sister, believe it or not."

"That's convenient."

"I know, right? Well done with that lie."

"Shh." I looked around, but Gran was far away. The only people nearby were in the kayak with the kid determined to donate his belongings to the sea. "Did I get anything else right? And don't bother saying *career plans*. You want to be an optometrist as much as I want to. I mean, you don't want to be one."

He made a huffing sound.

"What?"

"Nothing."

"No, you meant something. Say what you're thinking."

"If I said what I'm thinking, it would be insulting to your family, and they've been nice to me this week. I just think they should pay more attention, and they would notice how you would be a terrible optometrist."

"Hey."

"Not because you aren't smart enough. Because you're completely uninterested in it."

"Of course I'm interested. It's the family profession." My back stiffened. "Besides, we're not talking about me. We were talking about what else I made up that's true about you."

He hummed and waited a few strokes before replying. "I suppose it's safe to confirm things you've already said. You also got it right that I'm handsome and incredibly smart and definitely good for you."

I splashed him with the paddle.

He laughed. "Seriously, though, it seems like the guy you made up isn't your type."

"How would you know what my type is?"

"You're saying past boyfriends have been studious and dull like Jacob? I need to understand my competition."

"Let's just say none of them would have received invitations to Maui."

"Poor taste in guys, Kenz?"

I splashed him again. "I thought that was obvious."

"I know you're trying to insult me, but I'm choosing to ignore it because I want details."

Telling him wouldn't hurt. It might make him understand why I'd made Jacob the way I had.

"Do you want to know about Brady the lacrosse player, who asked me what was happening every five minutes throughout the superhero movie because he was legitimately confused? Or Anthony, who was in a band, and said he wrote a song about me, and then sang another girl's name when he performed it? Or the guy I went to homecoming with, who vanished halfway through the dance, and I found out later he'd been arrested for covering the principal's car with chicken nuggets?"

"How did he do that?"

"Apparently barbecue sauce is fairly sticky."

Jake was silent. Then, "Wow, you really do have poor taste in guys."

"Now you see why I made one up." To be fair, none of those guys had seemed terrible at first. And to my credit, I had been the one to nix any possibility of a second date.

"What about you? You don't have a girlfriend, do you?" I hoped I sounded casual.

"I would never fake date someone if I did."

A burst of unexplained happiness shot through me at that news, but I shoved it aside. "Anyway. *My* type doesn't matter. I made up Jacob because he was my parents' type."

"Trying to compete with Neal?"

"Hey, don't mock him."

"I'm not. He's a good guy. And he'll be a good doctor—wait, sorry, I know, not an official doctor. I just mean the calm bedside manner. I'd trust him with my eye health."

"Yeah." My reply came out like a sigh. "Exactly."

"Ah. So you wanted your parents to see you the way they see Alana, and you thought Neal Two Point Oh was the way to do it. Why create a fake boyfriend at all, though?"

The plastic seat and my damp legs and this tiny boat were suddenly very uncomfortable. "You wouldn't understand."

"Try me. I'd like to know," he said. "So I can make this more convincing, of course."

Of course. Why had I thought, for a split second, that he'd meant he truly wanted to understand me?

How had we gotten onto this topic, anyway? If he wasn't going to open up about his mystery boat, I certainly wasn't going to share all my secrets.

Maybe it was better if we didn't talk.

CHAPTER FIFTEEN

We kept paddling, and passed an unopened granola bar floating in the water. Probably from that serial litterer in the making. Jake drew it closer with his paddle until he could grab it.

Then ahead I saw a ripple on the water's surface. I stared. Was it a rock?

No. It moved.

"Turtle," I breathed.

The shell was dark like wet rock, but too smooth for stone, and it was definitely moving. A head poked up.

I froze. A thrill shot through me.

"Here," Jake said, and the kayak rocked gently as he leaned forward to press something into my hand.

It was a GoPro, the same model as the one I had at home, with an identical floating hand grip.

"What's this?"

"I thought you were a photographer. You have a better angle. Hurry, before it swims away."

I propped the paddle on my thighs and snapped several pictures. The turtle swam around, sometimes floating so I could only see its shell, but sometimes raising its head.

"Circle around to our left," I said.

Jake expertly steered us close but not too close, and I took more pictures and a short video. Some photos would look like nothing more than a rock, but we were close enough that I got a few good ones of its head, and the water was so clear, you could see the shell under the surface.

Another kayak came near, and we watched the turtle swim around before it dove. When it didn't immediately resurface, we moved on. I twisted to try to see it again.

"I'm sure there will be more," Jake said.

I hoped he was right. One wasn't enough.

We rounded the point, and ahead lay a quiet bay with calm turquoise water. The shores were lined with trees so green that the colors looked like they'd been Photoshopped. A few larger boats floated in the bay.

Why was every new thing I saw in Maui more perfect than I could have imagined?

Everyone paddled their kayaks until we were in a row, and we tied them together. Gran and the guide were at the far end, and she waved to us.

Jake and I gathered the shoe, hat, and granola bar and passed them to the dad in the boat next to us, who apologized six times and thanked us. I didn't care about the apology—he didn't need to say sorry to me. He needed to teach his kid to respect the wildlife.

Jake cleared his throat. "Hey, buddy. Did you see the turtle?"

The little boy stared at him and nodded.

"You know they live in the ocean, right? So we don't throw

things into the water, because it's their home and the items might hurt them. Does that make sense?"

The kid nodded again.

"Can you say sorry to the turtles?"

The kid just stared.

"Like this. Sorry, Mr. Turtle," Jake called.

"Sorry, Mr. Turtle," the boy yelled, and everyone stared.

"Good. Now, you know how we show we're sorry, right? We don't do it again?"

The boy bit his lip. "Okay."

The father watched with his head ducked and his face red, and hurried to prepare his kids for the water when Jake finished.

I sat sideways, my legs dangling over the edge of the kayak, and stared at Jake as the dad helped his sons into the water.

"What?" Jake asked.

"That was kind of amazing."

"It was your idea."

"It didn't occur to me to make him do it."

He shrugged. "Like I said, I wanted to see it. Plus, he needed to learn."

I returned his smile. It was nice to have someone who shared my views.

We took masks and fins from our bag.

"Let me guess," I said. "You've done this before, too."

"Have you?" He pulled the mask on and left it atop his head.

"Nope. We weren't supposed to go until Friday." I'd been looking forward to it, after spending an hour convincing my mom that snorkeling wouldn't lead to the entire family drowning in a coral reef, our decomposing corpses becoming food for tropical fish.

"Focus on breathing evenly through your mouth." He held up the mask. "And be careful to keep the tube above water."

"Super helpful. Thanks."

I put the goggles over my eyes and tightened the rubber straps, which caught on my hair.

"Ow." I tried to tug the mask off and managed to yank out a chunk of hair.

"Here, let me."

Before I could reply, gentle hands covered mine and moved them away. Jake slowly and carefully untangled my hair from the straps. He was close enough that I could feel the heat from his body. His hands were gentle.

The tugging stopped, and he handed me the mask. Then his hands returned to my hair, smoothing out the knots and brushing it back.

"How . . ." My voice squeaked. "How did you manage not to yank out half your hair?"

"Practice. Here." He took my mask again and slid the strap over my head, then adjusted it, the mouthpiece dangling. His fingers brushed my cheek. Then he tightened the straps. "How's that? You want it tight enough to keep the water out."

"Good. Yeah. Thanks."

I couldn't look at him. He was only being nice, right? He didn't mean anything by it, beyond making sure I didn't choke or go blind underwater. So why was my heart pounding in my throat?

And why was he frozen with his face so close to mine, staring at my eyes through my mask? His attention dipped to my mouth, and my skin felt electrified.

He blinked, cleared his throat. "Mouthpiece. Um. Yeah. That's all that's left." He shifted away, the kayak rocking.

I swallowed hard and tried to calm my breathing.

"Ready?" he asked.

"Yeah."

I peeked at him, looking funny in the mask, and tried to pretend he hadn't left me feeling warm and gooey and tingly with . . . whatever that had been.

We slid over the side of the kayak into crystal water. I slipped the mouthpiece in and tried breathing, which wasn't too hard. We put our faces down and drifted away.

Beneath the surface was a new world, everything tinted blue-green and slightly fuzzy, though the water was clear. Coral grew in knobby formations, dotted with spiny sea urchins. Fish darted in and out, yellow-and-white-striped, red, bright electric blue, squarish yellow ones with polka dots. Parrotfish with their weird beaks made snapping noises. Some fish were alone, but some flowed past in whole schools, moving together in formation. I glimpsed an eel darting into hiding. I'd read about many of these species.

It was crazy that there were so many. All these creatures living unique lives, in a world completely unlike mine. I loved the ocean, how much there was that we didn't know about it. Humans were only just beginning to see it, but it had been there all along.

I floated, suspended, silent except for the sound of my breathing in the mouthpiece. Rays of sun shot through from above.

And then there was another turtle, soaring along the coral ahead.

I stopped. It looked cooler underwater. Flippers moved gracefully as it propelled itself toward the surface, like it could have been flying.

Jake floated next to me, and I grabbed his hand. He looped a strap around my wrist and pressed the camera grip into my hand.

Autopilot took over. Remaining as motionless as possible, I snapped photo after photo of the turtle as it nosed around the reef, floated, surfaced for air. It studied us, and we moved away as it came closer, so we wouldn't touch it, but we slowly edged around it to get good views. I loved its little face. I switched to video mode and captured it swimming.

As the turtle swam away, it took part of me with it.

Jake pointed to an eel, and I followed that to a school of yellow-and-black fish. I drifted, taking pictures of them, too, until Jake tugged my arm.

I surfaced.

"Time to head back," he said. "Sorry."

It wasn't his fault everyone else insisted on keeping to schedules. If I ever came back, I would buy myself a kayak and snorkel gear so I could spend all day out here.

We swam to the kayaks, and I was sad to emerge from the water. It had felt so peaceful and right, a whole other world, where nothing existed except me and the fish.

After we climbed in, I handed the camera to Jake even though I wanted to cling to it.

We were silent as the boats separated and we began the paddle back to the beach.

"What did you think?" he finally asked.

I didn't know where to start. "It was amazing. There were so many kinds of fish. And coral is fascinating. Did you know it's an animal, not a plant? And the turtle!"

"Do you like turtles or whales more?" Jake asked.

"That's a supremely unfair question. They're so different. Whales are huge and majestic and impressive. But actually swimming with the turtle was amazing. I might need to swim with whales to decide for sure." And I was rambling again. "Why, what about you?"

"I like them both. I mostly wanted to hear your thoughts."

A light feeling swelled in my chest, before I remembered he was only saying that because he had to. "You don't have to pretend to be a good boyfriend when my family isn't here."

"Listening to someone talk about what they care about isn't a fake-boyfriend thing, Kenz. It's a decent-person thing."

Was Jake just trying to stay on my good side? Or was he right, and I should have been expecting more from my family all this time?

After returning to the beach, we dried off and Gran drove to a nearby restaurant for brunch. It was called the Gazebo and had gorgeous views of the bay. This entire outing was so much better than golfing. To think, instead of swimming with turtles, my family would rather swing a stick around for hours. So. Weird.

We ordered the most interesting dishes we could—macadamia pineapple pancakes with coconut syrup, a towering mountain of fried rice, French toast covered in whipped cream—and shared them.

"So, Gran, what did you think of snorkeling?" Jake asked.

"Oh, it was lovely. So many interesting things. Do you know, I had never been?"

"You didn't travel much?"

"My late husband rarely took time off. It was hard work, establishing the practice."

Jake leaned forward. "Tell me about that. How did he start? Did you work with him?"

Gran's expression grew fond and distant. "He grew up poor after the war. We both did. My father died overseas and left my mom alone. Kenzie's grandfather and I met in community college and fell in love. He was determined to make something stable for us. He worked so hard, in school, then building the practice. I learned the business side of things and ran the office for him. We never did get to travel. Taking days off meant no patients, which meant not getting paid. And then he got so used to always being there for his patients, it became a habit."

This explained my dad's desire for the family to work together. His own dad had wanted roots, something stable for the whole family that made them part of the community, where they could help others.

"Why optometry?" Jake asked. "It's a great field, but it seems like there would have been easier ways."

"There would have. But his parents couldn't afford glasses,

and his older sister had terrible eyesight, even as a child. He saw the problems that caused her in school and life and wanted to be able to help. For years, he supported charities, provided free clinics for people who couldn't afford care. My son has continued that work."

"I like that, remembering where you came from. Honoring your family and not being ashamed of your roots." Jake's voice sounded wistful, like he was thinking of more than Gran's story.

Gran sighed. "I loved my husband very much, and I was so proud of him. I have no regrets. But looking back, there were many things we should have talked about first in terms of what we wanted out of life. That's important in a relationship, sharing your goals and your hopes. You can't know everything about a person, but you should get to know them as well as you can before you commit."

How had she kept her spark, her zest for life, in a family so focused on work? Or had she waited until my grandfather was gone to let her true self out? I had trouble remembering what she'd been like before my grandfather had died, when I'd been too young to think about it.

The server came to refill our coffee, and when he left, Gran had a twinkle in her eye.

"So. What do you like most about Kenzie?" she asked.

"Gran," I said.

"It's okay." Jake smiled at me. "I like that she's dedicated and hardworking and loves her family."

"Hmm." Gran didn't seem to like—or believe—that answer. Probably because, though he sounded sincere, those were not the first adjectives that came to people's minds when they thought about me.

"Also," he said, like he realized he needed to sell it better, "she's creative and passionate and curious, and she inspires me."

Gran nodded, apparently satisfied.

His attention on me was piercing.

My breath caught. I didn't know what to think. It was exactly what I hoped a guy who was supposed to like me would say. But surely the words had only been to convince Gran, who didn't believe the boring version of me as easily as my parents did, and who had been looking doubtful. Jake couldn't know me well enough to believe those things about me, could he?

"And what do you have in common?" Gran asked.

"Oh. Um. Well, we both value career and education and helping others."

Again, it was exactly what Jacob should have said. Except, Gran didn't care. She had never minded my tendencies, had supported my photography enough to buy me the camera.

"We both like being outside," I said. "Seeing and trying new things. And we love the water."

She smiled.

Jake met my gaze. "Exploring," he added. "Adventure."

We hadn't really talked about it, but it was true. For both of us. The food. The spur-of-the-moment surfing. Today's change of plans. Was it too much? It was everything I had tried to move away from. And yet, it was *me*.

I shouldn't have been wishing he meant the words. My stomach squirmed, and I blinked first.

Gran studied me. "What about the future? I know, I know. You're young. But what do you want out of it? Not necessarily together, just in general?"

What was this, a grandmother matchmaking service? Except we were already supposedly dating, so we didn't need help. Not that kind, anyway.

I needed to get things back on track, not let the fresh air and the new experience and the joy of the day derail my plans and my new image.

"A fulfilling career," I said. "And someone who shares my values."

Not totally a lie.

Something in his eyes shifted, seemed to recognize that I was done. "Exactly," Jake said.

Gran studied us, then nodded. She paid, and we explored a rocky trail to a nearby beach.

"So, if I want to take a picture of this, how can I make it good?" Jake asked.

He snapped some with his phone that I could tell would be terrible—with people blocking the beach, or the pointy roof of the restaurant half hidden, or straight into the sun.

"If you want a nature shot, you generally start by making sure people aren't blocking the best part of your view." I pointed to the interlopers. "Try to frame the main subject. Items in the foreground are helpful, like a rock or a tree, to give a sense of the distances. Check the lighting, where the sun is, and don't look right into it. Make sure shadows aren't casting some parts in darkness. If you want a wave, don't take it when the water's flat.

Wait for it to start breaking. Clouds are more interesting than a clear sky. The rule of thirds is good—usually you don't want the main subject right in the middle. Pretend the image is divided into a grid—"

And I was giving a full-on lecture. I stopped.

Jake wandered away and took more, then handed me his phone. "Better?"

I scrolled through them. "Are you naturally bad, or are you messing with me? Like that first day at the whale lookout point."

"I don't know what you mean." His dimpled smirk emerged, and he took his phone from me and strolled down the beach.

I glared at his back. He was definitely messing with me, *and* he'd made me geek out over photography.

Gran appeared beside me and linked her arm through mine, watching Jake.

"Kenzie girl," she said, her voice serious. "We need to talk."

CHAPTER SIXTEEN

The solemn tone of Gran's voice was rare and sent a shiver through me despite the warm sun.

"I know we don't see each other often, but I've heard enough about Jacob from your parents to know one thing. That boy"—she pointed to Jake, who was several yards away, out of hearing range, walking through the shallow water—"is not who he says he is."

My stomach hardened. I swallowed. "He actually is . . ."

She raised her eyebrows and pursed her lips, which were red again. Apparently, after the snorkel mask and brunch, she'd re-applied lipstick.

I'd been half thinking she knew about Jake and was the one who'd told him to come here and pretend. But apparently not.

"Has he been lying to you?" she asked. "Or to us? Because he's nothing like the boy you've been telling us about. And no matter how nice he is, a liar is not the kind of person my grand-daughter should be dating."

I could have thrown him under the bus, let her think the worst. Said that he'd misled me, or the distance meant we didn't know each other as well as I had thought. But that was unfair when I was the original liar.

If anyone would understand, she would. She was the best possible family member to learn the truth. And maybe she could help somehow.

I sighed. "His name *is* Jacob Miller. But he's not my Jacob."

"I don't understand. You invited someone other than your boyfriend to come with us?"

"Not exactly. I kind of . . . made up my Jacob. I don't have a boyfriend."

Gran stared at me. Then turned to look at Jake, standing in the waves. "So who is he? An actor?"

"Not exactly. He's a guy named Jacob Miller, pretending to be my boyfriend."

I didn't want to admit the whole truth, that I didn't know who he was or how he'd gotten here. She was fairly understanding, but that might be pushing my luck.

She blinked a few times. And then laughed. "Oh, Kenz. Of all my grandchildren, only you would end up in a situation like this. Tell me everything. Where'd you find him?"

I gave her the abridged version, of how I'd made up a boyfriend to impress my parents. Then said, "Jake and I . . . have a mutual friend. And Jake had a reason for needing to visit Maui. So we agreed to help each other."

Not technically a lie, though I didn't know who that friend was.

Her face was serious again. "How well do you know him? Is this safe?"

I shrugged. "Well enough. He's not a criminal or anything." I hoped. "He's been perfectly polite."

"Hmm."

I gripped my backpack straps. "Do you think everyone else has figured it out?"

"I can pretty much guarantee that no one would ever guess what you just told me." She chuckled lightly and shook her head.

"Yeah . . ."

"What is his reason for being here?"

"Um. It's secret?"

"As in, you can't tell me because it's his secret to tell? Or as in, he kept it secret from you?"

I didn't answer.

"You need to get the whole truth, Kenz. As amusing as this is, we have to make sure it's safe for the family. Who knows what he could be up to. I hate to be the adult here, but . . ."

"No, you're right. I'll talk to him."

"Good. Tell me when you have. Now." She studied him. "He's cute. And much more fun than the guy you made up."

"Yeah." I sighed.

"And you."

"Me what?"

"You seem happy."

"I'm in Maui. Of course I'm happy."

She waved a hand. "Today. During the surfing. Helping your sister on the cruise last night. It's you again, my adventurous, free-spirited little Mackenzie."

I tried to ignore the clenching in my chest, the tightness in my throat. Tried not to think about how happy it made me, these things I would do every day if I could. Those pictures, the wildlife, the gorgeous views. Sure, everyone enjoyed views of

Hawaiian beaches. But it was something deeper, a longing for this to last, to be my life.

Better to focus on getting a very cute and very secretive boy to talk.

By the time we returned, the others were at the condo. Tyler was in his room. Had he even come out while we were gone? Weirdo.

I'd tried to act normal on the drive, so I could better ambush Jake when the time was right. Which meant I had to get him alone, away from my family, who were recounting every hole of a riveting golf game—and continuing to give Neal pointers it sounded like they had repeated many times.

It did sound like the views had been nice, but that was no substitute for seeing the water up close.

When they asked about our morning, we gave a version they would like—quiet kayak to a reef, saw turtles, stopped for brunch. No mention of the photos I took. No gushing about the underwater paradise and how I was ready to build an airtight house and live in a reef for a month to photograph the fish.

Definitely no Gran uncovering the partial truth about Jake.

I glanced at her, then the others. I hadn't meant to, but I'd made her complicit in my lie. By playing along, she was lying to her son. I swallowed any misgivings. Couldn't change things now.

Mom decided to take a nap, while Neal and Alana were happy to read on the lanai, though it seemed Alana was looking at her new ring as much as her book.

It was truly a mystery how I was related to these people.

"I'm going to the pool," I said. "Jacob, want to come?"

My tone did not leave refusal as an option.

He blinked. "Sure. I mean, I would love to join you."

"The pool sounds nice," Dad said.

"Why don't we let them have some time together." Gran jumped in before I had to.

"Oh. Right."

A twinge went through me. This was our first real family vacation in . . . well, a long time, and I was so distracted by Fake Jake, I'd barely talked to my parents.

"Maybe sometime this week, the two of us can hang out," I said to Dad.

His face lit up. "That would be great."

Jake and I grabbed towels and went to the pool, where we located two free chairs under a row of palm trees, away from the crowded area.

I was trying to figure out the best way to say, *Hey, my grandmother knows you're a fraud, so you'd better tell me why you're lying,* when Jake turned to me.

"What's the deal with you and photography?"

"What?" My thoughts couldn't shift.

"You're talented and knowledgeable. You wanted to camp out in that gallery in Lahaina. And you clearly love it, since once you started today, you couldn't stop. But you've barely taken any pictures in one of the most photogenic places on the planet, and when others bring it up, you change the subject."

"That's not . . ."

Okay, did he have to be so observant? And today had been a onetime thing. It didn't mean anything.

I plopped onto a lounge chair. "No. No distractions right now. We need to talk." I pointed to the chair next to mine.

He sat, crossed his hands behind his head, and leaned back.

"My grandma figured it out."

"Figured what out?"

I waved a hand between us. "This. You. Us. That we're faking."

He sat up abruptly. "What? How?"

"I don't know. Those questions at brunch today. Or the fact that you're nothing like the Jacob Miller I invented."

"The rest of your family seems to be buying it."

"They're not as observant. You've been doing a decent job, but today was . . . I don't know. Too much like the old me."

A slight frown creased his forehead and his lips twitched, but he blinked, and the expression was gone. "What's Gran going to do about it?"

"I don't know. She told me to get the truth so she knows we can trust you."

He tilted his head back, closed his eyes, and exhaled hard. "Fine. I'll tell you everything. But you first."

"Excuse me?"

"Answer my question about the photography. Then I'll tell you why I'm here."

"This isn't a negotiation."

His eyes opened and met mine. "I know. But it's hard to talk about. I need a minute."

My determination faltered at the serious tone of his voice. "Fine. The photography is tied to why I invented a boyfriend. I used to be really into it."

"Used to?"

"My family thought I was spending too much time on it. I would vanish for entire days in a park or on a trail or at the zoo. And you've probably noticed that I'm not an organized, well-prepared go-getter like everyone else."

"There's nothing wrong with that."

I snorted. "Tell that to my parents."

"I will."

"I didn't mean . . . Don't say anything."

His determined face indicated that he would march upstairs right now. A flock of hummingbirds fluttered through my chest.

I cleared my throat. "They never approved of me wanting to make a career of nature photography. Or to delay college to travel, or get an internship or build a portfolio. There was this local photo contest that I was certain would convince them it was a legitimate career goal."

A weight settled on my shoulders, that same feeling from months ago slamming into me full force. I tried to keep my voice light, like I didn't care, like admitting this aloud for the first time wasn't reopening the wound that I'd hidden but that had never healed, was still raw and throbbing.

"What happened?"

I swallowed and stared up at the palm leaves, the pattern of sun and shade and green. "I made a deal with my parents. If I won the contest, they'd consider that I might be able to make photography work. But I didn't win, so we mutually decided I'd shift my energy to something more suitable and stable long-term."

"Optometry?"

"Why not?"

He sniffed. "Was that really a mutual decision, or did they dictate, and you didn't argue?"

"There's nothing wrong with making them happy. My life is much easier now."

"If *easier* means 'more miserable.'" He shook his head. "I'm sorry. About the contest. That sucks." He took my hand. "When was that?"

"Last summer. So since I failed, I had to—"

"Hey." His voice was sharp. "That's not failing. That's one contest, one opportunity. Failing is when you give up."

I huffed. "Well, then, I did fail. Because I figured I'd reinvent myself. Become the Kenzie they wanted me to be. Optometry was as good as anything else. I joined a science club and that future healthcare professionals thing. Went to that weekend conference where I supposedly met you. Jacob. Whatever. Tried hard to be more organized, less distracted. Put the camera away. And it made everyone so happy."

"Did it make *you* happy?"

I avoided his gaze. "I like that they aren't frustrated with me all the time. Or constantly criticizing me. I like that they seem proud of me."

"So you're going to fake it for the rest of your life? Go to school for something you don't care about, for a job you don't like?"

It sounded like he was trying to carefully keep his voice neutral, and I ignored the squirming in my stomach at his accusation. I cared. It would be fine.

I watched the pool instead of him. "The world needs more women in STEM."

"That's true. But that means making sure they have opportunities and encouraging the ones who want to pursue those careers, not forcing women into the field to make other people happy."

I fiddled with the edge of my towel. Whatever. Time to shove the tangled mess of feelings from all those confessions back into their cave and focus on him.

"We're done talking about me. It's your turn. I made up a boyfriend who was part of that image. Like you said, Neal Two Point Oh. When I got home from that dreadful conference, Alana and Neal were talking about their future, and the lie just slipped out, so I went with it. But how did you know about it? And those details to fake? What are you doing here?"

He studied the water. "I know something about trying to keep up appearances. My family is big on that. It's one reason I hate to see you do it, because trust me when I say, eventually it's more work than it's worth."

He seemed to be thinking and preparing to continue, so I stayed silent. Then he set his jaw.

"I have a half brother." The words were abrupt. Awkward.

"Um. Okay?"

"That's the first time I've said it out loud."

I twisted to face him. "What, seriously?"

He glanced at me, then away. Swallowed. "I found out at Christmas that apparently I'm not my dad's oldest son. That they've been hiding it from me my whole life."

"Oh, wow. That must be weird."

"Yeah. Like I said, my family is big on looking good. My parents own a real estate business. Similar to your family, they took over from my grandfather. They're considered community leaders, attend charity events, donate, and make sure people know about it. Everyone knows them because they have commercials. They always dress nicely, and my mom won't leave the house without makeup. She led the PTA, and my dad turned down a request to run for mayor. As the oldest— I do just have the younger sister. Well, I thought I did. Anyway. I was expected to set an example, work hard, be a good role model, be polite."

"You're very good at being polite."

Dimples flashed in his cheeks but vanished quickly, and he shook his head. "But it was a lie. I'm not the oldest. My dad had another kid. With his assistant. Less than three years *after* he married my mom. A kid they never mentioned in nineteen years."

"Wow." It was hard to imagine finding out that your parents had this whole other secret life. Easy to forget they'd been young once, done things before having kids. "How'd you find out?"

"I overheard my parents one night when they thought I was asleep. When I asked more, they refused to tell me anything, said that was behind them." He snorted. "Like you can put an actual person out of your head forever. All I learned was that he'd recently started working on a boat called the *West Wind* on the island of Maui. They wouldn't even tell me his name."

His shoulders were tense, and bitterness laced his voice.

"I'm sorry. That must have been hard to process."

"Still is. And it's ridiculous that they hid it. But apparently they didn't want to risk any damage to their precious reputation." He shook his head. "Was the charity work real? Did they care about helping others? Or was it only about maintaining that perfect image?"

He paused while a family trooped past us. By the time they were gone, Jake's posture had drooped.

"Is that why you're ignoring their texts?"

He slid me a sideways look. "I knew you were spying on me."

"Can you blame me?"

"I'm honestly surprised you haven't done more."

"Maybe I have and you just don't know about it."

That elicited a faint grin, but it faded. "My parents tried to get me to forget about everything, too. But I decided, this guy, he's family. A brother. And I wanted to meet him. I'm an adult now. I can know him if I want to."

"You can. But that doesn't explain . . ."

He cleared his throat. "Right. Let me tell you my side, all of it, before you run off and . . ."

"And what?" A warning rose inside me.

"Speaking of brothers . . ." He looked at me.

"Tyler?"

"Tyler."

"Wait, what? What about him?"

"We know each other."

I half came out of my seat. "What?"

Jake reached out an arm as if to keep me in my chair. "We met the summer before last, at sports camp, when he was an incoming freshman. I was a senior counselor for the baseball clinics."

"I knew you played sports."

"I didn't technically lie—I'm not playing right now." He smirked slightly. "Checking me out again, were you?"

"Wait, so you've been pretending not to know each other all week?"

"At camp, we discovered we both liked the same online game, and we stayed in touch, playing once a week or so. When he told me his sister had started dating a guy with my name, he wanted to see if it was me. Obviously it wasn't—it's a common name."

"Yeah, that was the point." I was still having trouble comprehending.

"Clever," he said. "So, a few months ago, Tyler messaged me and said he thought his sister's boyfriend was fake. We had a laugh, joked about me showing up one day and pretending to be the guy. I didn't mean it, and I don't think he did, either. But then when I learned about my half brother . . . it offered me a way to come search for him. Like I said, paying for and managing the trip myself would have been impossible. So Tyler invited me."

"What?" Apparently that was the new extent of my vocabulary.

"I tried to convince him to bring you in on it, so I didn't blindside you at the airport. Which ended up being rather fun."

I scowled.

His smile twitched. He leaned toward me. "I really am sorry. He wasn't sure you'd agree to play along. You didn't know he'd figured out that you'd been lying?"

"I definitely did not know."

How had my nerdy little brother been the one to see through my lies? I'd been worried he would figure out the truth, but he'd known all along. The little jerk had been messing with me.

"He sent me a list of information, the details you'd made up about Jacob, so I could prepare. Stuff about your family, how to impress your parents. And connected me with your mom so I could say I was able to come after all and ask if we could surprise you."

"Who knew Tyler was so devious."

"I didn't—I don't—love lying to them. Your family has been generous and so nice to me. And I am paying them for as much as I can. But I needed to get here. This was unconventional, but it worked."

"So you already kind of knew me? What did Tyler tell you about me?"

"Just basics," he said quickly. "Enough to make it believable, but nothing bad, no embarrassing stories."

I wasn't sure I believed that Tyler would keep that to himself. Something squeezed inside me, like my heart. Jake had been a complete stranger to me, and on some level, I'd believed we were on an even playing field. How much had he already known about me? What was his opinion of me before he arrived? One thing he'd known, at the very least, was that I'd been desperate enough to invent him in the first place.

"You don't consider it embarrassing that I made up a boy-friend?" I asked.

"Well, okay, there is that."

I scowled again. I'd thought we'd been getting to know each other, despite his insistence that we not get personal. How many of the questions he'd asked me had he already known—or thought he knew—the answers to?

"How did Tyler figure it out?"

"I don't know. You'd have to ask him."

"Oh, I will."

In a way, both Jake and I had been victims of my brother's scheming. I supposed I couldn't be too mad at Jake, not for coming here. An opportunity he'd needed had landed in his lap, and he'd taken it. I would have done the same.

"He was trying to be a good friend," Jake said. "He wanted to help me. I'm sorry you got caught in the middle."

"Does he know why you're here?" I asked.

"I didn't tell him everything. It still feels weird to say it. I *am* a brother. I have a *sister*. But now I *have* a brother, too. I wanted to tell him. Someone. Everyone. Part of me thought my parents deserved for the truth to come out, and at first I was annoyed at myself because I couldn't do it."

"That's not a bad thing. You were loyal to your family, even if they didn't fully deserve it. Because that's what family does."

His shoulders lifted and sagged. "Yeah. I mean, now I'm glad I didn't act when I was mad. But anyway. I told Tyler I needed to come for a personal reason and I needed to find a boat. He used his computer skills to do some searching that gave me leads but nothing firm."

Something inside me softened. Jake trusted me enough to tell me, to let me be the one person who knew his secret. But . . . did he really, or had I simply left him no choice but to confess?

"So before I go threaten *my* brother with all kinds of creative torture, what can I do? To help with *your* brother?"

"What?"

"You're here. You want to find him. And you're helping me with my family by playing along, so what can I do?"

"I . . . don't know." He studied me like he couldn't believe the offer. "Tyler handled advance research online. I've searched the harbor in Lahaina, although there are berths that were empty both times. And I have two more harbors left. The island has three, so my plan was to somehow find a way to search them all."

"Where are the others?"

"Kahului, where the airport is. That one is mostly commercial, but I figure I should check to be safe. And one partway between here and there. Where we're supposed to snorkel from on Friday."

"If we don't search until Friday, that doesn't leave you much time. What else is nearby? Maybe we can go earlier. Gran might help."

"Really? You'd do that?"

"Of course. But I won't tell her if you don't want me to."

"She knows we're talking. She's going to want an explanation."

"I can tell her I trust you and ask her to trust me."

He sighed. "No, tell her everything. We could use the help of someone old enough to drive the rental car. Even if that driving is a menace to polite society."

We chuckled.

We. Like we were official partners in crime now, fully aware of what we were both doing. How we were using each other.

My insides felt tied in knots. I liked knowing about him and working with him more than I should have. This was a temporary partnership so we could both get what we wanted, nothing more.

"We'll find him," I said.

He leaned toward me again, and his hand twitched like he planned to reach for me, but he didn't. "Thank you, Kenzie. Really."

Hearing my name in his voice, earnest and sincere, sent a shiver down my spine.

"Of course." I swallowed, trying to hide the fact that he had any effect on me at all, and set my jaw. "Now I have to talk to Tyler."

CHAPTER SEVENTEEN

My brother was—where else?—in his shared bedroom on his laptop.

I marched up and yanked out his earbuds. "Let's go, Ty."

He squawked. "What? Where? Did I miss something on the schedule?"

"Yep. It says *talk to sister*." I grabbed the disgusting baseball hat from his bed and parked it on his head. "This is not optional."

In case he tried to argue, I took his arm, dragged him up and into the living room, and announced, "We're going in search of SPAM. Be back soon."

The one thing guaranteed to make no one else interested. Alana and Neal glanced over from the lanai but didn't move. Dad blinked at me drowsily from the sofa. We were out the door before they could reply.

"Really?" Tyler asked when we were in the corridor. "Are we finding SPAM?"

"If *SPAM* stands for *Speaking Plainly to Avoid Murder*, then yes."

He slowed, and I shoved him.

"Let's go, Sneaky Person about to Answer Me."

"Answer what?"

"I think you know."

"I don't know what you mean. Where's Jake? Jacob."

"At the pool."

I needed somewhere public where Tyler and I could talk but where he couldn't escape. I led him to the small miniature golf course on the resort grounds and picked up two clubs and balls. This was the kind of golfing I preferred, short and easy, with fun things to look at.

"You hate golf," he said.

"So do you," I said. "I don't think this counts."

We went to the first hole, where a large plastic hula dancer stood guard over a box the ball had to go through to reach the hole.

I waited until he was lined up and about to putt before I said, "Jake told me everything."

Tyler jerked. His ball sailed high and bounced off the hula dancer's face.

"What . . . what did he tell you?" He caught the ball with his club before it rolled past us, and lined it up again.

I let him hit, then followed, sending my ball through the box. "That you already knew him. That you set this up." I waved my club. "That you knew I made up a boyfriend."

He refused to meet my gaze, trudging toward the hole.

"Jake told me his side. I want yours."

"He wasn't supposed to say anything."

"Gran figured out we were lying, so he had to. How did you know I made up a boyfriend?"

Tyler sighed and we finished our turns, grabbing our balls and moving on. "Fine. One evening when you said you'd been video chatting with Jacob, I had found your phone in the kitchen, which meant you would have had to be on your laptop to chat, which meant you'd have to use the Wi-Fi. But the internet was out that night. I got kicked off my game partway through. Plus, since I wasn't playing, I had my headphones off, and I didn't hear you talking at all that night."

Wow. He was a full-fledged detective. I couldn't find words. My brother's addiction to the internet had been my downfall.

I hit my ball down a lane, this one lined with turtle statues.

"After that, I was suspicious, so I listened more closely. You did a pretty good job. I never knew you had it in you to be so sneaky. No one else even suspects."

I crossed my arms and glared at him as he hit his ball.

"That was a compliment," he said.

"Was it?" I marched down the green. "Thanks for making a stranger think your sister was desperate and pathetic."

"He's here, so he obviously doesn't mind. Why do you care what a stranger thinks about you, anyway?"

Because it was Jake. But I couldn't say that.

To reach the next hole, we crossed a wooden bridge over a pond with a plastic whale statue.

"Whatever," I said. "You could have blown it for me."

"But I didn't. Jake's good, and you played along. And you seem to be having fun again."

"Huh?"

"Come on, you've been miserable."

"Why does everyone keep doubting I'm happy when I'm in freaking Hawaii?" My voice rose, and I waved my club as if to show off Hawaii's brilliance.

"Not this very moment. You know what I mean. You hate science club."

"Actually, I kind of like blowing stuff up in the chemistry lab." It was usually on accident, but still.

He gave me a look before hitting his ball. "You have zero interest in optometry school. The job at the office makes you grouchy. You stare longingly out windows when you're stuck inside, and you constantly reach for your camera when you see something you like."

"What . . . wow." I had no idea he was so observant. No one else recognized those things. "You should be a detective."

"I'm not an idiot," he said. "And unlike Mom and Dad, I don't care what you like or don't like. I mean, I do care. I just think you should like what you like and ignore anyone who says differently. If Mom and Dad weren't so set on you and me becoming copies of Alana, they would see it, too. But I have to admit you're doing a bang-up job of giving them exactly what they want, which means they haven't thought to question it."

I wasn't sure if that thought pleased or disappointed me. I leaned on my club even though it was my turn. "So you knew I was lying about Jacob for weeks?"

"Yep."

"Why didn't you say anything?"

He shrugged. "None of my business. Until it was."

"What do you get out of this?"

"Besides helping a friend?"

I grunted. "You're not that nice."

"You think there isn't pressure on me, too? Especially if you follow Alana to optometry school? Then I'm the only one who isn't copying Mom and Dad."

"What do you mean? They love your computer stuff. And you're still helping, with that program you're writing for them."

"I finished that in, like, November. It was easy." He pointed to the green. "Are you gonna go?"

"Wait, so what have you been working on all week? All semester?"

"Some people might call it a video game . . ."

This time it was my shot that went wild, sailing onto the rocky hill above the pond, by a waterfall. I stared at Tyler, mouth hanging open, before clambering up to retrieve the ball. When I bent over, twisted at an angle to reach where it was lodged next to a rock, my hotel key card fell out of my pocket.

It floated down, caught on a breeze, and fluttered into the whale's gaping mouth.

"Oh, you're kidding me."

Tyler laughed. "I don't think that's coming back up for three days."

I studied the pond. Yeah, there was no way to get the key without jumping into water that was dyed a very unnatural bright blue that would likely stain my clothes and give me a rash.

I sighed.

"I guess Jonah is staying put." I climbed down with my ball. "So. Video game?"

"Yeah, a prototype for an RPG. Set on a spaceship. It only has basic features now, but it could be more."

I blinked at him. "That means you've been lying, too."

"Sort of. I did write their program first." He hit his ball, and we headed for the green.

"Why?" I asked.

"It worked so well for you. It made Mom and Dad more accepting of the fact that I want to do coding instead of healthcare, as long as they thought I was working alongside the family. But if they find out I'm working on a video game . . . You know how much they hate those."

"Yeah, but you get away with everything."

He didn't bother trying to argue. "Not this."

We finished the hole, and I sent one last look at the hungry whale that ate my key before moving on.

"You should be impressed," he said. "I put a lot of work into getting Jake here, same as you did inventing Jacob. First, I had to confirm my suspicion that you were lying. I got into your phone and checked your contacts, saw no actual texts."

"Hey. Not cool. That's, like, a felony or something."

"Then I made a list of every single thing you told us about Jacob. Like a dossier on a cop show. And I sent Jake basic details about you, and tips on how to charm Mom and Dad."

"Creepy. Did you give him my Social Security number and my passwords, too?" The squirming sensation returned to my stomach at the thought of Jake knowing more about me, which hardened when I thought of my own brother revealing secrets to a stranger.

He had a point, though—it was as impressively thorough as my deception.

"He has been convincing," Tyler went on, ignoring me. "He did the rest himself, I guess, researching optometry and Ohio State and all that. Immersing himself in the role."

"No thanks to you and your snarky comments this week."

We both hit our balls toward a green being guarded by a row of small plastic palm trees.

"Why didn't you tell me?" I asked. "You could have prepared me."

He sank his second shot. "I wasn't sure you'd agree to help. This whole new perfect-child thing might have corrupted you."

"Being a perfect child means I'm corrupted?"

He waved his club. "You know what I mean. Last year, I would have told you. I knew the old you would have helped. But I couldn't be sure if you would now, and I didn't want to risk Jake not being able to come."

My gut clenched. I wanted to be a person my brother could trust to help him. I didn't realize that the last several months had changed his opinion of me.

"What if I'd confessed everything at the airport when a stranger first showed up?"

"I would have acted like it was a joke, so you were forced to play along."

"Mature, Ty."

We moved on, and he hit his ball toward a tiny hole in the base of a volcano. It bounced off and came back at him.

"Why didn't you tell Mom and Dad you thought I was lying? When you first figured it out?"

"Like I said, it wasn't my business. Besides, would it have changed anything? Would you have denied it and then broken up with him soon after and gone on with the other lies you're living?"

"This is my life, Tyler. I can live it however I want." My voice came out harsh.

"But it affects me, too." His face was earnest. "And I do want you to be happy. Jake is good for you. You're more like your old self this trip."

"That's not a good thing. I remade myself for a reason."

"A dumb one."

"That's not your decision to make." I snagged his ball for him when he missed again.

"What are you going to do?" he asked.

"I obviously can't tell Mom and Dad. And Jake does have a good reason for being here, so I'm going to help him. And then . . . I don't know. But do me a favor and stop trying to help me? Because you've been lying, too, and while I might be able to keep Jake's identity a secret, you're on borrowed time with your project. Figure out your own life and stay out of mine."

Once we finished the hole, I marched off. I shouldn't have been so mean. He had been helping his friend. And maybe he thought he was helping me, too. But it wasn't the type of help I wanted. Everything had been going fine until this week.

I could still save the situation. I'd help Jake finish his search, work extra hard to stop letting him draw out the old Kenzie, and then leave Tyler to face his lies sooner or later.

It was fine. All under control.

Other than the fact that my key card was still sitting in the belly of a whale.

CHAPTER EIGHTEEN

We made it home in time to attend an evening cooking class with the whole family.

Storming off had been ineffective, since the front desk wouldn't give me a new key without parental approval. I wasn't about to confess I'd lost it, knowing my family practically expected that to happen. Instead I had to wait for Tyler, who unlocked the door, then handed me his key and entered, leaving me blinking after him.

As we shuffled out of the condo, I leaned toward Gran.

"Everything's okay with Jake. He's friends with Tyler. I'll tell you more later, but we can trust him."

She leveled a look at me. "You need to tell your parents the truth, Kenz."

"I will. One day." Like, when they were in a retirement home.

She held eye contact a second longer.

After Gran moved on, Jake sidled up to me. "How did it go with Tyler?"

Lingering anger toward Tyler was fading. It felt petty to be upset with my brother when Jake had never met his. "I'm only a little mad, but I need to make him worry for a day or two."

Thankfully, cooking involved no blender mishaps, and other than Tyler setting his SPAM on fire, things went fine.

The next morning, I was up before my alarm, bouncing with excitement for the day I'd most been looking forward to—our tour of the road to Hana.

My parents had been hesitant. Hana was on the opposite side of the island, and the road was famous for narrow switchbacks and one-lane bridges. Rather than gush about black sand beaches and waterfalls, I had simply said, in a reasonable tone of voice, that it was one of the most famous places in Hawaii and it would be a shame not to see it, because we might never have another chance.

I'd been rather proud of myself. And now a tour van was picking us up bright and early.

It wasn't exactly the way I would have chosen to see it—on someone else's schedule, with prescribed stops, a guide enforcing the agenda as strictly as Dad's spreadsheet did—but I'd take what I could get.

Mom rose to see us off, though she wasn't going. She had tried to insist that she'd be fine and we had to experience it together as a family.

"We don't want to experience it if you're puking all day," Tyler had said.

"I'm sure it's not that bad." She hadn't looked convinced.

"Over six hundred curves, many hairpins, and forty-six bridges that are one lane only," I said.

"It's a puke fest waiting to happen." Tyler's helpful contribution.

"But it's a whole day apart. I'll take medicine. It will be fine."

She'd need enough Dramamine for a whale for a road like that. Assuming the medicine didn't make her sleep for three straight days.

"Mom," Alana said gently, "we're spending the whole week together. Wouldn't you be more comfortable here? Have a quiet day to yourself. Read by the pool, get a massage, take a nap."

Dad placed a hand on her shoulder. "You work so hard. We just want you to relax."

"And we want *us* to relax," Tyler added, "not always worrying whose lap is getting spewed on."

"Tyler, seriously, enough," my dad said. Then to my mom, "But really."

Mom had sighed. "I guess it wouldn't be bad to take my book to the pool."

Now, though she wasn't coming, she was double-checking our bags, making sure we had medicine and water and sunscreen and hats and towels. She followed us downstairs to the tour van, reminded us to be safe, and waved us off.

Once we were out of sight, I relaxed. Not that Mom was inherently more stressful than anyone else in the family. But now today's adventure had begun.

The van was nice, with elevated seats, huge windows, and lots of room. We munched on muffins and juice, and the driver maintained a constant stream of chatter, narrating facts about the island. I perked up whenever he mentioned the wildlife and the habitats. My dad constantly interrupted to ask questions.

We passed through a cute little town with colorful, old-fashioned buildings, and then along the dramatic northern coast, where windsurfers cruised the waves.

Lush vegetation lined the winding road. We crossed tiny stone bridges over creeks. Several other cars had gotten an early start as well.

"Oh, we have good luck," the driver announced. "There's parking today. We'll make a stop to see the rainbow trees. Many people miss these. This is the second area, not as impressive, but the first is on private property. Here you can get up close. Everybody out!"

When we exited the van, I inhaled deeply, the tangy scent of eucalyptus in the air. A small grove of trees stood nearby in a grassy field. When I approached, I saw the reason for the name. The bark was striped in green and orange and pink and blue.

"It's peeling," Jake said as he placed a hand on the trunk and ran his fingers down the stripes.

"That's right," the guide said. "Each layer is a different color, changing based on the age. Maroon is the oldest, and green the most recent. They're actually not a native species."

He told us the history of the trees, what they were used for. Jake listened intently. When the guide finished, he left us some time to wander among the colorful trees.

They looked surreal, like I'd wandered into a fairy-tale land. The colors resembled melted paint or wax dripping down every trunk. A breeze rustled the leaves in a musical sound.

There were so many interesting and unexpected things to see in nature. This was exactly the kind of thing I loved to discover. I studied each tree, circling slowly. One trunk was perfectly illuminated by a beam of light that made the colors glow.

It would make an amazing photo. The lighting, the shades. But also, showing off wonders of the world that people might never imagine could exist.

I'd enjoyed taking photos on the kayaking trip, but my family hadn't been around then. I intended to enjoy today, but I needed to be careful.

Jake was walking near me, so I said to him, "Here, if you want a cool picture, try from this side."

Jake held my gaze, direct, and I wanted to squirm, but he looked away and approached to take the photo. He shot more close-ups, and I moved away before he could comment.

And then I spotted it. The perfect tree to climb, with a low branch about shoulder height, and more at well-spaced intervals all the way up. I glanced around. The driver hadn't said not to. Maybe it was implied, because normal people's minds didn't jump straight to, *Oh, a tree, I should climb it.*

Or maybe this was allowed.

No one was near to see or stop me, so I grabbed the branch and swung myself up. Sturdy, solid. With another branch beckoning me higher. Three more branches, and I found a perfect place to sit, leaning against the trunk, surrounded by the play of light through the leaves. The sharp scent enveloped me.

Properly hidden, I took out my phone and snapped pictures of the colorful bark and the branches and the bright green grass below.

And then voices reached me—specifically, someone saying my name.

"Where did Kenzie go?" My dad's voice, from right beneath me.

"I saw her with Jacob a minute ago." That from Alana.

I sat very still. *Don't look up. Don't look up.*

"He's been good for her," my dad said. "Or he reflects that she's growing up."

"From what I hear, he's much better than the other guys she dated."

My dad chuckled. "I didn't get to meet any of them. They didn't stick around long enough."

Hey. I wasn't a serial dater. I just liked to keep my options open. There was nothing wrong with that.

"I know I haven't been around," Alana went on, "but she does seem different. I thought this week we'd be constantly looking for her, and she'd make us late to everything, or she'd take five million photos and keep getting lost."

Rude. But fair.

My dad laughed. "She has outgrown that phase. Your mom and I were talking about how proud we are. Her grades are good, and she's been far less reckless and scatterbrained lately."

Ha. As I sat on a tree branch high above them, trying to remain motionless so I didn't shower them with leaves and chunks of multicolored bark.

"The optometry thing really might work out for her."

"I'm glad," Alana said.

"I am, too."

They were saying the words I'd been working for months to hear.

And yet, the compliments failed to fill me. Maybe because they were talking about someone who wasn't really me? Because if I'd been acting like myself this week, the real me, I would have arrived late everywhere, I would have gotten lost while tracking down photo ops, and I definitely would have taken a million pictures.

Was it too much to want them to appreciate who I was, instead of the person I had to pretend to be?

A perfect example—my current precarious situation. They were talking about how I'd outgrown my impulsiveness, when I had literally just climbed a magical rainbow tree without stopping to ask if it was allowed. And why? Because it was pretty? I'd wanted a better view? I'd thought it would let me connect with the tree in a deeper way?

Kenzie is definitely more mature than before. Other than the whole desire to be a squirrel.

And yet, all I'd wanted was their respect. Sure, I'd lied and changed myself to get it. But now, knowing I had it, maybe the last several months had been worth it.

So why did I still feel hollow?

CHAPTER NINETEEN

I waited a few minutes after Dad's and Alana's voices faded before peering down and easing myself to the ground.

When I rejoined Jake, he raised his eyebrows. "Where were you?"

I avoided his gaze. "Just admiring the trees."

He smirked, reached out, and plucked a leaf from my hair. "Nice accessories."

Great. I patted my head to make sure there wasn't any more evidence, and brushed off my clothes in case of incriminating bark, before returning to the van. The restlessness in my chest lingered, making me twitchy.

When we drove on, the scent of sunscreen filled the car as Neal slathered his exposed skin. Which wasn't much, since he wore long sleeves and hiking pants. And he'd been wearing a hat that shielded his face and neck.

"Ooh, look at that." Gran pressed her face against the glass.

The road had grown more winding. Groves of bamboo popped up, and water trickled down cliffs.

"Is it more trees?" Tyler asked.

Gran smacked him. "Show some respect for the beauty of the island."

I met Jake's twinkling eyes and bit my lip to keep from laughing.

It reminded me of my guilt over walking away from my brother. I should have asked Tyler more about his video game. He was lying, too, and like me, obviously found it necessary. I vowed to talk to him more, going forward. In case he didn't find encouragement from anyone else in the family, I wanted him to know he had it from me.

Our next stop was a botanical garden called the Garden of Eden, an appropriate name for how perfect and gorgeous this whole part of the island was. We were given an hour to wander the dirt paths. I set an alarm on my phone. I was not going to blow it right after my dad's and Alana's conversation. And this was exactly the type of place where I'd lose track of time and spend an entire day while my family wondered where I was.

Jake and I set off down a dirt path. It meandered through several types of areas, small forests and flower beds and green lawns. Leaves of brilliant green and deep maroon, bamboo towering above us, orange and red bromeliads, water lilies and orchids and hibiscus and flowers I didn't recognize. A peacock crossed our path, and ducks swam in a pond. One side offered views of the ocean, and then we came to an overlook that peered down on a hidden pool far below, with a waterfall pouring into it.

"Ooh, check out that shot." Orange flowers in the foreground framed the waterfall perfectly. "Ha. I sound like Gran. You should stand here."

"No," he said.

"No?"

His cheeks dimpled. "I refuse to be part of this any longer. Take the picture yourself."

I huffed and crossed my arms while I fake glared at him.

We had separated from the others. No one was around. . . .

I clutched my phone and stared at the scene.

"You'd be having a lot more fun if you did, and you know it." His eyes held a sparkle and a challenge.

I held his gaze. Bit my lip. Oh, fine.

I took a few photos from slightly different angles.

Capturing the waterfall led to taking close-ups of every flower, panoramic views of the ocean, interesting trees wrapped in vines, more rainbow bark, a peacock's brilliant feathers gleaming in the sun.

It felt like I was sneaking, doing something illegal or illicit. Like my phone was broadcasting a beacon from my pocket saying, *Kenzie took three hundred pictures when you weren't looking.*

My dad and Gran appeared ahead, and I quickly pocketed the phone.

"Okay, what's up?" Jake asked, speaking for the first time in a while. Whenever I'd glanced at him, he'd either been watching me with a half smile or studying a plant and not noticing my five million photos.

"Nothing."

"Something's wrong. You're fidgety."

"No, it's not. I'm great."

"Kenzie." He crossed his arms and stared at me.

I sighed and stared off at the green hills, the sea, the clouds. "It's working."

"That's great," he said. "What's working?"

I waved a hand at myself. "This. The reinvention thing. I sort of . . . overheard my dad and sister."

"You were spying?" His cheeks dimpled. "Seems to be a hobby."

"Not intentionally. They didn't know I was in a tree above them. And then I couldn't exactly climb down with them standing right there."

He laughed loudly.

"They were talking about how I've changed, how proud they are of me." My voice sounded flat. A melancholy feeling thrummed inside me. "That's why I did all of this over the last several months."

We had paused in a field with views of the sea, and I stared at the ocean.

"And yet you don't look happy," he said.

I sighed again. "I thought it would make me feel better. I convinced them. I've resisted the temptation this week. Okay, except with the turtles. And just now. But mostly resisted. And they're buying you and me."

"Maybe you're not happy because you don't really want them to buy this version of you."

"Of course I do. Why else did I work so hard?"

He gazed at me, those sky-blue eyes intense and probing. "So why aren't you satisfied?"

I chewed my lip and stared at him. Good question.

My phone alarm startled me. I broke eye contact and took a few steps, breathing hard. Glad to escape.

"Time to get back."

"Right. Can't be late because you like this place. You'd hate to let everyone down." His voice was neutral and held a note of . . . something. But he took my hand as we followed the path toward the exit.

I couldn't bring myself to look at him. He clearly had thoughts, and I didn't know if I wanted to hear them.

The next part of the drive was loaded with waterfalls right off the road, the van windows offering stunning views. Tiny bridges crossed flowing creeks and offered views of green pools. Cliffs overlooked the ocean with lush valleys, and on the other side, verdant hills stretched upward.

We had made two wise decisions today—not letting Mom and her car sickness join us, and not letting Gran drive. She'd have plunged right into a river or over a cliff.

If the road weren't here, nature would rule. The small strip of pavement was the best humans could do to make a dent in a wild, mysterious place we could never tame. It was satisfying, thinking that places like this existed.

"Is everyone okay?" Alana asked. "I have Dramamine and crackers. And don't forget to focus on the horizon or ask me to make it colder if you need it."

"Thanks, Mom," Tyler said.

"Can I see your sunglasses?" my dad asked the driver. "I'm not sure those offer full UV protection."

"Is there a phone signal anywhere on this road?" Tyler asked.

I fought the urge to tell my entire family we should take a vow of silence for the rest of the day. The lack of phone signal was part of the appeal. If I came out here alone, no one would be able to reach me.

The road continued, above little inlets where the ocean jutted in, forming secret bays. There was probably a way down if you were willing to hike, which I definitely would have been. Gran passed around chunks of banana bread until our next stop, Upper Waikani Falls. After Alana ensured we had our towels, proper shoes, and had reapplied sunscreen—Neal for the fourth time—we parked on the side of the road. It required a short walk to the falls along the narrow road, making Alana order us to stay in a single file and watch for cars. *Thanks for that genius advice.* We took the short but slippery hike down.

It came into view. A triple waterfall, cascading down a rocky cliff topped with trees, surrounded by lush vegetation, a blue-green pool at the bottom.

And the knowledge hit me as surely as a physical blow.

This was it. Right here. I faced a choice.

CHAPTER TWENTY

For ages, since I'd seen a photo shoot of Iceland's amazing waterfalls, my dream had been to take pictures from under, inside, or behind a waterfall. The way the light caught the water, how you could see the sky beyond the falls . . . it had captivated me. Made it feel like there was a secret world waiting.

People were swimming in the pool at the base of these falls. And it looked like there was enough space between the water and the rock.

My dad would freak out if I got too close. Alana, filling in for Mom, would be convinced the falls would drown me.

But we were going swimming, so that was a start. I didn't have to decide immediately. I could scope it out first.

We left our towels on a sunny boulder and waded carefully into cool water that was surprisingly clear. The bottom was rocky, proving the stupid schedule right once again when it had recommended water shoes.

Jake floated near me as I swam toward the center, where the water grew deeper. My ears filled with the melodic rushing of water as it cascaded down moss-covered stone. Lush plants grew around the edges. It smelled of growing things, and if not for the other people, I could have imagined I'd found a hidden magical glen in the middle of the jungle.

There might not have been space to get fully behind the falls, but the center one appeared to offer a nook. And the one on my right wasn't much more than a strong trickle, totally safe. Ish. Other than the slight possibility of falling rocks. But it looked fine.

A hand grabbed mine. Jake pressed the GoPro into my free hand.

"What's this?"

"How many times do I have to tell you it's a camera? Do I need to show you how to use it, too?"

"Yeah, if I want blurry pictures with no artistry whatsoever."

"I'll have you know I'm perfectly capable of taking good pictures."

"I knew it. It was all a ploy."

"I have no idea what you're talking about. Now. Get closer. You're staring at the waterfall like you were staring at my piece of meat. Except hungrier."

My head swiveled toward the others.

"Kenzie. Stop worrying."

I faced him fully. "Why do you care?"

He watched me steadily, focused as if we were alone in the world. "Because I care about you. Because I want you to be yourself and be happy and stop letting others define you. You deserve to do what you like, and I want you to stop listening to people who don't appreciate you."

I felt adrift, more like I floated in a vast, uncertain sea than a small pond. "Why, though? You don't even know me. Not really."

"I know enough to know you're special."

Our gazes held, his full of warmth that pooled in my stomach.

"And," he said, "maybe I want to know you. For real."

The words hung for a moment in the silence, rippling through me like waterfall waves through a pool.

He drifted a few inches closer. His hand brushed mine beneath the surface. "Tyler said you had a weird sense of humor, but I think you're funny. And he said you were always daydreaming, but I suspect you're thinking interesting thoughts that you don't share. What I've seen, I like, and it makes me want to know everything."

That warmth spread, and his words touched something deep inside me. This was flirting with danger, though. We were faking for my family, and nothing real could happen. But I wanted to know him, too.

"Does that go both ways?" I asked.

"Do you want it to?" His eyebrows twitched up. "And not just so you can expose me?"

"You were the one who said it was better if you stayed Fake Jacob in my head."

He tucked his hair behind his ears and stared at me. His eyes matched the sky.

I found myself holding my breath. Yes, it was dangerous. Yes, it might cause us to slip up. And yes, I knew we couldn't stay in touch after this week, not after all the lying. But I wanted to know this boy, who was cute and adventurous and funny and who saw me.

"Between my family and whatever Tyler told you, you know so much about me, and I don't know anything about you," I said. "It hardly seems fair."

"I needed to know about you to make this fake relationship believable. You don't need to know the real me. It will only complicate things." His voice was quiet, lacking conviction, with a note of . . . longing?

"Maybe I want to know you, too," I said. "Maybe I like complicated."

Which was ridiculous. Our situation was complicated enough. My *life* was complicated enough. A web of lies and half-truths and secrets. But as I stared at him, all I wanted was to study him like a photo subject, examine every angle, to know everything so I could capture his best parts and hold them close.

"Yeah?" His voice sounded hopeful.

"Yeah."

He blinked, his eyes locked on me.

"Okay," he said. "For real. Both ways. Let's do it."

Bubbles fizzed inside me, and I grinned. It was like plunging off a trail into the wild, and I couldn't wait to explore what awaited.

"Starting with, why do you look like you want to devour the waterfall?" His lips quirked.

I bit my lip and stared past him to the falls. "It's kind of a dream of mine, to photograph one from, like, inside."

"Let's check it out, then."

"But—"

"Just to take a look."

He was right. I was yards away from a dream. What could it hurt?

We paddled closer to the smallest of the falls. Definitely not strong enough to drown me. More like a hard shower.

I clutched the camera. Fought the urge to glance around like a criminal breaking into a bank vault. Droplets splattered me, and I ducked under the stream and closed my eyes, let the water pour over my head. Then took photos. Looking up at the falls, covered in spray, from right in the middle of it.

I didn't know if they would turn out. This wasn't like the caves behind the Iceland falls, offering carved-out spaces, interesting angles, and sprawling vistas. But it was fun.

Falls offered plenty of opportunities for playing, if I'd been here alone or with more gear. Shutter speeds and long exposure, different times of day so the lighting varied. But for now I'd work with what I had.

Jake was checking out the middle fall, and when he ducked into the stream and tilted his head back, I snapped a few photos of him. Then joined him. There was just enough space behind the water next to the rock wall that I could take photos outward, and a narrow ledge offered a place to perch. The mossy wall smelled of damp rock.

When I emerged, Jake floated nearby, watching me with a slight smile.

"What?"

"Aren't you going to say thank you? 'Thank you, Jake, for

encouraging me. It was so amazing. I couldn't have done it with-out you.'"

"First of all, I do not sound like that. Second of all, thank you."

He grinned. "So why waterfalls?"

I studied them. "I don't know, really. I think they're pretty. And the up-close thing. I always have this urge to immerse my-self in something as much as possible."

"Was it everything you'd hoped?"

"It was a bad idea."

He blinked. "What? Why?"

"Because now I want to find bigger ones, and ones with caves behind them, and ones high in the mountains, and—"

He laughed. "Oh no. I created a monster."

"Just fed the monster a little."

"That's even worse. Now the monster knows where to get food and will keep coming back. You're the nature expert. It's bad to feed wild animals, right?"

"We need to end this analogy, since you've now called me both a monster and a wild animal."

He laughed again.

"Your turn. I shared my random dream. What's one of yours?"

"Hmm. I guess . . . when we drove past those windsurfers on the north coast? That shot up high on the list."

"I'm surprised you haven't been before."

"Just regular surfing."

"Ha. I knew it."

He pouted. "But my wipeouts were so convincing."

"They really weren't."

"They were to everyone else. You just couldn't stop watching me. It's okay. You can admit it."

I splashed him, which made those dimples flash, which suddenly made the sun hotter.

When we waded out of the water, Alana was waiting.

"Kenzie, do you know how dangerous that is?"

I sighed. My sister had nailed Mom's Trying Not to Panic and Failing tone. Way to kill the mood.

"I was careful, Alana. I picked the smaller falls. The volume of water was more like a shower than anything else. I checked to make sure the rock wall was stable. And I made sure the current at the base wasn't strong enough to trap me."

She blinked. "Oh."

I swept past her and grabbed my towel, fighting to cling to the light, free feeling and not let her drag me down. Had I undone months of work? Did I care?

Next to me, Jake was toweling off, and the idea of getting to know the real him renewed the thrill inside me. I had so many questions. And that slight hesitation inside that said it was a bad idea? Yeah, I would just ignore that.

In the van, when Jake reached across the aisle to take my hand, I wound my fingers through his, leaned my head back against the seat, and tilted it toward him. And smiled.

CHAPTER TWENTY-ONE

After another half hour of twists and turns, trees and close calls on the road, glimpses of the sea and roadside stands and little houses, we exited the main road again, this time heading into the small town of Hana. It had a cute old general store, tons of trees, and wooden houses with porches.

"People live out here?" Tyler asked. "Do they have internet?"

"Can you imagine getting groceries?" Alana asked.

"Or needing medical care?" Dad added.

Living somewhere so remote sounded amazing.

The driver gave us the history of the town and, with what I was pretty sure was a hint of smugness in his voice, made sure to mention the fact that they had a medical clinic.

I fought the urge to apologize and tell him I wasn't related to these people.

We stopped for a picnic at a beach park. The giant sandwich was delicious because we were outdoors and it was beautiful here and I was starving. We topped it off with more of Gran's banana bread. I was starting to suspect she had a magical supply that replenished itself in her bag.

I wandered away from the picnic tables toward the water, and Jake joined me.

"If I ever come back," I said, "I'd stay in Hana so I could spend time at every single stop. All the ones we're driving right past that probably have amazing views and fascinating sights."

"Definitely," Jake said. "Seeing the highlights is fine, but to truly know a place, you need more time."

"Is that your travel personality?"

His eyes crinkled. "Is that a thing? I like that."

"It's definitely a thing. Like, do you want a color-coordinated schedule telling you what to do every hour of the day, or would you rather be spontaneous? Or not worry about what's next and enjoy the moment?"

"As grateful as I am to your family, if it were up to me, there would be more free time to explore and hike and do whatever caught your eye."

I nudged him. "I knew you were lying when you said you loved the schedule."

"It really is frighteningly thorough."

"I have nightmares about them. When I was a kid, we had a huge chore chart with colors and symbols. And a family calendar for lessons or classes or clubs. Alana's took up an entire wall. She gave me a binder full of lists with information on every class she took, plus study schedules for the SAT and AP tests. The night before I took the SAT, I dreamed that binder grew to the size of a *T. rex* and devoured me whole."

"That sounds terrifying. Not just death-by-binder, which is awful. But all of it."

At the end of the beach, there was a small jetty, so Jake and I walked to the end. No boats were docked here. On shore, clouds hovered at the peaks of green hills. The other direction was nothing but deep blue ocean that made it feel like we were at the edge of everything.

That ache formed in my chest again, like some desire inside me was growing, expanding, longing to grasp the enormous potential offered by a distant horizon and endless possibility.

Jake's shoulder brushed mine, and I shifted to glance up at him. He was looking at the unused pillars for tying up boats.

I let my arm press into his. "Sorry there aren't boats here. I guess it's too small and that's why it wasn't on your list of harbors?"

"Yeah. Boats can dock here, but it's not a permanent harbor."

"We'll get back to work tomorrow trying to find your brother."

He offered a slight smile. "I know. And it's hard to be upset about not being able to search today when we're somewhere so amazing."

He shifted his gaze to the ocean, and we paused, letting the moment envelop us. The sun warming my skin, and the damp sea air, the scent of life and his coconut hair, the sound of water surging beneath us.

"I have an idea for tomorrow, if you're willing," he said.

"Does it mean defying the schedule? Because I'm all in."

"Have you read it?"

"Not really."

"We have free time tomorrow. It's a perfect chance."

"Ah yeah. My parents love schedules, but ironically, they plan for rest time. Like, how often are we going to be here? We should take advantage of every second."

"More of your travel personality?" he asked.

"Yep. Speaking of families, what's your sister like?" I asked. "Are you guys close?"

"Is Jacob Miller close to his sister? Emma, right?"

I punched his arm. "I thought we were being real. No Jacob Miller. Not when it's just you and me."

"You and me." He took my hand, and a flock of birds took flight in my chest. "Her name is Audrey. She's cool. She's sixteen. We aren't super close. No one in my family is. No one's allowed to be themselves. We have to be perfect all the time. She does cheerleading and student government. We both keep busy and smile no matter what and don't really talk."

"That sounds stressful."

"Yeah."

I sighed. "I know that feeling, but mine's more recent. I just wanted not to be compared, judged. Be myself and have it be enough, no matter what."

We rejoined the others, with Jacob and new Kenzie firmly in place as we drove to another waterfall. After admiring the falls, we took a wooden walkway through a bamboo forest.

Our feet thudded on the planks, and dry creaking and rustling sounds echoed softly. The filtered light made everything a glowing green, and the straight angles of the bamboo and the shadows it made were incredible. So unlike a regular forest.

When I craned my head to look up while we walked, Jake caught me before I could fall off the walkway. I slowed to let my family get ahead so I could take a picture of the walkway when it was free of people. It left Jake and me alone.

"Tell me about what you look for in photos," he said as we shuffled forward slowly.

My gaze darted from one possible photo to another—one leaning stalk amidst straight ones, the view straight up a stalk into the sky, slants of light piercing the bamboo.

"How long do you have?" I asked jokingly.

His voice was serious when he replied. "As long as you want to talk."

I blinked, my stomach fluttering.

He took my hand. "I like your passion. I'm curious to see inside your head."

I gulped. "You asked for it." My voice didn't sound as teasing as I meant it to. "A lot of things. Colors, and composition, and angles. Lighting. Interesting textures. But . . ."

"But?"

"There's more than the technical aspect. Lots of photos are good pictures. They're aesthetically pleasing and capture the scene. But I want mine to . . . I don't know, tell stories or open someone's eyes to something new or make them think *Wow* or see the world in a new way." I bit my lip. "It's why I like nature. Not that family memories or weddings aren't important. But I want to inspire, to challenge, to bring far-off places a little closer."

He was watching me intently, and we could glimpse my family ahead though we remained behind, so I continued.

"Like, the first time someone sees a whale in person and

marvels at it, or sees a turtle and it makes them want to protect it. Or a picture of a grand landscape makes them consider travel for the first time, or they see a scene of a remote place and imagine a whole other way of life they'd never thought about."

His gaze was warm. "You're an artist. Would your dream job involve always traveling?"

Artist might have been too generous. Just because that was what I liked about photography didn't mean I had the skill or vision to accomplish it.

"A lot of it. Seeing new places, exploring, or spending a month somewhere, like you said, getting the feel for it, wandering around and taking pictures." I exhaled hard. "I mean, that was my dream. But . . ."

"But what?"

"My family thinks it's too risky. The physical risk of traveling to remote places or staying in the woods, but also the career factor. It's hard to be successful, and it's not financially stable until you're established. You heard Gran talk about their past, about having nothing. My dad's big on none of us ever going through what his dad did. And my parents don't see the value in it, don't think it contributes to humanity."

He hummed. "I'd think they would respect all your dedication and hard work. You're knowledgeable about nature, photography. Just because your effort is toward a goal your parents don't appreciate doesn't mean it's less meaningful."

It was the exact thing I'd wished my family could see, and this stranger had picked up on it in a few days. A soft ache gripped my chest.

"They never saw that. They focused on me being late or wandering off or getting lost in my camera and the world inside my head. But not the research, learning about the thing I wanted to shoot or the camera tricks that make a particular photo work. Or the hours of practice, or learning editing software, watching online tutorials and studying professional photos."

"Well, I'm impressed."

I shook my head. "It won't happen, anyway. They're right. It's hard. Enough about me. What about you? I don't know what you're really doing with your life."

"What if it was healthcare?"

I whipped toward him, to find him smirking. I smacked him. He grabbed my hand and kept it.

He paused and looked at me. Then stared up at the bamboo. "It's plants," he said.

"What about them?"

"What I want to do." He kept his voice low.

"Like botany?"

"I'm thinking about landscape design."

That made so much sense. "Gardens and yards and stuff?"

"Yeah. Or work in an official garden."

"That's why you didn't notice I was taking all those pictures at the Garden of Eden. You were busy studying the plants."

"I could have spent all day there." It was his turn for the shining eyes and passionate voice. "I'm taking community college classes now and working with a landscape company, planting things and helping with designs. I like the art aspect, but I might want to do more than that, like at a botanical garden.

Knowing what each plant needs, arranging them to look good but also to help the soil, or attract birds or insects. Something working outside, getting my hands dirty. Kind of like you said, I also want to help people appreciate the natural world around them. Be aware of it, so the world's not all buildings and concrete and cars."

His words stirred something inside me. "That sounds fun."

"I like it. I would hate to be trapped inside all day."

"Tell me about it," I muttered.

"I don't want to dread getting up every day, hating Mondays or whatever."

"And your parents . . . ?"

"As long as I go to college for something, they don't mind." He sighed. "I wanted to move out at Christmas, after the whole brother thing, but I don't earn enough. I'm trying to save up. I can't do the fake stuff anymore."

His desired career path sounded less risky than the one I wanted. Had wanted. It sounded like a stable, dependable field, people always needing that done, plenty of options and opportunities.

He reached his hand up like he was going to touch my face, but stopped.

"What?" I asked.

"Your face. What are you thinking?"

"I don't know, that I'm jealous? I agree with everything you said. Wanting to do something you love, something you're passionate about and look forward to. But I can't . . ."

He seized my hand. "Enter that contest."

"What?"

"Just enter. No one has to know. If you don't win, you don't win, but what does it hurt to try?"

"It hurts, trust me. How do you think all this started?" I waved a hand. "Besides, I haven't taken enough photos this week. You have to take hundreds to get a few great ones."

He studied me. "If you could do your dream job, take nature photos all the time, who would you work for? A company? Magazine? Freelance?"

"Yeah, any of those. Or work for a travel company or blog."

"Would every photo you submit get published or printed or accepted?"

"Of course not."

"So you'd face rejection."

"Yeah."

"Do you think . . ."

Unease slithered through me. "What?"

"Do you think partly you reinvented yourself because you were afraid? You didn't want to face rejection again in something that mattered, so it was easier to do something you didn't care about? Then if you failed, the failure wasn't personal. It wasn't really you, so it would hurt less."

Though his voice was kind, a flood of panic rose in me. The air left my lungs. Of course that wasn't the reason. I crossed my arms and shuddered.

"Think of the contest as preparation," he went on. "Do you truly want a career in photography no matter what, or do you only want it if it's easy?"

"I want it to be easy. . . ." Forcing out the words was a challenge. Why was a fist squeezing my lungs?

"But then wouldn't everyone do it? You take photographs because you love to. Don't let other people's opinions stop you."

My limbs felt shaky. "That's easy to say. But try living that way when you fail and when your family doesn't believe in you and when everyone in your life wants you to do something else."

He squeezed my hand. "Not everyone."

It was a nice sentiment, but he wasn't really in my life. Not after this week. He wouldn't be there to encourage me or convince my parents or stand up for me when I needed it or remind me I could succeed when I doubted.

No matter how much I liked the real him or was enjoying our honesty, we had no future.

Besides, I wasn't afraid. He might think he knew me. But my choices had nothing to do with fear. Of failure, rejection, or anything else. They made sense. That was all.

After our hike, the van turned around to head back, but we had one final stop—at a stunning black sand beach. There was a short hike down full of amazing color contrasts—the dark sand, the blue sea, the green trees. Seriously, why were the colors brighter here?

My fingers itched for my phone. But I'd done enough of that for the day. I didn't need photography to be happy.

Instead I knelt and picked up a handful of black sand.

"Black sand beaches are often short-lived," I said to Jake. "They're volcanic, and the sand won't replenish like regular sand does. But they can also be formed instantly in an event like a lava flow. It reminds me of photography. I love the idea that beautiful moments are just that—moments. They exist perfectly in that second, in your memory and nowhere else. But a photo lets you save it and share it, even though it's not complete, since pictures can't capture everything."

"That's kind of sad," he said.

"I think it adds to the beauty."

We were quiet, watching the waves eat away the sand.

"Did you research this?" he asked.

"Yeah, I read about everything before we came. All the highlights."

"Kenz, seriously. Your knowledge is impressive."

I shrugged.

"Are we going to have to have another lecture about not selling yourself short?"

"Nope."

The beach was a perfect reminder. Despite his inaccurate insights, I liked getting to know him. But I shouldn't get too attached. Like the beach, this relationship had an expiration date.

Today had been great, feeling relaxed and free and more like my real self, but that's all it had been—a day, a break, to enjoy an amazing place. It wasn't the real world, and like those memories I'd told Jake about, I would enjoy it in the moment, knowing it couldn't last.

CHAPTER TWENTY-TWO

"If someone's willing to drive, I'd love to go to the aquarium tomorrow," Jake announced that evening. "My sister loves them, and I told her I'd try to visit if I could. Since the schedule has free time."

He'd told me about his idea, and we'd decided he should be the one to ask, since my parents would be less likely to say no. It was the perfect opportunity, a rest day between our Hana excursion and the several-hour trip to the volcano the following day.

"I'll drive," Gran said, and winked at me.

After our cooking lesson the previous evening, I'd summarized Jake's situation, and she'd agreed to help.

"Is it indoors?" Neal asked. "I could use a day out of the sun. We'll come along."

He looked to Alana, who said, "Sure. Tyler, want to come?"

"More sea creatures? Nah. I need to work on my project." His eyes darted to me.

I wasn't going to snitch about his video game.

Yesterday hadn't given us an opportunity to talk again, but I'd decided not to be mad. I rolled my eyes at him.

He blinked and nodded.

Enough for me. We were good.

When Jake and I went to the lanai to watch the twilight sky, I asked, "Does your sister really like aquariums? Or do you want to go because it's near the harbor?"

"It is near the harbor. And *you* like them, which is why I picked it specifically."

A tendril of warmth curled through me. "Did Tyler tell you that?"

"He didn't have to. A whole selection of animals in one convenient place, unable to swim away. A captive audience for as many pictures as you want to take. It was an easy guess, Kenz." He nudged me with his elbow.

Something fluttered in my stomach, manta ray wings and tiny darting fish and bubbles.

"Hey, sorry about earlier." His fingers brushed my forearm. "It wasn't my place to say that stuff about your photography. I'm too blunt sometimes."

"It's okay."

"Is it, or are you saying that to keep the peace?"

I was over it. Didn't need to keep thinking about it. "It's fine. Really."

"We're good?"

"Yeah."

The door opened, and Neal and Alana joined us.

Jake slid his arm around me. I sucked in his tropical smell and leaned against him. To play the part. So my sister thought we were enjoying a romantic view. Not because the way Jake stroked my arm and breathed in my hair was making my insides sparkle, like light on water.

My hesitation from earlier lingered, lurking inside like a half-hidden creature. A constant, necessary reminder that this couldn't work. Not with how it had started on a mountain of lies.

"So what did you guys like the best about today?" Neal asked.

Taking pictures. Getting to know the real Jake. Feeling like myself for the first time in months.

Not that I could say any of that.

"There were so many great sights," Jake said. "That road was wild, wasn't it? And the guide was so knowledgeable. What about you?"

And there was Jacob again, confirming that I was right to be cautious.

"You're right," Neal said. "There were lots of great things. Those trees were like something from a fantasy novel."

He looked at me, and I returned his smile, since I'd had the same thought.

"Do you like fantasy novels, Jacob?"

"I'm not a big reader. Of fiction," Jake quickly added when Alana opened her mouth.

"I'll give you the series I'm reading, if you want," Neal said. "It might change your mind."

"Thanks."

Jake's arm stiffened around me. Was it for the same reason I was currently feeling nauseated? Neal was trying to get to know him, being nice. And we were lying to his face.

After being so honest with each other all day, our roles felt odd. His role. Hearing him be Jacob.

Not that I was . . . Oh fine, I was playing a role, too. But that was permanent. The stuff with Jake was temporary. Just like the lying. It would all be over soon.

The aquarium was going to be my downfall. Utter and complete ruin was imminent. I'd vowed that I would walk around, enjoy it, snap a picture or two, and move on. Like a normal person. Coo at the seahorses. Be impressed by the turtles. Shudder at the sharks.

Technically the place had won before we left the condo, since I couldn't resist wearing my *Save the Chubby Mermaids* shirt with a picture of a manatee on it, which earned a grin from Jake.

But the situation only grew more precarious once we arrived.

The first building was dedicated to the reefs. A deep sense of peace settled on me. There was something magical about the lighting in aquariums. Dim overheads combined with glowing blue tanks made you feel like you were underwater, suspended in some between-world. Displays told of habitats and sea creatures. Huge tanks contained colorful fish and fascinating coral.

I'd read about many of these creatures, and seeing the variety, the colors and different species, the interesting shapes . . . I'd never get tired of this.

I snuck pictures of everything, concealing my phone until my sister wasn't watching. Waiting for a fish to swim directly in front of me, making sure no people were reflected in the glass.

"Are you going to take a picture of every fish here?" Jake asked.

"Ooh, I should. They could have an animal yearbook, with their names and info and stuff."

"Which fish would win Most Likely to Succeed?"

"The sharks, definitely. Apex predators always win."

He laughed. "What about Class Clown? The clown fish?"

"Too obvious. That angelfish, I think. He looks like he's up to something."

"Most Likely to Become a Rock Star?"

"Um, the starfish that cling to rocks. Duh."

"And that's not too obvious?" He poked me, and I laughed.

I felt light, free inside. The joy of spending time with someone I could trust with all sides of me—the silly one, the dreamer, the adventurer.

"What about you?" he asked. "What category would you win?"

"Probably none. My high school is big and I'm not that social. I bet you totally got voted for something. Most Likely to Play Thor?" I flicked his stubby ponytail.

"I'm taking that as a compliment. I knew you liked my hair."

"I do." The words slipped out before I could stop them.

He smirked. "Most Likely to Get Elected to Office."

"What? Wait, really? Yeah, I can see that. You can be kind of charming."

He put a hand on his chest. "*Kind of?* I'm hurt."

The others had gotten ahead of us, so we hurried after them—once I had taken more pictures.

We rejoined my family near the exit. Outside, the sun felt extra bright, and Alana used the sunlight to make her ring sparkle before giving Neal genuine heart eyes that would have made Jake proud. We stopped at the tide pool where you could touch starfish. A waist-high rock wall held a pool with a variety of species in different shapes and colors. We stuck our hands into the salty water and rubbed the starfish's rough tops.

"Take a picture of me?" Jake asked. "For my sister."

I wiped my wet hand on my shorts and tried to take my phone from my small backpack. The zipper caught, and I twisted, tugging on it.

And the hotel key card Tyler had given me tumbled out. I lunged. Missed. It sank into the pool and landed next to a bright orange starfish.

My heart lurched. I was going to poison the poor creatures. Contaminate their home. Destroy the ecosystem of this entire tank.

My wide-eyed gaze jumped to Jake.

His lips were pressed together to contain laughter.

"Help," I mouthed, and tilted my head toward my sister a few yards away. I didn't need a lecture. And I had to get that key. Not only to save the animals but because I could not lose another one.

Jake moved closer to Alana and Neal and positioned himself to block their view of me. I leaned over to touch the starfish guarding my card. Just as it inched sideways, covering the edge.

Seriously? Who knew starfish were such jerks?

"Ouch," Jake called.

My gaze darted to him, then to the card.

"It bit me," he said.

"I don't think starfish bite," Alana replied.

"Are you sure?"

I plunged my arm in again, half leaning over the rocky edge. My fingertips brushed the edge of the card.

"Oh, you might be right. It seems okay." Jake again. "Hey, Neal, your nose looks pink. Do you need sunscreen?"

This led to fussing, which let me grip the edge of the key card and wiggle it. I didn't want to yank and make the starfish mad. I tugged. Wobbled. *Don't fall in.*

And then I had it, was pulling it free with a splash that sent water down the front of me.

Take that, thieving starfish. Also, sorry I littered in your tank.

I shoved the card into my bag as the others approached. That had been close. I'd almost lost another key to Maui's sea life.

Alana studied my shirt. "Why are you all wet?"

"Is your nose okay, Neal?" I asked. "Gotta be careful with this Maui sun."

I linked my arm through Jake's and strolled away, and he shook with silent laughter.

"Was the rescue mission a success?" he asked.

"It was. How's your starfish bite?"

"I'll live."

I laughed as we came to a giant tank of turtles. We watched from above, then circled to view them through the clear tank below, where you could see them swimming underwater.

Again, that tightness gripped my chest. One soared past right in front of me, smooth and graceful. They were amazing. Something about their faces was so cute, and yet so ancient.

"Wow." Neal stood beside me. "They're pretty cool, aren't they?"

I just nodded.

When he and Alana left, I waited patiently for another one to pass. After I got the picture I wanted, I spun to join the others and crashed into Jake.

He steadied me with hands on my arms.

"What are you doing?" I peered around him.

"Guarding you. From killer starfish."

With his position, he would have also been guarding me from the view of the others, perfectly blocking me as my phone and I lay in wait.

A tingle shot through me.

Our next stop was a building with information about the history of Hawaii and its culture. This time, Alana stopped to read.

Next came the deep-sea exhibit, offering a peek into that mysterious world you couldn't reach with snorkel gear, deeper and more unknown. Beams of light shone through the surface. Manta rays sailed past, their adorable faces on the undersides brushing against the glass.

I barely fought the urge to press my face to the glass and imagine I was being sucked in.

And then there was a person in the water with the circling sharks.

Where did I sign up for that?

Jake leaned close to my ear. "You totally want to do that, don't you?"

I nodded without taking my eyes off the person.

"Have you been scuba diving?" I asked. "That sounds like something you'd like."

"I haven't, but I'd love to learn."

"Me too. But the one time I mentioned it, my mom freaked out. And that was to get certified at a local pool, no sharks involved."

"Maybe one day?"

"Maybe."

The glimmer of hope faded. It might be possible, once I moved out. If I never told my parents. Plenty of optometrists had hobbies, right?

"I'm guessing you aren't afraid of sharks?" Jake asked.

"Nope, I think they're amazing."

"What are you afraid of?"

"Wow, going deep, huh?"

"Seemed appropriate in the deep-sea exhibit." His cheeks dimpled. "And you agreed to the real getting-to-know-you stuff."

"I did." I stared at the person in the tank, calmly floating as the creatures swam around them. "Hmm. I don't love public speaking. And we've established my terror for spreadsheets and schedules."

He snorted.

A manta ray soared past, graceful and sleek. But no matter how beautiful it was, it would never know true freedom.

"I guess being trapped," I said softly. "Not so much physically. Like, I'm not claustrophobic. But trapped, I don't know, in life. One reason I don't like being in charge or making decisions is, what if I make the wrong one and can't get out of it?"

"Huh." He frowned at the tank. "So you basically forced yourself into a situation you're terrified of and have been pretending it's fine?"

I blinked. I hadn't thought of it that way. "In a way, it's easier, though. I'm letting someone else make the choice."

His jaw tightened, the dark lighting making his face look sharper. I sensed he wanted to speak, but he was restraining himself.

"What about you?" I asked.

"Definitely also your dad's schedules."

It was my turn to laugh.

He, too, watched the tank. "I don't know. I felt confined for so long, by my family. Being controlled, I guess. Not having freedom."

"Like, your parents were controlling you by having high expectations?"

"I guess so, yeah."

"Would you have done anything differently if they hadn't?"

"I don't know. I liked baseball. I didn't hate the charity work or the school radio station. I would have skipped Future Business Leaders, which I imagine is about as fun as your Future Health-care Professionals."

"It sounds like it could have been worse. Not that I'm saying it's okay for them to control you, but did you get to pick the things you liked?"

"I guess I did. It was just that quitting wasn't an option. And it was definitely hard to keep up my grades to the level they wanted, along with all the extracurriculars."

We entered a walk-through tube, with water on every side. These were the best. The closest I could get to being in the deep sea without buying a submarine.

I only ran over two people and a stroller when I tried to stay directly beneath a swimming ray.

Next there was a huge white spherical building with so many displays about whales—the building was the actual size of a whale, which was genius. The floor showed a map of their migration from Alaska to Hawaii and back. Interactive screens and a keyboard that played whale song offered hands-on options, and I was like a kid, touching everything.

"You're not very musical, are you?" Jake smirked.

To be fair, my whale song did sound a bit like one was mating with a bagpipe.

We ended in a theater, where we received special glasses and reclined to face a huge screen that arced above. The 3D show about humpback whales made it appear like we were submerged beneath the surface while a giant whale swam right at me. I reached out and connected with Jake, who took my hand and gripped it throughout, like an anchor as my mind floated away.

The images were so real. I might have truly been in the ocean, able to run my fingers along the whale's face or shake its flipper. I swore it made eye contact, and my heart expanded so that I thought my chest might burst. Tears pricked my eyes. Whales were just so incredible.

When the show ended, I blinked hard before removing the glasses.

"Well, that was impressive," Neal said.

Alana nodded. "It really was."

I couldn't speak.

Gran watched me, a gentle smile on her face, as we exited.

I'd rather take pictures of animals in their native habitats, be in the ocean for real, but working somewhere like this wouldn't be a bad alternative career. Would my parents agree that environmental education and conservation was important work, or say I should focus on helping humans, never mind that helping the planet helped us, too?

We moved outside, and Gran pulled out her phone. "There's a gift shop, and then I found one more thing for us to do nearby."

"I wish my grandparents were as cool as you with technology. They don't even have smartphones," Jake said. "My parents have to mail them actual pictures of us, and they check email once a month."

Alana stopped. "Kenzie said your grandparents were gone."

CHAPTER TWENTY-THREE

I froze, and Jake blinked.

"Right," he said. "I meant before they died."

Alana was frowning at him.

"I sometimes forget for a moment. I'm sure you understand, like when you lost your grandfather."

"Yes," I added quickly. "I do that, too. I miss him, you know?"

Alana's face softened. "Me too."

Neal took her hand, and I spotted Gran's face. Her red lips were pressed tight.

I hated that my lie had hurt her. I wrapped my arms around her. "I'm sorry, Gran."

She patted my back. "You need to come clean to your family, Kenz," she said in a low voice only I could hear. "This is going to hurt everyone in the long run."

I gulped and pulled away, avoiding her gaze.

"Think about it," she said.

"I feel like I just murdered my grandparents," Jake muttered when I rejoined him.

"Same. Sorry. It was easier to say you didn't have much extended family than to have to make up stories about all of them. Shouldn't that have been in your notes?"

"It was. I forgot."

"I think my sister bought it."

He nodded, and we followed the others to the gift shop, but the earlier joy had turned sour.

The shop door had a sign for the photography contest. I slowed to look, then kept moving inside.

"I still think you should enter," Jake said softly into my ear. "Just saying."

I glared at him, and he shrugged.

"You've taken lots of pictures today. The contest was about the natural world, for a group working toward conservation. They'd probably love a sea creature picture."

The urge grabbed me to immediately scroll through all the photos I'd taken and see if any were good enough, but I resisted. I didn't have to do anything with the pictures to simply have fun taking them. I would enjoy the process, and they would remind me of the day, and that was enough.

Besides, I doubted photos from an aquarium were sufficient. I needed animals in the wild, in their real habitats. Or scenery. Not something anyone could take with a phone.

Jake lifted a shoulder and drifted away.

Alana and I examined the usual shirts, mugs, and magnets, in addition to locally made wooden products, local coffees, and honey. I spotted a T-shirt with a jellyfish that said *Go with the flow* that I had to have.

The gift shop also had fudge in multiple flavors, and of course Gran bought five different kinds.

When I approached the register with my shirt, Jake had bought something and was pocketing it.

"For your sister?" I asked.

He smiled. "Cool shirt. It suits you."

"Thanks. I think. Wait. Is being a jellyfish good or bad?"

"You're the expert. You tell me."

"Hmm. Well, they don't have brains. But some of them are super deadly, so I guess there's that."

He laughed.

Once we exited, we walked to a shopping area next to the aquarium that overlooked the harbor. Despite having bought approximately seventeen pounds of fudge, Gran led us straight to a cookies-and-ice-cream shop that I suspected was what she had been Googling.

"Shouldn't we get a real lunch?" Alana asked. "It's after noon."

"We can eat when we get back," Gran said. "Life's short. Enjoy dessert first."

"Yeah, because her driving might kill us before we eat lunch," Alana muttered.

As we entered, Gran winked at me and angled her head toward the harbor.

Sneaky, Gran. I'd almost forgotten the real purpose of today's excursion—to help Jake, not to indulge my obsession with ocean life.

Inside smelled heavenly, like fresh cookies and the sugary scent of waffle cones.

"It's not shave ice, but it will do," Gran said, and ordered three scoops, plus bags of their cookie mixes.

Knowing Neal would want to stay indoors, I asked, "Want to go for a walk while we eat?"

"We'll stay here," Gran said. "If that's okay with you, Alana? I could do to rest my feet."

"Of course. Kenz, you two go without us. We'll wait with Gran." They took a seat at a table under a shaded walkway outside.

Happily eating my melting cookies and cream ice cream nestled between two chocolate cookies, I aimed for the harbor with Jake.

"What was your favorite part of the aquarium?" he asked as he licked his towering cone of chocolate and peanut butter.

If it had been anyone in my family asking, I would've played it cool. But this was Jake, and I could be honest.

"That's hard. I love the turtles. But we got to see those while snorkeling, which was cooler because they were in the wild. The sharks? The whale show was awesome. Oh, and I love the jellyfish, those tanks where they swirl up and down. And the manta rays. Their little faces are so cute."

Jake smiled. "Your ice cream is melting."

Oops. "Sorry."

I licked my fingers where my dessert had oozed down my hand and hurried to eat the softest parts.

"Don't apologize. Not to me, not for caring about something." His voice was gentle. "And the sharks are definitely the coolest."

"You're just saying that because they sound big and tough."

"Anything that can eat you is impressive." He grabbed my hand and lifted my forearm to his mouth and pretended to chomp.

I yanked away, laughing. "Am I supposed to be impressed?"

"Are you not? I'll have to try harder."

We grinned at each other, and it was easy to forget the lies, the awkwardness, the way we'd almost been caught.

We reached the harbor's edge and stopped, finishing our ice cream and looking at the boats.

"Are you ready?" I asked. "Are you worried?"

"Why would I be worried?"

"I don't know, that we might not find the boat? Or that we will find it? Like, are you nervous to meet your brother? Do you think he knows about you?"

"I don't know. Probably? It sounds like he's in touch with my dad. But we've established that my dad is a world-class liar, so . . ."

"It must be hard for your brother. I wonder where he grew up? If he knew he was basically being sent away?"

Jake blinked at me.

"What?" I asked.

"You're a good person, Kenzie Reed. You're right. I keep thinking about how my dad lied to me, and how mad I am, and how my life might have been different. But my brother is a real person, too."

"Who was probably just as hurt as you, if not more. Imagine being the one who was essentially abandoned?"

"You're right," he said. "Thank you for reminding me."

I grabbed his hand and squeezed, our palms slightly sticky from the ice cream. "Does your sister know about him?"

He shook his head. "She thinks I'm here with a friend this week. But I gave my parents until I get home to tell her, or I will."

"Hmm."

"What?"

"I don't know. Do you think that's unfair?"

"She has a right to know."

"Maybe so. But is it your decision to make? Would she want to know?"

"Why wouldn't she?"

"I mean, I don't know her. But not everyone is like you, wanting to tackle problems head-on."

He looked unconvinced.

"I'm just saying, be gentle or cautious or at least think about how you approach her." I waited until he nodded to ask, "Do you think your parents will do it?"

"Hard to say. I think they're hoping I'll fail this week and forget about it."

I grunted.

"Yeah. Like I said, they're good at pretending. And living in denial."

Hands clasped, we made a circuit, starting on the shore side and inspecting all the boats. Many slots were empty, out for tours or excursions. Jake made notes on his phone.

"You don't know what kind of boat it is?" I asked.

"No. That would be much more helpful. When I confronted my parents about what I'd overheard, they tried to deny everything at first, even though I'd obviously heard them. When I insisted, they still wouldn't tell me anything."

The anger mixed with hurt in his tone struck something deep inside me.

I hummed. "You hated always having to be someone you're not, which means you hate lying, secrets. No wonder you were so rude at first. It must be frustrating to once again have to pretend to be someone else. I'm sorry I'm adding to it, making you lie more."

He raised his eyebrows. "I'm sorry, *I* was rude?"

"Um, yeah, super judgey."

"While you were plotting my death."

I waved a hand. "Only hypothetically."

"No, I'm sure you had lots of vivid scenarios in mind." He swung our hands. "But you're right. I was judging you. I'm sorry for that. I thought you were like my parents, but you aren't."

The hugeness of what I'd done was sinking in. I'd had good reasons, but I was doing the same thing his parents had—concealing the truth, putting on a happy exterior to please everyone else, hiding anything real as long as I looked good.

"I kind of am like your parents." My voice was small.

"Hey." He stopped and tugged me to face him. "You're not. They care what everyone thinks. Strangers, the public, whatever. You just want to please your family."

My stomach twisted. It was nice of him to say, but what was the difference?

"And I'm obviously doing it, too, since I'm going along with it." None of the judgment from earlier this week showed in his face, only sympathy.

"Does that make us horrible people?" I asked.

"Maybe it makes us desperate ones? Confused ones? Ones without a lot of options?"

"Or ones who took the easy way out."

I recalled his words about fearing failure and rejection. Was that what I was doing with life? My parents weren't wrong—travel photography was hardly a field to guarantee success and stability, though it was difficult to imagine optometry school as the easy way. Had I used their disapproval and our bargain as an easy out, an excuse?

We headed onto the jetty that extended into the water, with cars parked along it and more boats docked on the inside, and he continued to check his phone.

"Are you making a list?" I asked.

"Yeah. Some of the slip numbers are listed online, with the bigger ships you can charter. Tyler found those. But the website didn't include all of them, so I'm checking the others and marking them off the list."

"Let me guess, the list is from Tyler?"

"Ding, ding, ding, we have a winner."

I snorted. "You can always count on my family when you need organizational help."

When we reached the end, we stared at the shore. Bright green trees lined the base of brown hills. A row of buildings sat along the water, and the deeper sea glistened in the sun. The sun was warm, the breeze strong, whipping at my hair.

"Several spots were empty, like in Lahaina," I said. "I guess we can search again when we come snorkeling?"

"Yeah, but I have one more plan."

He kept my hand as we started back, and he stopped every person we passed to ask if they knew of a boat called the *West Wind,* or what boat was usually in the empty spot next to them. Now I understood what he'd been doing in Lahaina.

A few people recognized the name, but none knew who owned it or worked on it. One man said the regulars weren't here this time of day and to check in the evening. I didn't see how we could swing that without raising more suspicions, but morning would be possible in a couple of days, when we returned for our snorkeling tour.

Jake's shoulders were slumping as we left to rejoin the others.

"I'm sorry," I said. "We have one more harbor, right?"

"Right."

We paused and studied each other, the sky bright, the water lapping, the warm sea air enveloping us. Waves bubbled inside me, light and frothy and full of hope.

A boat motor revved nearby, and we laughed and looked away.

"We should get back," I said, trying to cover how breathless I felt. "We'll keep searching. We'll find him. We have three more days."

Jake nodded but didn't look convinced. Then said, "Kenz?"

His voice sounded rough over my name.

"Yeah?" Mine sounded high.

"Thanks."

"For what?"

"I feel . . . relaxed with you. Like you aren't judging me for everything. And that's been rare in my life."

I bit my lip and met his intense gaze, which felt like it was physically touching every inch of my face, leaving thrumming in its wake.

We had three more days to search—but also three more days to keep pretending, something that didn't feel very pretend anymore.

And then what?

CHAPTER TWENTY-FOUR

"**R**eady to go?" Dad asked.

I had nearly forgotten I'd suggested that the two of us spend quality time together. I forced the fake smile which had been getting lots of use this week. "Of course, Daddy. Can't wait."

In the lobby, the hotel had a list of cultural programs they offered. I wanted to laugh at the idea of my dad twirling a fire stick, painting coconut shells, or taking a hula lesson.

"What about lei making?" I said. "It starts in fifteen minutes."

"We could do that."

We joined the group on the lawn, in the shade. Tubs of yellow, white, and purple flowers covered a table, along with assorted greenery, thread, and needles. I wanted to dump the flowers out and take photos of them.

Jake would know about the flowers and how to grow them. Ugh. *Stop thinking about him.* Our relationship wasn't real. But something about the truths we'd shared the last two days made him feel like a friend, or at least a step above co-conspirator. That's all he would ever be.

Speaking of growing them . . . where *did* they grow these?

I'd love to see a garden filled with nothing but purple orchids and—oh. The instructor had started. I needed to pay attention so I didn't accidentally stab anyone.

She showed us how to thread a long, hooked needle, stack flowers onto it, and gently push them onto the string. Simple enough. Especially since half the people in the workshop were kids.

I couldn't imagine doing this when I was younger. When we were children, our curiosity was directed. My parents deemed certain activities important and others not. Vacations were rare, but educational outings were popular—for things my parents thought worth the time.

Wouldn't you rather go to the science museum than yet another zoo?

No, actually, that's why I asked about the zoo in the first place.

Why couldn't it be enough that I simply enjoyed something? Why did everything have to contribute to the betterment of mankind? And didn't art do that, adding depth to life, and beauty and new perspectives? Like I wanted to do with my photos.

I needed to shift my thoughts away from topics that made me angry while I was holding a large, pointy piece of metal.

I decided on a pattern of purple orchids and white plumeria with a touch of greenery. Dad was staring helplessly at the bowls of flowers as the kids attacked them like hyenas tearing apart a dead antelope.

"Mom likes purple, right?" I asked. "That's classic. You can't go wrong with that."

"Right. Good call. Is that for Jacob?"

"Gran." I hadn't thought about it, but that felt good.

We slid flowers on, one by one.

"Are you enjoying your time with Jacob? I admit, he isn't exactly what I expected, but he's a nice young man."

Yeah, he wasn't what I'd expected, either. "I am. And you know, it's hard to do someone justice to people who haven't met him."

"He seems to make you happy. Is it serious?"

The clenching in my chest suspiciously resembled regret. "I don't know. I'm young. I like him, but I'll be in college soon, and he's far away. We'll see what happens."

The idea of not seeing him again felt like a needle through the heart. But we couldn't keep up the lie. It would only hurt the fragile new relationship I'd built with my dad if I kept lying about something so important.

My dad hummed. "I do like that he's interested in the profession. I always dreamed of my kids and their spouses working alongside me one day, eventually taking over."

"Spouse?" My needle slipped and stabbed my fingertip, and a tiny drop of blood appeared. I swallowed a hiss and hid it from Dad by pressing it to the underside of the tablecloth. "Dad, I'm in high school. I don't know if Jacob . . ."

"I know, I know." He smiled. "Just let me enjoy the idea, sweetie. I know you might not marry another optometrist. And I know Tyler wants to pursue his computers."

Boy, was Dad in for a shock.

"But it will be nice to have you girls with me, the way I was with my father. I'm so proud of you."

It echoed his comments to Alana from the day before and

didn't feel any better today. Everything he was proud of was the stuff that wasn't me, stuff I copied from my sister. Apparently, all it took to make him proud was being exactly like her.

Which hurt even more after yesterday, how much I'd felt like myself and enjoyed—in secret—everything Dad thought I'd let go.

When we finished, we donned our leis and I had someone take a picture of us.

Dad watched me pocket my phone. "The pictures you took for your sister turned out well."

"They did. Alana was happy."

"It was nice of you to help."

I waited for more. For him to say he'd noticed me sneaking photos this week. For him to ask if I'd enjoyed photographing Alana. For him to fondly—or even not-so-fondly—remember how much I loved it.

But there was nothing further. No comment on how I never took pictures anymore, or how he was glad I was past that, like my parents used to say in the first weeks after I'd stopped. Those comments had become more and more infrequent as my family gradually believed the lie I'd built, the new me convincing them I'd changed.

And while that had relieved me at first, now I found unexpected anger welling up. Shouldn't the people who loved me care enough about me to encourage my dream, not be happy I'd let it go?

We might have been very different, but he was a good dad. Who wanted to enjoy his chosen career with the kids he loved. I might enjoy working with him.

But the future was a snake tightening around me, one of those boas that slowly strangled you to death before swallowing you whole.

"Good news, Kenz," Jake said when we walked in the door. "Neal found Clue."

Neal held up the board game box. "I remembered you saying it was Jacob's favorite, and they had it in the library of games and puzzles for resort guests. I thought we could play."

Jake met my gaze, his eyes wide. "Wasn't that nice?"

His expression said it wasn't nice at all and he was panicking on the inside, which I was guessing meant he didn't know how to play.

"I have to warn you, though," Neal said, "that Alana is good at uncovering people's secrets."

I gulped. He meant in the game. It was fine.

But we'd barely covered up the grandparent thing. I didn't know how we'd fake our way through a complicated game Jake was supposed to be good at.

"That's so sweet, Neal. Thanks. Maybe later? We were talking about how we wanted to take a stroll on the beachwalk for sunset tonight, and that's coming up fast."

I was glad I'd read about it earlier, a long path along the beach, passing through several resorts.

Neal nodded. "Oh, of course."

"I'm looking forward to it, though," Jake said. "Thanks."

We made a quick escape, through the resort grounds and onto the path. The route led past restaurants where people sat outdoors, and the sun was sinking in the sky.

"How do you not know how to play Clue?" I asked.

"Why would you make up a boyfriend who loves a game centered around murder?"

I rolled my eyes. "You better read up on it, in case we can't get out of it again."

"I'm a pro at reading up. How do you think I learned so much about optometry and Ohio State? But really, you couldn't have given Jacob one sport he liked instead of documentaries?"

"There was an unfortunate incident with a lacrosse player who ran over our hydrangeas when he came to pick me up for a date. It turned my parents off of me dating jocks."

"Those poor plants." He clicked his tongue. "Again with the questionable taste in guys."

"Shut up," I said, but I was smiling. "Does it count as *taste* if I wasn't really interested in any of them? They seemed fun, we went out once or twice, and I never got to know them much. It was like, after ten minutes, I knew they weren't right, but since I didn't want anything serious, it didn't matter."

"Sounds like the girls I dated. One or two dates, and I could tell I didn't need to get to know them better. Not like—"

He stopped, and I snuck a glance, my face getting warm. Did he mean not like with me? It was safer not to pursue that line of thought.

We continued on, our fingers brushing occasionally, but he didn't reach for my hand. Until I had to edge sideways as someone passed. I bumped into Jake, and his arm came around me to steady me. When we moved on, he linked his fingers with mine.

A thrill shot through my core.

The people-watching was as interesting as the scenery. Most of the walk was like a mall, except there was an ocean nearby. Palm trees and bushes bordered the path, but there were also hotels and booths and decks with tables.

"How was the time with your dad?" Jake asked. "Gran liked the lei, though I'm trying not to be insulted that I didn't get one."

"I wasn't sure if you wanted one. Do you only like growing flowers? Is it, like, plant murder to wear them around your neck?"

"It's actually good for flowering plants to cut them."

"Oh. Cool. What did you do while I was gone?"

"Neal wanted me to tell him about my plans for classes over the next three years, but I managed to turn it on him and get his advice." A slight wrinkle flickered across his forehead.

"What's wrong?"

"I feel bad lying to them. Neal's nice, and he wanted to help."

"Yeah." I thought of the time with my dad. "I know what you mean."

His grip tightened on my hand.

"Gran was upset earlier." I bit my lip. "She thinks we should tell everyone the truth."

"What do you think?"

"It's been too long now. They'll be mad, and hurt. Maybe we should continue on like we planned."

"And then break up and not see each other again?" he asked, and I couldn't read the tone of his voice.

I swallowed hard. "It's probably for the best."

He didn't reply, and we took a short path from the walkway to the sand.

We passed a couple posing for a selfie.

"Hey," Jake said to them. "My girlfriend is a great photographer, if you want her to take a picture of you."

He said *girlfriend* easily, and it sent a pang through me. I took the phone the woman handed me, and moved around until I had the best angle.

She offered to take one of us, and it felt so natural to let Jake put his arm around me. I leaned in and smiled.

As they moved on, Jake was studying the ocean. More specifically, people jumping off a cliff into the ocean.

"No way," I said. "If we go back soaked, my parents will wonder why."

"We can say we went for a swim. I mean, not if you don't want to," he said quickly. "I would never force you."

I was tempted. But night was falling, and it was a long way to climb up there, then swim to shore, then walk back.

"Do you do everything you want to, no matter what others might say?" I asked.

"Yep. Mostly."

"Were you always like that?"

"Sort of? I guess I used to be more cautious. Only because I knew how much trouble I'd be in if my parents found out I did something that might look bad."

"So not because you might hit your head on a rock?"

"Nah. I might get hit by a car while walking across the street. I don't believe in living in fear."

I hesitated before continuing. "Do you think you're more likely to give in to those ideas now as a way of getting back at your parents?"

His jaw tightened.

"Not that anything you're doing is wrong or bad. Just that, now that you know what you know, it's like your way of rebelling?" I held still, hoping I wasn't getting too personal.

"You . . . might have a point."

Instead of throwing ourselves off a towering rock of death, we sat in the sand at the edge of the waves, touching at shoulders, arms, hips, legs. The water was like liquid silver as the brilliant colors of sunset flared and slowly began to fade.

He shifted, and I turned to look at him. We studied each other, our faces close. His blue eyes matched the ocean.

"I didn't think I was trying to cause problems," he said. "But when I learned the truth . . . I don't know. I was angry, not just about what my parents had done, or that they'd lied. But also how everything else seemed like a lie. I started to question myself, what was really me, who I was."

I shifted my hand to rest atop his in the sand. "That sounds like fear."

He stared at the waves. "Maybe it was. But I let it become anger instead. I ignored my parents when we were alone. Didn't even tell them I was coming here until the plane was about to take off, sent them a text right before I shut off my phone. And the last few months, I think I was trying to be more *me,* if that makes sense. Doing everything I wanted, when an idea hit me, without hesitating. It made everything feel more real if I didn't stop to think."

"That makes sense, actually. It gave you a feeling of control." I tried to picture confident, determined Jake doubting himself, and the idea made me sad.

"I also felt, I don't know, relieved? That I no longer had to be so perfect." Jake's dimples flashed briefly. "I wouldn't have considered any of these feelings if not for you."

"I'm sorry you're having to deal with the whole situation."

His eyes softened. A tendril of his hair brushed his cheek. We reached up at the same time, me to tuck his hair back, and him to do the same to mine.

I froze, a breathless laugh huffing out. Our hands hovered near each other's faces.

My heart skipped. I swallowed hard, and his gaze dipped to my lips. My stomach plunged like I had jumped off that cliff.

This was a bad idea.

I swayed toward him. His fingers trailed down my cheek.

Water surged over my toes, and we scrambled to our feet. My heart was racing. What was that? Had I been ready to kiss him?

That couldn't happen. I couldn't like the real Jake. My family knew him as a different person. We had to "break up" soon. All of us was built on a lie, not a firm foundation, and like a sand-castle, we would soon be swept away.

CHAPTER TWENTY-FIVE

Mom refused to let Gran drive the convertible up the volcano in the middle of the night. We'd gone to bed early and were now up at an hour that could not be considered morning. Watching the sunrise from the top of the volcano required a long drive, but it would totally be worth it. Mom was driving the van. She said being behind the wheel would help prevent car sickness, and she'd brought a gallon of coffee, which I hoped would stay down.

After much complaining on Gran's part—and pouting of lips that were bright red even in the middle of the night—Dad took over the Mustang. And immediately closed the roof.

"That's a tragedy," she said.

"It's going to be freezing up there. And it's pitch-black outside."

"It's still a tragedy. I'll ride in the van."

Dad rolled his eyes. Alana and Neal ended up with him, while Gran took the van's front seat with Mom. Tyler sat in the middle, and Jake and I crawled into the back.

Dad was right—it was pitch-black. Tyler's phone glowed briefly, but then he put in earbuds and slumped against the window, leaving us in darkness once more.

The humming engine and the gentle bumping made my eyelids droop.

And then Jake slid next to me. We had each taken a window, leaving a seat between us. But he closed the gap, his leg pressing against mine. He took my hand, twining his fingers through mine, tangling and then untangling, his thumb rubbing my palm.

Every nerve was now electrified, alert. My heart pounded loudly in my ears.

This wasn't a show. No one could see us.

The darkness made the contact feel secret and thrilling.

When Jake clasped my hand and went still, I slowly settled into a lull. My head drifted to his shoulder. His leaned against mine, a stray lock of hair tickling my forehead. He was warm and solid, and that familiar, comforting tropical smell enveloped me.

The next thing I knew, I was blinking awake as the car hit a bump. I rolled my head, which had been resting on something comfortable. Oh. It had been against his chest.

My gaze met Jake's, his eyes inches from mine. There was just enough illumination for me to see his smile emerge. I was too sleepy to be embarrassed and too comfortable to move. His arm was around me, and mine had circled his stomach, and it was incredibly nice.

He shifted, causing me to nestle closer and press against him once more. His other arm came around me in a hug and held me close.

No matter how comfortable it was, I was so far from sleep now.

My pulse tripped and skipped. His chest rose and fell beneath my cheek, his heart thudding.

I inhaled slowly, tried to calm my heart. I might have to break up with him soon, but that didn't mean I couldn't enjoy this a little longer. . . .

We rose up, up, up the side of the volcano, the road pitch-black and winding. I hoped Mom had taken the correct meds, to keep her from getting carsick or falling asleep behind the wheel. Gran might have been a better driver choice, since it was too dark for her to slow down and look at anything.

After we checked in and parked, it was time to untangle myself from Jake. I slowly shifted away, pulling my arm back and sitting up. I immediately felt cold, except a flush of warmth in my face. Our gazes snagged and held.

What was he thinking? Had he enjoyed that as much as I had? A storm churned inside me, not unpleasant.

We bundled up in jackets to fight off the chill at the high elevation and grabbed the blankets we'd brought from the hotel. From the parking lot, it was a short climb to the summit. Dad and Alana lit the way with their phone flashlights. Several other people had made the trek as well and joined us.

Jake took my hand, and I let him.

"Ugh," Tyler mumbled. "Why did I think it would be easier to stay up all night? How far is it?"

We took positions along a fence. The wind was cold, sharp, and Jake took a blanket and wrapped it around us, leaving his arms circling me to hold it in place. I nestled into his chest again. Purely for show. Since my family was now watching. Not because I liked the way his chin rested on my head.

Stars twinkled above, though they were fading. Nearby, an

older man was fiddling with a fancy camera on a tripod. A second tripod sat next to it.

Mom sniffed and moved around him, muttering about people taking up too much space.

"Nice cameras," I said. "Are you doing time-lapse?"

"On this one, yes. Then photos with the other."

My neck suddenly felt naked, where my own camera should have been hanging.

"Are you using a wide-angle lens?" It's what I would have used.

His eyes lit up. "I am. Are you a photographer as well?"

"Not really. Just for fun sometimes."

Jake's arms tightened around me.

"You don't have to be a professional to call yourself a photographer," the man said. "If you like to take pictures, I say, claim the title. None of that 'aspiring' stuff. I'm hardly a pro. But I am a photographer."

"Do you . . . do anything with them? Or are they just for you?"

"I've had a few accepted by small magazines. Lots more rejected." He chuckled. "But I keep sending them, everywhere I can find." He didn't seem bothered to admit that.

"That's brave."

Wait, by calling him brave, was I admitting I wasn't, since the idea of that rejection made me not want to send a photo to anyone, ever? If I had pursued the career, I would have had to learn to handle rejection. That was part of the job. But I wasn't doing that anymore, so it didn't matter.

"Eh, I'm a stubborn old fool. Taking pictures makes me

happy, so I might as well keep trying. Already covered the walls of my house with my pictures, and my kids and neighbors are sick of receiving more for gifts."

We laughed.

"I hope you get some good ones today."

"You too," he said, which was interesting, since I didn't have a camera.

The sky was turning dark purple, the stars fading, and a row of mountains was sharpening in the distance, below a strip of pink sky.

I watched the man tinker with his settings.

"Take some," Jake whispered into my ear. "It's a Hawaiian sunrise. It's strange if you *don't* take pictures."

My hand went to the phone in my jacket pocket.

As the sky continued to lighten, we could see that beneath us was nothing but clouds. The volcano and the rest of the island were hidden by the fluffy, silvery bank. Above, the sky glowed with a stripe of gold. We were on top of the entire world. Nothing existed up here, no cities or beaches or jungles. Only peaks and clouds and a vast, vast sky that called to something deep in my soul, the infinite touching this one place, here and now, where I stood.

I took out my phone. Mom and Alana and Neal were taking pictures. They couldn't judge me for this. Photos could never do this scene justice, but I pulled away from Jake to find a better position.

The world grew brighter, the sky shifting to brilliant shades of pink and orange above the silver bank of low clouds. Then the tip of the sun appeared, and everything was fire, the edges gilded in gold and orange and red. The peaks and valleys of the clouds resembled a fluffy mountain range.

Everyone else was so focused, they didn't notice me taking picture after picture.

The sun rose higher until the sky turned pale pink and blue, the clouds white. And then the sun was up.

This was totally worth not sleeping. I could have stood there, motionless, every morning, over and over again. The one thing that could always keep me focused and settled—watching and waiting for the right shot. It reminded me of the old Kenzie days, when I would go to a nearby trail to watch the sunrise, or drive to San Francisco and sit on the beach for two hours for sunset and twilight. Nothing made me so calm and yet purposeful as those times. Focused, but relaxed, and totally at peace.

I let the enormity of the sky, the vastness of the landscape, envelop me, until I was a small part of a grand world, filled with wonder at the fact that I got to be here to experience this.

It was over too soon. I pocketed my phone, and Jake's arm came around me again, and we stared at the clouds.

A voice intruded, and I dragged my gaze from the clouds. Dad. Most of the people had gone, and he was herding us to the cars. I sighed and trudged down the hill after my family.

We sat in the van with the doors open, eating the muffins and bananas we'd brought.

My mind replayed the scene over and over. Conversation buzzed around me, but I didn't hear it, reliving the most glorious sunrise I'd ever seen.

A hand on my back made me jump, and I blinked to see Jake leaning close.

A half smile lit his face. "Ready for our hike?"

"Oh. Right."

We were the only two left in the van.

"Don't worry. I told them you were tired. But you were daydreaming about the sunrise, weren't you?" His eyes sparkled.

I ducked my head and grinned. "That doesn't sound like me at all."

He laughed. "Come on."

He climbed out and offered a hand to help me, and kept hold as we joined the others. Alana was staring at her phone but looked up at our approach.

"Great. The trail is this way."

"Did everyone bring sunscreen and water?" Mom asked. "I know it's early, but we want to be prepared."

Her gaze went straight to me, but I had carefully stocked my backpack, proving I was capable of taking care of myself in some things—and the outdoors and hiking, I could do.

"See?" Jake said. "Dedication and planning."

At least someone recognized it.

"Watch your step, everyone," Mom called. "Don't want to turn an ankle."

The air was chilly, and we followed my sister down a trail leading from the summit into the volcano. The sky was a brilliant blue above, but clouds lurked in the crater below. The trail led down a hill of reddish-brown and black sand, with rocky outcroppings that were twisted and weird. My feet skidded occasionally on the loose dirt.

It looked like yet another alien planet, with fog floating among jagged rocks, blocking our long-range views, shifting and blowing, revealing strange shapes and then concealing them again. Like it was playing games. It left a slight dampness on my skin.

Jake stopped near a plant, squatting close but careful to stay on the trail.

Long silvery-green tendrils formed a round ball shape, and each leaf was covered in tiny hairs. It reminded me of a sea urchin. Or an alien being that might leap up and attach itself to his face.

I knelt beside him to take up-close photos, wishing for my fancy zoom lens.

"It's called a silversword," he said. "Incredibly rare and endangered. They're only found here at this summit. It looks like a succulent, but it's in the daisy family. They can live over fifty years, but they only flower once."

"You know a lot about plants," Neal said.

"Yeah, at the banyan tree, too," Alana added.

Jake shrugged. "I like them. I took a, uh, botany class. You know, for the bio major. And I found it interesting."

I could tell that, like me, he was trying not to reveal how much he cared. And trying to tie it to the person he was supposed to be, since Jacob would have no reason to know about rare plants found only in Maui.

"That's very specific," Alana said.

"My professor liked unusual plants."

"Huh." My sister looked at me. "I thought Kenzie was rubbing off on you."

"Would that be a bad thing?" Jake met her direct gaze with one of his own, and I wanted to tug him away.

This was Jake, not Jacob, slipping from lies about his college classes to wanting to defend me to anyone and everyone. And though a part of me appreciated it, we didn't need the potential conflict.

Alana held his stare. "No. It wouldn't." She smiled at me, took Neal's hand, and continued on.

As we moved on deeper into the heart of Mordor, I hung back with Jake. He was watching the plants along the trail and stopped to study another.

I took out my phone and circled the plant as much as the trail allowed, careful where I stepped, then took some zoomed-in pictures and some with the vast volcanic landscape in the background.

"So, other than because you like the outdoors, why plants?" I asked him.

He studied the alien plant that so far wasn't trying to latch on to his face. "I don't know, lots of reasons. I like the idea of bringing nature more places, even to cities. How gardens can offer a taste of nature no matter where you are, and there's something about it that feeds our souls in a way cities can't."

"That is true," I said. "I love finding a park or just a nice shade tree, or flowers, those bursts of color where you don't expect them. It always cheers me up."

"Exactly. Like your pictures. I want to forge that connection between people and nature. And I like that there are so many kinds of plants and combinations. It's a fun challenge to find the right mix. Every project is different."

That reminded me of what he'd said about looking forward to a job, not simply enduring one. How excited he was to talk about it and the idea of him attacking each new plot of earth with purpose, bringing life and color and potential to it.

My heart expanded in my chest. With Jake, I had someone who understood me, who saw what I wanted to do and thought it worthy. Who shared a similar outlook.

We were only a few feet apart on the trail, mist swirling around us in this strange land. We couldn't see the others. Might have been alone on the planet.

"Can I see your pictures of it?" he asked.

I hesitated. Then stared at the phone. Why did I care? Because he might not like every single image?

I stared at the weird little plant. "You . . . might have been right."

"I'm right about lots of things. You'll have to be more specific."

I rolled my eyes. "I think I do fear failure. Or rejection or whatever."

"Why do you say that?"

"I don't know if I could handle all the rejections that older guy faced. If I would have the courage to keep trying."

He grabbed my hand and waited until I looked at him. "I bet you would. It might be hard at first, but if you really want something, isn't it worth the struggle?"

"Maybe I didn't want it badly enough?"

"I don't think that's true. Anyone who knows you for more than five minutes can see your passion."

I swallowed. "Then I guess reinventing myself was the coward's path. A way to keep my heart safe."

"Or, it was a small setback in your journey, a single moment of weakness, and nothing more. Not something you can never undo."

But did I want to undo it? Was I strong enough to return to the path that not only offered the potential for my work to get rejected but also for my family to constantly disapprove and criticize *me*?

"What if I try it and don't succeed?"

He held my gaze. "But what if you do? Don't let the reason it doesn't happen be because you didn't try."

Voices reached us through the fog. I pulled away and hurried to catch up to the others. But his words stayed with me— I'd made a choice, possibly in a moment of weakness, and that choice could be undone.

If I wanted it to be.

CHAPTER TWENTY-SIX

The climb up was much harder and warmer than the climb down. By the time we reached the cars, though it was barely midmorning, I was sweating and my thighs burned. The feeling was invigorating. I was ready to see more.

"That was a lot of rocks," Tyler said. "And half of them are in my shoe."

"I wonder what the UV index is up here," Neal said.

So more hiking was probably out of the question. . . .

For the drive down, Gran was allowed in the Mustang again and offered to take me and Jake—probably because we were the only ones who didn't complain about her driving. My dad did insist that she go first so he could stay behind her in case she had trouble. I guess he trusted her not to drive away so fast that he wouldn't be able to keep up. Which I wouldn't have put past her.

Now that we could see everything, the views were amazing. The green hillsides of the volcano, the banks of clouds, glimpses of the rest of the island spread out below us.

Ahead, vans were parked in a turnout area, along with some bicycles.

"Ooh, bikes," I said.

"Want to check it out?" Gran was already parking next to them.

"Hello," she called, and a man approached.

"Can I help you?"

"Is this . . . Can you bike down the volcano?" I asked.

"You sure can. You missed the guided tour, but we have a few bikes left for self-guided trips, where you go at your own pace."

The van pulled up next to us, and Dad rolled the window down.

"What's going on?" he asked.

"Kenzie and Jacob want to rent bicycles," Gran called.

"That doesn't sound safe," my dad said.

"It sounds amazing," I muttered.

"Right?" Jake said.

"Do you know how to use a hand brake?" the guy asked.

Jake and I nodded.

"Then it's as safe as any other bike ride."

"I ride my bike all the time, Dad. I'm good at it. And I've never had a problem."

Zooming down the side of a volcano sounded way cooler than a high school senior riding her bike to school. And way more thrilling, no matter what the guy said.

"Oh, come on, Richard," said Gran. "Let them try it. I'll wait at the bottom to take them home."

"I thought Jacob didn't like to bike?" Alana asked.

Had I said that?

"Not the way Kenzie does, but partly it's the Ohio weather," Jake said easily. "I'm good enough."

"Are you sure?" Mom was frowning at me. "Don't let her talk you into something that makes you feel unsafe."

Jake took my hand. "Thanks, Dr. Reed, but I'll be fine."

"If you're sure . . . But be careful."

They waited while we scrambled out of the car, signed waivers, and grabbed our jackets.

"I got directions, so I'll meet you when you're done," Gran said. "But don't hurry. Just have fun."

I hugged her. "Thanks, Gran."

She patted my back. "You deserve to do what you like on this trip, too, dear."

She waved and drove off, my dad following her, leaving me, Jake, four wheels, and the volcano.

The guy gave an overview of what to expect—descending sixty-five hundred feet over twenty-three miles, ending in the small town of Haiku. My pulse skipped and tripped as he rolled two bikes over. This was going to be amazing.

"That was close back there," I said to Jake. "Nice save."

"Why would you make up a guy who doesn't like to ride a bike?"

"I don't know. I couldn't make up a guy who liked all the same things as me. That would have sounded suspicious, and it sounded dreadful to ride a bike in Ohio in the winter."

"Worse than in Sacramento in the summer?"

"Why didn't you know that?"

"It wasn't in the notes Tyler gave me. He must not have heard you say it."

"Honestly, I don't remember saying it. Curse my family's

good memory. Between that and your freakish knowledge of plants, we need to be more careful."

The guy was looking at us strangely, so we quickly donned helmets like motorcycle helmets, gloves, and our jackets. He also gave us a backpack with a repair kit, water bottles, and a first aid kit. Good thing Mom hadn't seen that.

The bikes were sturdy mountain bikes, much more heavy-duty than the cruiser I rode around town.

We rolled them to the road.

"Are you ready for this?" I asked.

He grinned. "I feel very unsafe."

"You like it."

"I really do. Is that bad? Am I acting out of anger toward my parents again?" His cheeks dimpled.

I rolled my eyes. "I didn't say you should stop doing everything fun. I like that about you, that you go after what you want. It makes me a little braver, too."

"Well, then, let's be brave."

And we were off. I barely had to pedal, thanks to the constant descent. Anyone could have done this.

Though, we did share the road with cars and had to listen for them. One veered too close. There were more gravel areas where we could stop and enjoy amazing views of the island.

It was hard to watch the road, and I had new empathy for Gran's driving habits.

On some of the straightaways, our speed increased easily, and the rush of wind, the road blurring beneath me, sent my heart soaring.

When we paused for water, after drinking and taking in the view, I said, "Race you to the next stop," and shoved off before Jake could argue.

We passed a group on an official tour, and I recalled Jake's and my discussion about how we preferred to do our own thing, without someone else telling us where to go or when to stop.

Except we were going to have to stop. Not just today's ride, but all of this.

The lower we got, the more trees popped up. It was fully warm now, and I was sweating, but I sailed on, the wind blowing in my face, like we could outrun the inevitable.

We found Gran waiting in town, wearing enormous cat-eye sunglasses covered in rhinestones. We turned in the bikes and other gear at a shop and grabbed fish tacos at a food truck.

"We're making a surprise stop on the way home," Gran said. "Well, two of them. One is for me, but the other is for Jake."

"What's that?" he asked.

"Kahului harbor."

He blinked. "Really?"

"Of course." She patted his arm, and he smiled.

"What's the other?" I asked.

She winked at me over the top of her sunglasses. "Shave ice, obviously."

We drove along the north shore and into the city, the buildings strange after several hours of nature, and stopped at a park next to the water. This harbor was nothing like the others, with their small walkways, boats to rent, and ads for tours. Two huge cruise ships and several cargo ships were the only vessels. It didn't appear to have permanent berths.

"Could it be a cargo ship?" I asked.

"Probably not. I guess it's possible, but if he worked on one of those, he'd be moving around a lot, not living here."

"What else can we try?" There had to be some way I could help him. "Ask the harbor boss—what's that called? harbormaster?—about the boats here?"

He shook his head. "There's an online database of boats registered in Maui. I paid for an account that lets you see owners' names, but I didn't find my brother's boat listed. But that database is just where the boat's registered. It doesn't always mean the boat docks there. The *West Wind* could be registered on another island or in LA or Tahiti. And it's not an uncommon name."

"You said Tyler's been helping. Maybe he can search every harbor on the West Coast."

Jake's mouth quirked. "We might be at a dead end for now."

Gran sighed. "I'm sorry. I thought this would help."

"It did. Thank you. Now I know."

"But we still haven't found it," I said. "And we're running out of time."

Jake took my hand and squeezed. "Hey, it's okay."

"I should be the one telling you that. We can check the other harbors again. Try a different time of day?"

"I'll help however I can," said Gran.

"That means a lot to me. Thank you both. Maybe it wasn't

meant to be. Not now, anyway. It doesn't mean I'll never meet him. And hey, I got to spend an amazing week with all of you."

I could tell he was trying to sound positive, and I didn't want to push, but between the three of us, we could figure something out.

"We're going snorkeling tomorrow. Maybe we'll see something then."

"And I'm stopping in Lahaina for that excellent shave ice," Gran said. "You're welcome to look around there."

When we parked in town, Jake headed for the harbor, and I stayed with Gran down the main road toward the shave ice place. I slowed in front of the photo gallery.

"Go in," she said. "I'll bring you something."

"No, that's okay . . ."

"Kenz, you love sunsets, right?" She was staring thoughtfully at the door with the contest flyer on it, not at me.

"Yeah . . ."

"I think I heard you say once that you like that each one is unique, not another like it?"

"Right."

She shifted her attention to me. "Doesn't the same apply to people? What makes each person beautiful is that no one else is like them. So why are you trying to be someone you aren't instead of being the unique you that you are? The one that only occurs once in history and is meant to do things that no one else ever could?"

I opened my mouth. Shut it.

"Seems simple to me. You either embrace that idea and live to be your fullest self, or you don't. But those who don't are usually unhappy. Not only that, but they're depriving the world of something only they could have offered."

I'd never thought about it like that before.

I twisted my hands together. "How do you do it?" I asked. "Hold on to who you are when those closest to you don't approve?"

"Oh, Kenz." She took my face in her hands. "Your family will always be a part of you. It's wonderful that you care about them, and their feelings matter. But yours do, too. If you're constantly living for others, you'll miss out on so much. Don't let other people decide what makes you happy and fulfilled, not even your parents."

She released me, and my heart swelled.

"Don't wait until you're retired to enjoy your life. Eat that dessert, bike that mountain." Gran opened the door and gave me a shove. "Seize that day."

I let the momentum propel me inside as she continued on.

I took a few steps into the room. Gran was wise, and obviously happy. Maybe I should consider her advice. The owner I'd talked to, Rob, probably wasn't working today. He was likely off on an amazing adventure, and some clerk would try to convince me to buy artwork I couldn't afford.

But before the photos could pull me in, Rob was circling the desk to approach.

"You're back," he said.

"You remember me?"

"I remember everyone who gets the look you had when you were here. Wanderlust."

I huffed. "Yeah, that's me."

"Can I help you with something?"

"I don't know. Not really? I just wanted to look again."

He let me browse, and I paused in front of multiple photos to study them. An image of lava flowing into the ocean under a starry sky caught my eye.

"How'd you get the lava not to be so bright that it overpowers the stars?" I asked. "High ISO and a slow shutter speed?"

"Exactly. Are you into cameras?" he asked.

"Um. Sort of?"

"What about that one?" He nodded to an amazing image that showed a turtle swimming underwater as well as a rocky, palm-tree-lined shore above.

I studied it. "Split-level. I love those. The quality is excellent. Underwater housing for your regular camera? And the trees are blurry, but the turtle is sharp. Did you experiment with the settings?"

"I did indeed. Split-level photos often take experimenting and lots of patience."

"I'd love to try, but I don't have the equipment." I imagined spending an entire day on the water, in the reef, taking tons of pictures, playing with my camera, waiting for that one right image. I sighed.

Rob moved to stand in front of a huge picture of waves flowing into a cave. He had to have been standing at the rear of the cave, the water surging toward him, and the water was blurred. "And this one?"

"Long exposure. Maybe a neutral density filter? Since the sky is sunny. And a smaller aperture."

"You know your stuff."

Warmth surged through me. It felt weird but good to talk about this with someone, like a colleague. He didn't treat me like a kid or a student.

We paused as a couple came in, looked around, and left.

"Did you get any good shots while you've been here?" he asked.

"Oh, I just used my phone. I didn't bring my nice gear."

"If it's a new phone, lots of those have good cameras on them."

I swallowed. Showing him was much different from showing Jake. Rob was a pro. What if he thought I wasn't any good? That my photos were amateur. Mundane. That the one and only unique me wasn't anything special.

I pulled it out and scrolled through the ones I'd favorited. Would it make me see them any differently, remember the moments any differently, if he critiqued the images?

"They're not edited or anything."

I inched my phone toward him. He waited patiently, as if sensing my indecision, like I was a wild animal and he was letting me get comfortable enough to approach. Then I thrust it into his hands and stared at a panoramic sunset on the wall behind him so I didn't have to see his face.

"Interesting," he said. "You have an eye for details. Decent composition. Definite potential."

My heart stuttered.

"You have rather a variety. I know that's normal for vacation, but is there a subject you particularly prefer? Animals? Land-scapes? Close-ups?"

"I like all of it? I know it's good to have a specialty, but I kind of just focus on things that, I don't know, inspire me? And I hope they might inspire others, too. You have a lot. How do you pick?"

His lips lifted. "Well, in this gallery, I choose the ones that people might want to hang on their walls."

I smiled.

"But in general? I guess I prefer landscapes that bring out the character of a place. When the scenery is stunning and the lighting is just right."

I sighed again. "That sounds amazing."

"What do you want to do?" he asked.

"I don't really know. I want to travel lots of places. Maybe freelance or work for a travel company."

Wait. No. I was going to optometry school.

Rob handed my phone back. "You have potential. You know your equipment. Don't be afraid to experiment and take lots of bad photos until you find what works. And remember that successful photography isn't only about the technical side. It's about the heart. Figure out what drives you. For me, it started with wanting to show off the natural beauty of my islands."

Did that mean he thought my photos lacked heart? Or was this general encouragement?

A professional was giving me tips. I'd be an idiot not to listen. And he didn't say I was hopeless.

A strange mix was brewing in my stomach, excitement and fear and nerves, and I thought I might explode.

"Thanks. Can I ask one more thing? How did you convince your family to let you do this?"

"I wouldn't say I did."

"They didn't support you?"

He smiled sympathetically. "Oh, they did. But I didn't have to talk them into it or anything."

"Huh."

"It's risky and difficult, I won't lie. Especially at first. I met my wife while traveling, after I'd had a small amount of success, so she knew what she was getting into." He laughed.

"Yeah, my parents don't love the idea."

"If it's what you're meant to do, I'm sure you'll find a way. No career is easy. Each one has unique challenges. But I believe in finding the path where those challenges are worth it. Where they don't feel like insurmountable obstacles or impossible tasks or fill you with dread, but rather stir determination inside you to overcome them no matter what."

So, optometry versus photography. That couldn't have been any more black-and-white than the leaping whale watching me from the wall.

"Thank you for talking with me. Mahalo."

"Are you going to enter the competition?"

"Maybe."

"I hope you do. I'll watch for your name . . ."

"Kenzie. Kenzie Reed."

I took one more look at the walls before I left.

CHAPTER TWENTY-SEVEN

The volcano, like the whale, had eaten my hotel key. I swore I had it when we left in the morning, but now it was nowhere to be found, probably lying forlorn along the roadside halfway down the mountain or stolen from my pocket by a creepy creature in the Mordor-lands of the crater.

"You have bad luck with keys," Jake said as he pulled out his.

"The one that vicious starfish tried to steal was Tyler's. I lost the first one on the mini golf course. Well, it's not lost, but I didn't think they wanted me jumping into the pond and sticking my arm down the whale's throat. I didn't want to ask my parents for a new one, and my brother gave me his."

Jake smirked. "The starfish was only vicious in your imagination."

"He was totally going to eat that thing, and then I was going to have to explain how I gave a starfish indigestion."

He laughed again and opened the door.

"We made it," I announced when we walked in. "No broken bones or broken bikes."

Jake hadn't found anything at the harbor, and I hadn't

mentioned my talk with Rob to him or Gran, which meant I definitely wasn't bringing it up now.

"Was it fun?" Neal asked. He and Alana were on the couch. No sign of anyone else, which hopefully meant they hadn't been sitting around worrying about us for hours.

"It was. You guys should have joined us."

Alana shook her head. "I like to keep my workouts on my own two feet."

"And I like to work out as infrequently as possible, unless you count lifting a book." Neal raised his current read, the second in the series. "You're right. This one is better."

I smiled. "Where's everyone else? What have you been up to?"

"Mom and Dad went to the beach." Alana looked at Jake. "How'd it go, Jacob? For real?"

"I had fun," he said.

"I could have sworn she said you didn't like bicycles."

"Maybe I learned to like them because of her." Jake flashed his dimples at me. "Her adventurous spirit is good for me."

I swallowed a snort and held his gaze. I wasn't supposed to have an adventurous spirit anymore. I was supposed to have a nice, boring spirit that didn't get into any trouble or do anything spontaneous or risky or rash.

"Want to cool off in the pool?" he asked.

"Sure."

He headed to his room, so I went down the hall to ours. Alana followed me.

"You're really okay? And Jacob did have fun?"

"We're fine. It wasn't as terrifying as you're imagining."

"Mom and Dad were worried the whole drive down. At every sharp turn, they kept picturing you taking the corner on a bike and worrying you would crash and tumble down the mountain."

I rummaged through my bag for the striped two-piece I wanted. "It's not my fault they worry about everything."

"You don't have to make it worse for them, though. I thought you'd outgrown being so reckless."

The excitement from the ride, from talking to Rob at the gallery, was suffering the quick, painful death that all my dreams did when my family got involved. Were they completely incapable of letting me enjoy anything?

I fought hard to keep my voice level. "It wasn't reckless. It was perfectly safe. Just because it's something you wouldn't do doesn't make it automatically wrong. Heaven forbid I'm not exactly like you in every way, as if I haven't already tried hard enough."

"What does that mean?" she asked.

My nostrils flared. There was no point. She would never understand. "Nothing. Forget it."

"Why would you try to be like me?"

"I'm not. Don't worry about it."

I grabbed my cover-up to go with the swimsuit and slammed the bathroom door behind me.

It was good to know that even if they did think I'd changed, all it took was one decision to convince them I'd gone right back to my old ways.

Why was I bothering, anyway? Pretending was growing increasingly difficult. Did I want to continue? Nausea rolled through my stomach, but I didn't know if it was at the idea of continuing the charade or giving it up.

I waited until I heard the door close beyond to emerge from the bathroom, and Alana was gone. I stuffed everything into my bag and entered the hall, where I bumped into my brother.

"Whoa, sorry," I said. "I didn't realize you knew where the door to your room was. I thought you might have been trapped in there."

"Ha." He peered down the hall toward the living room. "Going swimming?"

"Yeah. Want to come?"

"Nah. You and *Jacob* are getting awfully close." He lowered his voice. "Don't forget who he is. And don't hurt him."

"Thanks for the family loyalty, Brother."

"I told him the same thing. The two of you seem to be forgetting what's real and what's not."

"You'd know all about that, since this was your idea in the first place."

I swept past him, and my family's comments hounded me all the way to the pool.

Jake and I found chairs in the shade to drop our stuff on, and immediately dove in. The water washed off the sweat and dust from the hike and the bike ride and was instantly refreshing.

I was going to ignore my family. Enjoy the cool water and the waving shadows of the palm trees, the soothing noise of the waterfall, and the cute boy. Let the worry wash away.

Jake and I ended up leaning against the pool edge next to the waterfall.

"Sorry if I dragged you onto a bike against your will."

He laughed. "It was terrible. I had no fun at all."

I poked his arm. "I know you had no fun when I beat you."

"I let you win."

I scoffed. "Yeah, right."

"Okay, fine, I didn't. You're freakishly good on a bike."

"I don't have a car, so I get lots of practice."

He smiled. "I like the idea of you riding around on a bike. So you can stop and take pictures, right?"

"Yeah." I ducked my head and smiled at the fact that he knew me so well. "You obviously aren't bad."

He tucked his wet hair back. "I don't ride much anymore, since my job and campus are kind of far. My parents bought me a car when I graduated from high school last year. Perfectly selected—used but newer, safe and sensible, but not too cheap. Apparently there's a whole science behind buying your teenager a car that projects the right image."

"Ugh. I'm sorry. Wait. I'm apologizing that you got a car . . ."

"I thought about selling it to finance this trip. But it's jointly in my dad's name, so I couldn't. Thankfully I was able to save enough from my job for the plane ticket and the amount your parents and I agreed on."

"Wow." His determination was impressive. Would I have been so persistent? I liked to think so, but I wasn't sure.

"Plus," he added, "selling it would have made them mad, which would have been an added bonus."

I bit my lip and trailed my fingers across the surface of the pool. "I get that you're angry with them. You have a right to be.

But . . . they're still your parents. You'll talk with them eventually, right?"

He lifted a shoulder. "If they'll let me. And not keep ignoring my questions."

"The way you're ignoring their texts?"

"Touché."

I continued to twirl a finger, watching the water instead of him. "I don't know what makes them the way they are, and I know you said you don't see me like you do them, but in some ways I have been acting like them. You were able to get to know me and hopefully judge me a little less."

I peered at him briefly before plunging on.

"You should give them the same chance. There has to be a reason for their image thing, right? Something with their parents or in their past. Did you ever ask them?"

His shoulders were tense now, and he looked at the waterfall. "We don't talk about real stuff."

"Maybe you should try?"

He grunted. "Maybe. One day. I might have to lock them up and force them."

I was making him uncomfortable. I lightened my tone. "I have lots of ideas about how to get someone to talk to you." I raised my eyebrows.

His eyes glinted. "Like dragging them behind waterfalls?"

"That was the kindest option I came up with."

"It's okay. I know you were only pretending you wanted to talk while thinking about kissing me."

"I was not!"

"If you say so."

I was thinking about it now.

My smile faded. "I'm sorry you didn't find anything today."

He sighed. "Yeah. What did you do in town? Eight more flavors of shave ice?"

"I actually . . . stopped at that gallery."

His eyes sparkled. "Good for you."

"Yeah. It was . . . informative, I guess. I showed Rob my pictures, and he didn't think they were completely awful."

"Of course he didn't, because you're talented."

"I don't know about that. But I think . . . I want to take pictures again. For fun. If I can find a way to not do it obsessively. Like a hobby."

Surely my parents would accept that, right? I could keep taking pictures in my free time while pursuing a nice, stable optometry career.

Jake's eyes flickered. "That's a start."

I sensed he wanted more, for me to yell to the world that I was a photographer, to chase my dream against all odds. Gran probably agreed. But I wasn't sure I could do that. Images flashed through my mind, of how disappointed my dad would be, how disapproving my mom would be. Of the chaos it would cause in my family. Jake didn't know what it had been like before, had only seen glimpses this week of how my family could be. I couldn't take that again.

"Well, if you enter the contest," he said, "you'll have to let me know what happens."

I swallowed hard. Because if I did enter, by the time I had

results, we would be home. He would be far away, and I would have invented some reason why we'd broken up. Something vague that placed no blame on either of us, like the distance and the fact that we wanted to live in different states.

"I mean . . . Never mind, I know we weren't going to stay in touch."

His rare display of uncertainty twisted my stomach. The idea of not talking to him again made the sensation worse.

"It's safer not to." I lifted my eyes from the water to find him studying me intently.

His gaze held mine.

"Neither of us cares about safe," he said. His hand found mine under the water.

My fingers tangled with his. He squeezed and pulled me closer.

We had drifted right next to the waterfall, and spray was misting my face. Jake smoothed my hair back and ran a hand down my neck, leaving a trail of goose bumps in its wake. My free hand came up to stabilize myself against his chest.

"You said no kissing," he murmured. "It was a PDA rule."

I watched his mouth form the words, and all I wanted to do was feel it on mine.

"We both suck at rules," I said, and lifted onto my toes to press my lips to his.

He responded instantly, holding me against him. My hands went around his neck.

A surge shot through me. It felt inevitable, like I was meant to be doing this. It was the thrill of plunging under a waterfall or racing a bike or surfing a wave. The heat of a sun-drenched beach. The deep hum of satisfaction from capturing a perfect sunrise and knowing the moment couldn't possibly get any better.

We kissed to the sound of the waterfall, in the tropical air. His mouth and chest were warm, and the water against my skin was cool, and as we kissed, there was only the water and Jake.

No past, no future, no lies or secrets. Just us.

CHAPTER TWENTY-EIGHT

We walked into the condo to hear my dad saying, "Where's all the cheese? We were supposed to use the rest for dinner tonight."

"I ate it," Tyler said from the couch.

"I had the food carefully planned for the week."

"You should have planned for me being hungry."

"So you thought you'd eat slices of cheese?"

Tyler shrugged, and my dad frowned.

Jake and I were lingering in the entryway, our hands clasped. After our kiss in the pool, I was exhilarated and breathless, like when I'd been rushing down that volcano. I snuck a peek at him, to find him looking at me, and we glanced away with slight smiles.

Dad and Tyler turned toward us. Tyler glared at our hands, and I twitched, starting to pull away, but Jake held on.

"Oh good, you're back," Dad said. "Your mother will be relieved."

"We were at the pool. What did she think was going to happen?"

Jake and I held hands all the way down the hall to our rooms to change, and he tugged on mine. I faced him, and his attention was on my lips. My heart stuttered. I swayed toward him. And remembered my family in the next room and made myself lean away.

At dinner, I moved to the end of the table to sit as far away from Tyler as possible, only to realize I'd taken the seat across from Alana, and the last thing I'd done was close the door on her face. To distract her, I asked a bunch of questions about her yoga, which was a bad idea. She was going to think I wanted to learn, and send me daily exercise spreadsheets.

Mom kept looking at me.

"What?" I finally asked.

"Just making sure you weren't hurt."

I hid a sigh. "I'm fine. Jacob's fine." The full name felt weird in my mouth. "There were no crashes, wrecks, accidents, incidents, or close calls with cars."

It helped that Gran hadn't been on the road with us.

I focused on eating, and on the way Jake's lips twitched upward whenever he glanced at me, and the way that expression made my stomach swoop.

After eating, Neal produced Clue. I swallowed hard, and Jake winked at me.

He must have studied like he said, because he won the first two games. I came nowhere close to winning and didn't care, because we were sitting close and his knee was pressed against mine, and when it wasn't his turn, he would drop his hand under the table and rest it on my leg, which made it feel electrified.

Bedtime was a repeat of longing looks in the hall that ended with my lips feeling far too lonely.

The next morning we were up early again, this time to the harbor in Maalaea for a snorkeling excursion. Neal wore his swim shirt and hat, Mom had triple-checked which medication she'd taken, and Gran's swimsuit was *Baywatch* red, matching her lips.

When my eyes met Jake's, my neck heated up and I smiled. His cheeks dimpled, and his eyes locked on to me. We sat close in the van, holding hands, and I ignored my brother's glare. My insides were dancing, and I felt alive and buzzing.

I also ignored the tiny voice in my head that had started whispering when I woke up, that said this was going to end badly.

After we reached the harbor, Jake and I split up to make a quick circle of the other boats.

"Where are you going?" Alana asked.

"Don't worry, we won't be late," was all I said.

I didn't find anything, and as we rejoined the others, I shook my head. Jake's hunched shoulders said he'd had no success, either. I took his hand again.

We got in line to board and posed for a group photo holding a life preserver ring. Mom clung to it too tightly. I was pretty sure they'd have real ones on board and the photo prop wasn't her last line of defense to ward off all of us drowning.

Inside the cabin, we found coffee, muffins, and giant squirt bottles of thick sunscreen. As we cruised offshore, the crew demonstrated how to use the gear and we lined up to get flippers.

Mom's medicine must have worked, because she was awake and not vomiting. In fact, she was feeling so much like herself that she and Alana insisted on wiping everything down with their own wipes, not trusting the sanitary quality of dozens of masks soaking in one huge vat of supposed cleansing liquid. All I knew was, I didn't want to mix up my mask with Gran's, because her mouthpiece was going to be covered in ruby lipstick.

"Everyone, make sure to test the fit of your goggles," Mom said. "The salt water will dry out your eyes."

That made me recall Jake fixing my mask on our first snorkeling trip, his hands on my cheeks, his face close to mine. A tiny school of fish darted around in my stomach.

Once we were fully equipped and sanitized, Jake and I stood at the rail as the boat cut across the dark water. It was calm this early, dark blue, and the island next to us glowed in the morning light. The breeze was pleasant, the air fresh. Jake put his arm around me, and I rested my head against his chest, and I would have been happy if we'd simply kept sailing forever.

We stopped at Molokini Crater, where a crescent-shaped island guarded a quiet cove. Though life vests were optional, Mom insisted we each wear one, and as we pushed off the steps and plunged into the water, she reminded us to stay close to the boat.

For the first two minutes, we did stay close. Dad immediately lost a flipper, and Jake had to chase it down. Gran kept coming up, mumbling "Did you see that?" without removing her mouthpiece.

Jake and I slowly edged away from my family. He handed me the GoPro, and I didn't hesitate before I started using it. This trip was as amazing as our first, with the colorful fish and the interesting coral and the magical, otherworldly light.

Rather than simply filming or taking pictures of every fish I saw, I considered Rob's advice. This time, I didn't want to just capture the moment. What did I want to focus on? What was the purpose? Some photos would be to remind myself of the day, but I also wanted to make Lucia feel like she'd been here. Or make Gran smile when she looked at the pictures later, and fondly remember the trip. Or show my mom the beauty of the natural world and convince her it was valuable for pure enjoyment.

Ha. That would have to be the most brilliant photo ever, developed with a bit of sorcery.

I kept my mind focused, trying not to think about returning to real life soon.

When he saw something cool, Jake tapped my arm and I joined him, and each time we surfaced, we beamed at each other through the masks.

After we boarded the boat, it cruised to another stop at an offshore place called Turtle Town, which, hello, awesome name. I imagined cities made of coral with little turtle homes and a city square.

"You're picturing an underwater town with turtles in suits carrying briefcases to the turtle office or stopping at the turtle day care, aren't you?" Jake asked.

"Turtle coffee shops and high-rise coral apartments and city hall," I said.

He laughed, and I warmed at the idea that he understood my brain. And found it amusing, when my family would have rolled their eyes.

Alana and Neal joined us at the rail.

"What are you guys talking about?" my sister asked.

"What turtle towns look like."

"I think it's metaphorical," she said.

And I think you have no imagination.

Buildings lined the shore, and the volcano rose above it, the top wreathed in clouds. Several other boats were anchored nearby, and lots of people were in the water.

We prepared for another swim.

"No punching a fish this time," my mom said to Tyler.

I whirled on him. "You punched a fish? Not cool, Ty."

"It was an accident! It startled me."

"You weren't expecting to see fish while you were swimming underwater in the ocean?"

"It was going to bite me."

"I don't think that's a thing. Keep your hands to yourself."

My brother's gaze darted to Jake. "You too."

I scowled at him.

"So are you ever going to tell Mom and Dad?"

"Shhh." I glanced around, but the rest of my family had moved toward the ladder. "No. I'll break up with him soon, and that will be that."

My brother scoffed. "If you say so."

He strolled off.

A weight settled in my stomach.

Yesterday had been the best kiss I'd ever had. I sensed Jake and I had a true connection. But I didn't know what to do about that. If I wanted to keep seeing him, we had two choices—continue to lie about everything, which sounded exhausting and also not like the kind of person I wanted to be. Or confess the truth to my parents and hope they didn't ban me from seeing Jake ever again, assuming they let me out of the house.

Would Jake want that? He had come here to find his brother, not a girlfriend. Definitely not a girlfriend who came with so many complications. He wouldn't want to keep lying, and knowing how much he hated it, I wouldn't ask him to. But if I told my parents everything, they'd partially blame him, and I'd be right back where I was before, with them not approving of a guy I was seeing. Except this time, I actually cared about the guy, and that would hurt even more.

There were no good solutions except what we'd planned all along—a fake breakup to end a fake relationship. The kiss didn't matter.

Jake came over, and I fought the urge to stare at his lips. "Was Tyler glaring at me?"

I sighed. "Probably. He's mad at me, I think. And he asked the same thing Gran did, if I was going to tell my parents the truth about you."

"I'm not saying you should or shouldn't. But if you want a healthy relationship with your parents, it might be good for them to know eventually. Secrets just lead to problems."

He had a point. The problem was, the truth would lead to more, bigger problems—at least right now. Maybe I'd tell them one day. But that didn't solve the problem of not being able to see Jake again.

We jumped into the water a second time and swam around until I spotted a parrotfish and followed it, flippers moving in a steady rhythm, my attention locked on the fish. When it vanished into a coral formation, I was breathing hard. I lifted my head out of the water, pulled up the mask, and sucked air. Then studied my surroundings.

Jake had remained beside me, but we were alone. Three smaller boats were anchored nearby, but we'd swum a long way from ours. Whoops. My mom was probably freaking out.

Then my gaze latched on to one of the boats as the words on the side registered.

I grabbed Jake's arm and pointed.

The boat was called the *West Wind*.

CHAPTER TWENTY-NINE

Jake froze.

We stared at the craft, not huge, but with a mast and a cabin. The script name was clear on the back. Or whatever the proper ship term was.

"We could totally swim to it."

Jake tugged his mask to the top of his head, like mine. "Are you sure?"

He didn't take his eyes off it, like it might sink to the bottom of the sea or get swallowed by a kraken at any moment.

"Absolutely."

Then his hands were on my arms and he pulled me toward him for a kiss. Our lips were wet, and the kiss, though brief, tasted of salt and wild freedom. It sent a shiver racing through me, straight to my flipper-clad toes.

I grinned. "What was that for?"

"Because you're amazing."

"No one's near us. You don't have to say that."

"I'm saying it because it's true."

Another shiver, this one making my insides warm and gooey. "Let's go."

The boat was farther away than it appeared, but with the flippers and the life vests Mom had insisted on, it didn't take us long to approach the people swimming nearby.

"Excuse me," Jake said to someone who came up for air. "Did you come on the *West Wind*?"

"What?"

Jake pointed. "Did you come on that?"

"Yeah. Why?"

"I'm looking for the guy who owns it. Is it like a tour?"

"It's a private charter. Came with a guy who captains it."

"What's he like? Can you describe him?"

I sensed the hopeful tension coming off Jake in waves.

"I don't know, fifty?" the lady said. "That's him on deck."

We turned. The man was too old to be Jake's brother.

"Any other crew?" he pressed.

"No, just the captain. He maybe has a crew sometimes? But there are just a few of us for a couple of days. We stayed off Maluaka Beach last night."

"Thanks."

The lady floated away and plunged under the water.

"Come on," I said. "Let's talk to the captain."

We swam closer, and Jake lifted his mask again and called hello.

"Excuse me? Sir?"

The man moved to the rail and looked down at us. "Can I help you?"

"I have a question about the boat." Jake swallowed. "This is going to sound strange, but I'm looking for my half brother, who

I didn't know existed until a few months ago. All I had was the name of a boat, this one. We've been searching the harbors, and this was the first I've seen it. I don't know if he's crew or what, but he'd be about twenty-three or twenty-four?"

"Oh, yeah, you want Ethan."

"Ethan," Jake repeated. "I have a brother named Ethan."

I squeezed his hand.

"He's not here?" Jake asked.

The captain shook his head. "Not this trip. I'll head back to Maalaea tonight to clean for a new group tomorrow afternoon. Ethan lives in Kihei. I can't give you his private info, but he'll be joining me, so you can find us at the harbor late tonight or tomorrow morning. Slip forty-seven."

Jake's eyes lit up. "I can't thank you enough."

"Want me to mention you to him?"

"I don't know if he knows I exist. I mean, I think he does, but he might not. Since I just learned about him."

The guy scratched his neck. "That's weird."

"Trust me, I am well aware. Can you tell him you met a guy looking for him but not who I am? My name's Jake. Then if he knows about me, he'll understand, but he won't be blindsided by a stranger. I know from experience that that's rough."

"Sure, why not."

"Thank you, sir."

"Mahalo," I added.

We swam away from the boat, and I grabbed his arm.

"Jake, this is amazing! Gran will totally bring you back tonight or tomorrow morning. And it's just in time."

He had a dazed expression on his face. "I can't believe this might work."

"It will. And I bet he'll be excited to meet you."

"I hope so. I hope he doesn't think I agreed with my parents' decision, that I knew about him all this time and never reached out."

"If he knows your dad, he'll understand. Are you nervous?"

"I don't know. I'm having trouble believing it's real." He checked his waterproof watch. "Oh man. We need to go."

We tugged our masks into place and ducked into the water, kicking fast. When we arrived, everyone else was on board and the crew was waiting, watching the water and scowling.

Oops.

We scrambled up the ladder onto the deck.

"Sorry," I said, water dripping from my hair.

Mom was also hovering. "Kenzie, where were you? We were worried. Anything could have happened to you."

According to the clock on the wall, we were only seven minutes late.

"These people have a schedule to keep," Dad added. "It's rude to keep them waiting."

As Gran would say, hang the schedule. Jake might have found a way to meet family he didn't know he had, and my family was worried about a few minutes' delay?

"I'm sorry, Dr. Reed. It was my fault," Jake said.

Something in me snapped. "You're sweet," I said, "but you don't have to take the blame. It was me. I was following a turtle, and we got farther away than expected."

Mom sighed. Dad shook his head.

"No, really, Kenzie." Jake touched my arm. "That's nice of you, but she's covering for me. It wasn't her fault at all. I'm very sorry."

I didn't want to ruin this for Jake. I was used to my parents being disappointed in me. I could handle it. Better to take that off him and let him enjoy our unexpected success.

"Go sit down," Dad said. "The boat needs to leave."

Jake and I shuffled inside and sat on one of the benches away from the rest of my family, wrapped in towels, our shoulders pressing.

"You didn't have to do that," he said.

I shrugged. "The best lie is one people believe, right? You saw them. No one was surprised."

"Yeah, but you don't have to . . ."

"What? Make them think something they know is true?"

"Haven't the last several months been about convincing them it's not true?"

"It is, though. That's totally something I would have done. Would still like to do. Follow a turtle for hours until I'm halfway to Australia. Don't worry about it. You should be enjoying the moment, celebrating the lead, not worrying about my uptight family. And you didn't have to try to take the blame, either."

His shoulder lifted. "It's better if they're upset with me. They can't get too mad because I'm an outsider, and they won't see me again, so it doesn't matter what they think of me."

That thought hurt the most, and his statement was a blast of cold water to the face.

We leaned back, and as if pulled by our own gravity, our

heads fell so they rested against each other. The scent of sunscreen and salt water seeped into me. My hair, or Jake's, dripped onto my neck.

A shiver shot through me, warm and buzzing. Thoughts of my family faded. It was hard to worry about them after an amazing morning and when Jake was here.

"You got a lead," I said. "That's what matters. I'll talk to Gran later, and we'll find a way to get you there, just in time."

"Thank you." His voice was quiet.

"Of course." I hesitated. "What if . . . my family did see you again?"

"I thought we agreed it was better not to continue."

"Yeah. It's just . . ."

He shifted and pulled away to look into my eyes. "I know."

His voice was gentle, understanding, and his eyes were soft, and it cracked something inside me.

"But how would it work?" he asked. "Do you want to keep lying to them indefinitely? Because I'm over the pretending."

Pretending to be Jacob? Or pretending to be with me?

The idea of losing him made my throat tight, but he was right. I didn't want to force him to keep living the way he had before, the way he hated, full of fakeness and appearances and not being his real self.

I'd needed this reminder. Both of us were getting what we needed. But our trip—and our relationship—was almost over.

CHAPTER THIRTY

I hoped the promise of giant cheeseburgers in the nearby town of Kihei was enough to distract my parents from their extreme disappointment in me. After drying off and changing, we made the short drive.

I would simply redouble my efforts to be good. I resisted the urge to scroll through the photos I'd taken, and I contained my desire to ramble about every fish I'd seen. I definitely didn't mention the burning desire to learn to scuba dive so I could go deeper, spend longer, immerse myself further in the magical underwater world.

I just ate my meal and listened to the others.

"It wasn't as bad as I thought," was my mom's ringing endorsement.

"My back got sunburned. But it was impressive." This from Neal, despite the fact that he'd used sunscreen and left his swim shirt on.

Tyler's helpful contribution was, "Too many fish."

"Well, I thought it was incredible," said Gran. "All the colors and the variety."

I smiled at her.

"Are you going to eat, or just stare at your ring all day?" Tyler asked Alana. "It's been almost a week. It's not going to disappear now."

She blushed and stuffed her hands into her lap.

My dad cleared his throat. "Time to share the good news."

Intriguing. Mom was smiling, but everyone else looked curious.

"One of the optometry magazines contacted me this week," Dad said. "They want to do an article on our family and the practice. They'll interview all of us—including you, Mom." He nodded to Gran. "About Dad getting it started. And talk to Alana and Kenzie about continuing the tradition, and Tyler about using his skills to help."

I choked on a French fry. Jake patted my back.

"That's great, Dad," said Alana.

Tyler had set his burger down. The unease on his face mirrored the churning in my stomach.

What was I supposed to tell those people? How excited I was to follow in my family's footsteps? How I couldn't wait to work with them?

My lies would be in print, captured forever.

Dad glanced at Mom. "One more thing. Kenzie, your mom and I have been talking."

That rarely ended well for me. I braced myself for the giant tidal wave of renewed disappointment or a lecture about being tardy.

"We were thinking, when we get home, it's time to get you a car."

Wait, what? I blinked at him.

"A used one, obviously, but you've proven more responsible lately, and you'll be starting college soon. You'll need to get to classes and a job."

Was this a bribe? A reward? A reaction to me liking my bicycle too much, as if the ride yesterday had reminded them of yet another unconventional thing I loved and another way they needed to force me into a boring mold? Or a test after I'd supposedly briefly lapsed into my old, irresponsible ways today?

It was nice of them. Alana had gotten a car before her senior year of high school. Something about me running out of gas twice, accidentally locking the keys in the car, and that small incident during driver's training when I chose to run over a trash can instead of risking hitting a stray cat had convinced them I wasn't a great driver. Though, I had improved lately, the times Mom had let me borrow her car. I hadn't hit anything in months.

But I liked riding my bike. In addition to being able to stop if I saw something to photograph, I enjoyed the fresh air and exercise and feeling of freedom.

If I didn't go to a four-year school and study science and keep talking about optometry—if I mentioned that I might start taking pictures again—would the offer stand?

I'd been silent too long.

"That's great, Dad. Mom. Thank you."

I pulled out the wooden smile again.

"Neal and I were talking about me getting something new soon," Alana said. "She could have mine."

Hooray. Another part of her life for me to copy.

"I'll Bubble Wrap our mailbox," Tyler said. "And post warning signs on the street. I don't have to ride to school with her, do I?"

"Yes, Tyler, part of the responsibility that comes with a car is helping out, so Kenzie will drive you sometimes."

"Why can't I just have a car, too?"

"Let's wait and see where Kenzie goes to school next year."

Or Kenzie could go on a backpacking trek through the Alps next year, and Tyler could have the car. . . . No. Optometry magazine. Office job. College. It would be great.

Ha. Not even the thought of a car could convince my brain of that.

Jake grabbed my hand and squeezed. "Too bad Ohio is too far to drive in a weekend."

"What's halfway?" I asked, hoping I sounded like I was joking. "We could meet there."

I held his gaze and found I sort of meant it, because halfway between Sacramento and San Diego might be doable.

But that was impossible. I looked away.

After confirming that Gran was happy to take us to the harbor first thing the next morning, before our final beach day, Jake and I went to the pool. Mom and Dad wanted to watch a movie, but I fully intended not to waste a second of the beautiful day. I was surprised when Alana and Neal decided to join us.

We took seats by the water, and I sighed as I savored the breeze, the trees, the flowers. I was going to miss this place.

"I bet you'll be sad to go back to Ohio after all this sunshine, won't you, Jacob?" Alana asked.

"Oh, definitely. Winter always lasts too long." His tone was distracted, and we soon dove in, leaving my sister and Neal in the shade.

Jake's posture was stiffer than normal.

"Everything okay?" I asked. Then, since the nearby waterfall would block our conversation from Alana, I added, "Are you excited about meeting your brother tomorrow?"

He lowered himself so only his head was above water, and leaned against the wall. "I guess so."

Such a guy answer. "What do you think he's like?"

Jake lifted a shoulder. "He works on a boat and lives in Hawaii, so that's promising."

"I wonder if he grew up here."

"I couldn't tell from what I overheard."

"It seems like you'll have some things in common. I hope he won't blame you for your parents' choices."

"Thanks for that," he said wryly, and flicked water at me.

I ducked. "I mean, I'm sure he won't. And if he does, you might not want to get to know him anyway."

His dimples flashed briefly, and his posture relaxed. "Thanks."

"The captain was nice," I said. "That's a good sign."

"I guess I'll find out soon enough." His grin slowly faded. "Speaking of . . . Are you going to do that article your dad mentioned?"

"Ugh." I plunged my head under the water and came up spluttering. "Yes. I guess? I don't have much choice."

He used gentle fingers to wipe water from my face. "There are always choices, Kenz."

"Yeah, but most of them end with lengthy lectures and disappointed glares."

He tucked my hair behind my ear and let his fingers trace my jaw. We gazed at each other, shadows from the palm trees flickering across his face, the scent of chlorine and the gushing of a waterfall filling the air.

I was the first to look away.

He cleared his throat. "I'm going to get a drink. Want something?"

"Sure. Something sugary to make Gran proud."

"You got it."

He climbed out of the water, exchanged words with Alana and Neal, and then grabbed his wallet from his bag. I ducked beneath the waterfall while I waited. When he returned, he plopped a drink onto the edge of the pool next to me, frozen and pink and topped with cherries.

He tossed his wallet into his bag and joined me in the water. There was no repeat of the kissing, even though I wanted there to be. But with my sister watching, it would have felt too much like a performance. Part of the roles we were playing. Besides, the reminder of optometry school and the car and the distance between us, both physical and metaphorical . . . There was no point. No matter how much I wished I could change that.

When Jake and I climbed out of the pool, my parents had joined Alana and Neal. All four of them were reading. Of course they were. At least they were outside.

Jake and I went upstairs and found Gran dozing on the lanai.

We sat on the couch, and I let Jake scroll through the pictures I'd taken. He pulled my feet into his lap, rested his arms on them, and I wished this could be normal, permanent. Spending the day together, relaxing at the end of it. Me capturing it all in photos. It was comfortable, and yet the brush of his skin against mine set my skin on fire.

"Can I see the one you sent to the contest last year?" he asked.

My stomach lurched.

He must have felt me tense, because he squeezed my leg gently. "Only if you want."

I studied him. He'd been nothing but supportive. And if I meant what I'd said about taking up photography again, it would be good for me to show someone. I loaded my now-private Instagram account, that had all my favorites from the last few years.

"The latest one was for the contest. I sort of stopped posting after that . . ."

I rested my head against the couch and watched his face as he studied the pictures, lips occasionally curving upward. Then he would turn the phone so I could see the screen, and give me a thumbs-up when he saw a picture he liked—animals and trees, sunsets and flowers.

"Wow, Kenz."

That was all he said, and combined with his focused expression, it was enough to make my heart warm.

The front door banged open, and I flinched at the sudden noise.

Mom and Dad stormed in, with Alana and Neal trailing behind them. Alana had a strange look, like she might be ill.

My parents stopped in front of us.

"We need to talk," Mom said.

I yanked my feet from Jake's lap and sat straight. "What's wrong?"

"Mom," Alana said. "Let me—"

"Get your brother."

Alana mouthed, "I'm so sorry," at me before she went down the hall.

A heavy feeling formed in my stomach.

My sister returned with Tyler, who had draped his earbuds around his neck. Gran came inside, blinking herself awake. They took seats, but my parents remained standing.

The weight in my midsection turned to ice.

"What's going on?" Gran asked.

"That's exactly what I would like to know." My dad crossed his arms.

Mom tossed a wallet onto the coffee table and then a small notebook.

Jake straightened, suddenly tense.

"Your sister had an interesting theory," Mom said.

Unease churned in me. I'd seen that wallet. Earlier today.

"Alana found this and decided it offered a chance to test that theory. Imagine our surprise at what she found." She shifted her glare to Jake. "We recognized the face on the driver's license right away. But would you care to explain why the state says California? Or the middle name isn't the one Kenzie told us? Or the school ID is for San Diego Community College, not Ohio State University?"

Adrenaline surged through me, and a fist seized my throat. "You went through his things? That's so invasive!"

"You're mad at *us*?" Alana asked. "I was worried about *you*."

She picked up the notebook and flipped the pages. It contained her tight, neat handwriting, perfect columns in three colors of ink. From what I could see, in blue she'd written phrases like *Ohio State, dead grandparents,* and *doesn't like bikes.* All the things I'd made up. In black were words like *surfing* and *knows lots about plants.* Little red arrows and question marks decorated the lists.

This was not good.

She ran a finger down one column. "He's been lying to you about who he is and his family and where he's from."

"You should be thanking your sister for looking out for you," Mom added.

I shot Alana a scowl. "He hasn't been lying to me. Why didn't you just ask me?"

So much for sisterhood.

"He's been lying about everything," my mom said.

My insides were a jumbled mess, my face hot. I wanted to do nothing except grab Jake's hand and make a run for the door.

"He's definitely not who he said he was." My dad glared at him.

"No, he's not who *I* said he was," I said.

Jake cleared his throat. "It's my fault. Kenzie is just trying to help. Again."

"Who exactly are you? Are you my daughter's boyfriend?"

"I'm not."

The simple, straightforward answer sent a spike through my chest.

Mom looked at me. "And what about your Jacob?"

I ducked my head. "There isn't one. I made him up."

Mom paused. "So you invited a stranger to stay with us?"

"He knows Tyler," I said. "He's not a stranger."

"Thanks a lot," my brother muttered.

Alana's gaze darted to me and away.

"Someone start at the beginning," Mom said. "Right now."

Considering the way she was glaring at me, I figured *someone* meant me.

The attention on me felt like a burning spotlight. Tension hung thick in the room.

I eyed the door again, but they were all watching expectantly. I met Gran's sympathetic expression and took a deep breath.

"I was never dating a guy from Ohio named Jacob Miller. After that conference last year, I made him up."

Several people spoke at once, and I caught "Why would you do that?" from Alana, "You've been lying for months?" from Dad, and then, from Mom, "Are you seeing anyone at all? I sure hope it's not that lacrosse guy."

My gaze darted to Jake. Seeing someone and having it be him was even more impossible now.

"I'm not seeing anyone. I never was. I just wanted you to be impressed, and it kind of . . . slipped out."

"We taught you better than to lie," Dad said.

They had no idea of the full extent. I didn't know what to tell them about not knowing Jake until this week. It was bad enough that they thought the two of us had conspired to make him sound like someone else. It was a lot bigger issue that we hadn't actually met.

"So who is this?" Mom asked. "What did you do, hire a fake boyfriend for a week?"

"Don't make it sound so scandalous," said Gran.

My dad whirled on her. "It is scandalous, Mom! We spent a week with a stranger. Wait, you knew about this?"

"Ah, not exactly," she said.

The tightness in my chest was making it hard to breathe.

Tyler sighed. "That's where I come in. Like Kenzie said, I know him."

I shifted to face him. "Tyler, you don't have to—"

"Yeah, I do. We wouldn't be in this mess if I hadn't tried to help." His face was resigned.

"We wouldn't be in this mess if I hadn't lied in the first place."

"Well, yeah," he said. "But this week is definitely on me. You had nothing to do with it."

"Explain," Dad said.

"I knew she lied about having a boyfriend. And Jake's my friend. We met at sports camp. I'm the one who invited him to come this week, to play the role of Kenzie's fake boyfriend."

"And he's been nothing but polite," I added.

Mom's face was dark. "Except the part where he lied about who he is."

"He didn't . . . exactly. He is Jake Miller. Just some of the details are different. And he has a good reason for being here. He isn't trying to rob us or con us or anything. I promise."

"We've seen that your word doesn't mean much these days, young lady." Mom's I'm Very Disappointed voice had resurfaced.

I sagged. "You can trust him, is all."

"And how can we trust you?" Mom asked. "How do we know you aren't lying about anything else?"

"I'm not," I said. "Just the boyfriend."

Jake tensed next to me. This was so not the time to go into other topics, even if he wanted me to be honest about myself. I certainly wasn't going to talk about photography or optometry or my future. Those lies weren't relevant to this situation. They would only make things worse.

Jake cleared his throat. "May I?"

My parents turned their angry glares on him.

"My name is Jake Miller. As you saw on my license, I'm from San Diego. And I met Tyler at camp, like he said. A few months ago, I told him about a . . . family situation I was having. I have a half brother who lives here, and I wanted to meet him, and Tyler invited me to come. Since my name matched Kenzie's boyfriend's, we thought it would work if I pretended to be him. But we shouldn't have lied to you about it. I apologize for taking advantage when you've been so kind."

"That doesn't explain why you lied to all of us, lied to Kenzie."

"I mean, I knew he was lying the whole time," I said. "So he never really lied to me."

Other than the first two days, when he pretended to be a figment of my imagination.

"Because you were lying, too," Dad said. "You're not off the hook, young lady. We should have expected something like this from you."

Right. Because wild, irresponsible Kenzie always let them down.

Mom's shoulders tensed. "Please leave, Jacob."

The newly calm tone of voice meant it took a second for her words to sink in.

"Seriously?" I squawked. "You can't kick him out. He's in a strange place with no car and nowhere to stay. Where's he supposed to go?"

"Yeah, Mom, don't do this." Tyler leaned forward. "He's a good guy."

"He's been with us all week," Alana said. "I don't think one more day would hurt. . . ."

But she didn't sound very sure, glancing from me to Jake with a frown. Traitor. It was too late to try to help now, after she'd been the one to expose him.

"Let the boy stay," Gran said.

Mom shook her head. "I just can't have him here. He said he has family on the island. He won't be alone."

"But he doesn't—"

Jake stood and cut off my reply. "It's okay, Kenzie. I'll go. I'll get an Uber. I'll be fine."

He trudged down the hall. I started to join him.

"Stay right there, young lady," Dad said.

I crossed my arms. "This isn't fair. If you're going to blame anyone, blame me, not Jake."

"You know what else isn't fair? Using a stranger to lie to us."

He had a point.

Awkward, heavy silence hung over the room, until Jake came down the hall with his bag. His gaze went straight to mine.

I stood.

"Sit," Mom said.

I did.

Jake nodded, gave me a sad smile, then turned to my parents. "I really am very sorry. Thank you for your kindness. I didn't deserve it. I'll leave this for you. It's the amount we agreed on." He set an envelope on the counter, then picked his wallet up from the table. "I wish you all nothing but the best. Kenzie, it's okay. We knew it wouldn't last, that it was only for a week. Thanks for everything."

And then he was gone.

CHAPTER THIRTY-ONE

Silence lingered after the door closed behind Jake. The condo suddenly felt cold and empty. I stared at the floor to avoid the judgment on Mom's and Dad's faces, the uncertainty on Alana's, the guilt on Tyler's.

A hurricane raged inside me. They knew I was lying, I'd just reaffirmed all their critical opinions of me, and everything was a mess. Not to mention they'd put Jake out onto the street. My thoughts whirled in the tempest.

I didn't know which was the worst. But no matter what happened to me, I couldn't let them do this to Jake.

My stomach hardened. I was already in trouble. Might as well make it worse.

"I'll be back." I rushed for the door before anyone could stop me, ignoring everyone yelling my name.

Jake wasn't in the hall, so I ran to the elevator and jammed the button a few times. When the door didn't immediately open, I raced to the stairs instead, and nearly tripped around the corners as I descended several floors.

I didn't even know what I intended to accomplish. I just couldn't let him leave without talking to him.

No Jake in the lobby, either.

"Did you see a guy about my age, blond hair, blue bag?" My words to the man behind the desk came out breathless, rushed.

He pointed to the front doors, and I ran again, flip-flops slapping on the stone floor. I slipped between the doors before they finished sliding open, and there he was.

Jake stood to the side, next to the driveway, probably waiting for his Uber. Streetlights formed pools of yellow, but he lingered just outside one, in the shadows.

"Jake."

My speed left me. Instead I inched toward him, cautious.

He turned. "Kenzie? What are you doing?"

"Don't go." It felt like a fist was squeezing my lungs.

"Your parents made it very clear."

"It's not fair, though." I shuffled closer.

"It is," he said. "They're right—I did lie to them."

"So did I, and they aren't kicking me out."

He gave me a look.

I stared at him. What was I hoping for? That he'd agree to defy my family with me? That he'd march upstairs and beg strangers for mercy or refuse to leave? That he'd argue with people he'd lied to?

A car pulled up.

I was half tempted to climb into it with him, to leave my family and the impending fight behind.

Like he knew what I was considering, Jake stepped in front of me, ran his fingers down my cheek, along my jaw. His gaze was solemn, resigned. "Let me go, Kenz. Everything will be okay."

"But where will you go?"

"I'll be fine. Don't worry about me. Be bold."

He pressed a kiss to my temple, so quick I might have imagined it, and then he was climbing into the car. I reached out as if to stop him, but it drove off, leaving me standing alone at the curb, frozen, watching until the bright red taillights disappeared.

The chasm inside me was as black and expansive as the sea at night. Like my chest had been scooped out, and there was nothing left inside.

Did he not think we were worth fighting for? I couldn't fully blame him—I didn't know if I'd stay after being told to leave. But I'd thought we had something rare and special.

I'd known it would be over soon. We'd made it clear we wouldn't stay in touch. He'd found what he needed.

Logic did nothing to fill the emptiness inside me. No matter what we'd had or hadn't had, it obviously hadn't been enough.

I stood in the twilight. The palm trees were black against the silver sky. The breeze fluttered my hair, and a sense of aloneness threatened to crush me.

Jake's final words echoed. *Be bold.*

Easy for him to say. Besides, I didn't have much of a choice about that. I had to face my parents. Unless I called my own Uber and didn't go back.

But that wasn't what he meant. He meant about all of it—being honest not just about him but about who I was. Taking a chance on the future I truly wanted. Like Gran had said, being my fullest self.

The idea was more terrifying than jumping off that cliff, yet also . . . oddly freeing? Like a weight was ready to lift from my shoulders and let me stand tall for the first time in months.

My hard work had been undone in a moment—if pretending even counted as hard work. Had I really expected to succeed? And at what, something I didn't care about? All I'd wanted was my family's respect, which I'd majorly blown. It hadn't been the real me they were respecting, anyway. Why had I been okay with that?

I wasn't anymore. After spending time this week with someone who accepted me, I couldn't return to lying about who I was to make others happy. No matter what the fallout, it was time to do what I should have done eight months ago—stand firm in what I wanted, even if my family didn't like it.

It would have been easier with Jake beside me, believing in me. But if I was going to do it, I needed to do it without him, for myself.

The sky had darkened to almost black, and no car returned. But I would be okay.

I set my shoulders and went inside.

Alana was waiting in the lobby, near padded chairs next to a planter full of bird-of-paradise flowers. Their little blue-and-orange plant faces made me think of Jake.

"I'm sorry," she said.

I paused several feet away. "For which part? Getting Jake kicked out or exposing me?"

"All of it," she said. "Are you okay?"

"Oh, yeah, great. About to get grounded until I'm eighty and everyone hates me, and Jake might have to sleep on the beach tonight while turtles nibble on his toes."

"I don't think turtles eat people."

"So not the point, Lana." I sighed and sank into a chair.

She perched beside me, shoulders hunched. "I didn't mean to tell Mom and Dad. I started doubting Jacob's story a few days ago, so I kept notes on things he said that didn't line up. I thought he was lying to you. When I saw his wallet, I figured I'd check it. It would prove me wrong and settle the matter. But when I opened it and saw the truth, I made a noise or something, and Mom heard me and freaked out, and then it was too late."

I made a scoffing noise. "You still spied on him."

"I wanted to protect my little sister, make sure some guy wasn't taking advantage of you. I would have talked to you about it first, if Mom hadn't gotten involved. I had no idea . . ."

"That I was in on the grand deception?"

"Why did you do it?" Her question was surprisingly curious rather than critical.

I poked my finger into the beak of a nearby flower. *Be bold.* "To make them think I was more like you. You've never known what it's like to be me. You always make them so proud, and I could never live up to that. Even your stupid hair looks great after a week of tropical humidity."

She reached up to touch it. "What's wrong with my hair?"

"I just wanted them to be proud of me for once, instead of criticizing everything I do. Inventing a boyfriend seemed harmless at the time, and it made them take me seriously."

A frown was etched between her brows. "I never realized I was putting pressure on you. I didn't mean to."

I sniffed. "If you could mess up just once, it would be nice. You and your spreadsheets and your good grades and your career plans."

"You don't like the spreadsheets?"

"They made me feel like I couldn't do anything myself. Like I wasn't free to make my own choices. My own mistakes. Any mistakes at all, ever."

She leaned forward. "Those lists and spreadsheets aren't to try to fix you. They're for me. Because I worry about things, but if I write them down, I feel like I can manage it all better."

That kind of made sense. "Like you managed your investigation into Jake?"

She bit her lip. "I really did just want to help you. With all of it. I'm sorry."

I nodded and continued poking the flower, in no rush to return to my parents.

"So what happened with Jacob?" she asked.

"Jake. Tyler invited him and didn't tell me, but I played along because I didn't want everyone to find out I'd been lying."

"You didn't think to talk to me about it?" Her forehead wrinkled.

"So you could go straight to Mom?" It was a low blow, and she winced.

"I want us to be the kind of sisters who help each other."

Would she feel that way when I told her I wouldn't be working alongside her for the rest of our lives?

"So he showed up," she said. "And then you fell for him for real."

"I did not."

She raised her eyebrows. "You just chased him through a hotel."

"Okay, maybe a little. But we were lying about so many things. And yes, I chased him, and he left anyway." I pushed down the tsunami of hurt, the tone of his goodbye, those vanishing taillights. "Besides, Mom and Dad will never let me near him again."

"You need to tell them all of it."

"Or I can stay here, let you all fly home, and go live in the jungle. I could gather coconuts and catch fish to eat and avoid people forever."

"Kenzie."

"Stop it. You sound like Mom."

"What else were you lying about? Other than Jacob?"

This was it. The first test of my new commitment to truth. If I didn't want my parents controlling my future forever, I had to say it. Alana would be my trial run.

"I don't want to be an optometrist."

She blinked. "You don't?"

"Sorry to ruin your dreams of the family business."

"I want you to be happy. Are you saying you haven't been?"

"Let's hope Mom and Dad share that sentiment. I'm not holding my breath, though." I eyed the elevator and sighed. I was in enough trouble without delaying much longer. "Are you planning to watch the disaster or hide down here until it's over?"

"I have your back, Kenz. I mean it. You're my sister."

She seemed genuine.

"Just be yourself," she said. "It will work out."

History made a strong case in favor of the exact opposite.

I nodded and hauled myself out of the chair, preparing to meet my doom.

CHAPTER THIRTY-TWO

I paused outside the room and braced myself. No backing down now.

Good thing Alana was with me, because I'd rushed off without a key. She squeezed my shoulder and let us in.

Mom was pacing, and Dad was scrubbing the kitchen counter. Not a good sign.

Tyler stared at me like he wanted to say something. I stared back. I didn't know what I wanted from him. Not necessarily an apology, and I was unlikely to get sympathy. He shrugged.

I glanced at Gran, who gave me an understanding smile. Maybe I could live with her if I got disowned. Her retirement community might be better than the jungle, since I had no idea how to cook a fish.

Mom pointed to a chair, but fire stirred inside me. Instead of sitting, I stood next to one of the barstools and grasped the top with a tight grip, keeping my chin high. "You can't run off like that." Mom frowned at me before turning to my sister. "Thank you for bringing her back."

I snorted. Like without Alana, I might have disappeared

forever. I wanted to explain, to stand up for Jake, but he'd chosen to leave, and I was in enough trouble.

"I'm sorry. And I'm sorry for lying to you," I said. "I knew it was wrong, and I never meant for it to come to this."

"Why start in the first place? We taught you better than that."

Here it goes. No turning back. Might as well rip the Band-Aid off.

"I have no interest in optometry."

Before that bombshell could lead to disappointment, I added fuel to the fire.

"I don't want to go to college, not full-time right away. And definitely not for anything that requires grad school. I'm a photographer. It's what I love and what I'm good at and what I want to do."

I could see gears turning in Mom's head, which meant she was preparing arguments. All of which I had heard many times. All of which I had pretended to agree with for eight months.

And all of which I was now done with.

"I know it's not an easy career," I said. "I know it's uncertain and unconventional and you think it's risky. But it's what I'm passionate about. Doesn't everyone deserve to find that and try it? I wanted so badly to not disappoint you. I wanted you to respect me, be proud of me."

"Of course we respect you." Mom looked offended.

Dad was still blinking at me like I'd spoken another language. I'd broken my father.

"Really?" I asked. "You did before the last eight months, when I started pretending to be exactly like Alana, exactly the person you wanted me to be? When I would take pictures all day and lose track of time or spend hours at the park or editing photos?"

Mom's jaw tensed. Dad remained scarily silent.

"We just want what's best for you," Mom finally said. "And when you don't make wise choices, it's our job as parents to help with that. As a kid, that meant teaching you to be responsible. And lately, it's meant guiding you into a secure future."

She hadn't even commented on the photography or the college thing. She disagreed so thoroughly that it wasn't worth arguing about.

"It's my future. My life. Don't I get a say in it?"

"Do you know why I never talk about my family?" Mom asked. "Why we never see them?"

I shook my head at the abrupt subject change.

"My father was a gambler. Couldn't hold on to money, always took a bet, and we not only suffered for it, my brothers grew up like him." The muscle in Mom's jaw jumped again. "I was determined not to let that happen to me, to my kids. I don't want you always worrying if you'll be able to eat or dodging bill collectors."

Many things about her personality that I'd always wondered about clicked into place. Her family situation sucked, but her past didn't get to define my future.

"Pursuing a career I love isn't like what your dad did. You made the choices you did to be happy. I want to be happy, too, and your path for me isn't going to do it."

Dad cleared his throat. Here it came. How I was ruining the family legacy. That article he was so happy about, that would have described his perfect kids joining him in his career.

"I can't deny that I'm disappointed, Kenzie. I don't know if you appreciate how hard your family has worked."

The familiar hurt sliced through me, but now annoyance accompanied it. Jake would have defended me. I needed to learn to defend myself, even if the confrontation made me nervous.

"I want to work hard at *my* thing, Dad. And I have. Studying and learning, online classes and research, practice. It might not be the subject you want, but that doesn't mean I haven't worked hard. You let Tyler pursue his programming. You obviously don't mind if all three of us don't join the family practice. Why is his choice valid and mine isn't?"

Dad frowned, and his head tilted, but he seemed to be considering my words.

"What about the deal we made?" Mom asked. "You agreed it was for the best."

"No, you thought it was best, and I went along to avoid conflict. I never should have agreed to it in the first place. I'm not blaming you," I added quickly. "I shouldn't have been so willing to give up on my dreams. But part of me was a coward, and scared of failing because I didn't win that contest, and tired of feeling like no one accepted me. But I shouldn't have pretended to be someone I'm not. Surely you noticed I haven't been myself?"

They were silent, processing.

Gran came to stand beside me, set a smoothie down on the bar, and patted my arm. "I'm proud of you, Kenzie girl. You're remarkable just the way you are. Did you know your grandfather's parents tried to talk him out of optometry? They thought it was too much work, too many years of school, and he should focus on something faster, easier, that would get him paychecks right away. But that's what he wanted, and he stuck to it. Richard, didn't I raise you to pursue your dream and work hard? Let Kenzie do the same."

"But . . . you want to take pictures of sunsets and birds all day?" Dad asked. "When you could be helping people?"

"You have so much to offer," Mom added. "Don't you want to contribute to society?"

My stomach clenched. Why was it so hard to breathe? I wouldn't be able to make them understand right away. But if I had hope of them ever seeing the value in what I loved, I needed to explain myself. In a way they'd respect.

"It's like . . . I want to help people see, too. Just not physically. Photography can make people see the world in new ways, open their eyes to what's around them. What if my pictures inspire someone to travel to new places, or think about the environment and protect animals and habitats, or make them feel wonder? Isn't that helping?"

Dad studied me longer before turning to Mom. Their eyes held a conversation I couldn't decipher.

"Give us a few minutes," Mom said, and they went outside.

My stomach was churning too much for me to drink the smoothie, which only reminded me of Jake making one the first morning. I finally sank into a chair at the table. Gran sat next to me, silent, and put her arm around me.

The others remained quiet, seeming to sense that talking to me would have made me sicker than Mom on the road to Hana.

My smoothie had nearly melted when my parents returned.

It was like awaiting execution. Were they going to make me walk the plank or keelhaul me, whatever that meant?

My dad sat across from me, folded his hands on the table. I couldn't tell from his expression what he was thinking.

"We're still not okay with the lying," he said. "But we understand why you thought it was necessary. Not pretending to have a boyfriend, which I don't get. But the rest of it . . . I may have put pressure on you in terms of a career."

"And we see how our behavior might have affected you over the years." Mom's voice was stiffer than Dad's. "Made you feel you couldn't be yourself."

It wasn't an apology, but it was better than nothing.

"Here's the deal," Dad said. "We're willing to let you try the . . . photography, to an extent." He made it sound like a dirty word.

Before I had time to process, Mom planted herself behind him. "But we're going to compromise."

I gulped. Was this one of those compromises where you ended up feeling like you lost?

"You'll finish your senior year as you have been, clubs and all that," Dad said. "You'll keep working at the clinic for the rest of the semester and the summer, and take some community college classes in the fall."

"Photography classes?" I asked.

"At least one general class, too," Mom said. "Plus ten hours a week at the clinic."

That was punishment, wasn't it? For the lying. One hour of filing for every lie I'd told.

I could survive a few hours a week if I was also allowed to spend time on stuff I liked, and I had told an awful lot of lies. Two more months of Future Healthcare Professionals was survivable.

"Okay. Thank you," I added, though I didn't feel much gratitude. Sure, they were letting me take small steps, but they weren't happy about it.

Dad was studying me, more contemplative than angry.

"We also want you to pick one of the four-year schools you applied to for the fall and see about deferred enrollment, so we can re-evaluate after a year." Mom's face leaned more strongly toward unhappiness.

Would a year be enough time for me to prove myself? I would have to make sure it was.

"I think it's cool that you want to be a photographer," Neal said. "The pictures you took for us were impressive."

I tried to dredge up a smile for him.

"I bet you can do it, Kenz." Alana nodded at me.

"Of course she can," said Gran.

"We'll see." Mom pressed her lips together.

Thanks for that ringing endorsement. My dad offered a sad smile, which was better than nothing.

Mom shifted. "Now it's your turn, young man."

I grimaced on Tyler's behalf.

"Like we told Kenzie, we're very disappointed. If your friend needed to come here, you should have told us. Instead you lied and you involved your sister in your lie."

Tyler visibly swallowed. He rarely received such a stern tone from her. "I was trying to help?"

They waited, apparently unsatisfied with that weak reply.

"Okay, and it sounded a little fun, to see what would

happen." He half smirked, but hurried on when no one smiled. "But mainly I was trying to help him, and I didn't know if any other way would work."

I sniffed.

He glanced at me. "I, uh, might as well confess something else, too. I haven't been writing a program for you. Well, I did. But it's been done for months. I want to develop video games. My teacher says I have a good eye for graphics and storytelling, in addition to the programming skills."

His words came out in a rush.

Dad blinked. Mom's nostrils flared, and she closed her eyes like we were giving her a migraine.

"You're a sophomore, so we can discuss that later."

Dad's tone meant many uncomfortable conversations for Tyler in the coming months.

"But for now, we'll address your lying and inviting a stranger on this trip. You'll be working in the office alongside your sister."

"We'll make a schedule for you both," Mom said.

I'd be willing to bet a great deal that it would be color-coded. We'd be spending plenty of family time together for now, just like Dad wanted.

Tyler sighed. "Fine."

When no one spoke, I grabbed my melted smoothie and escaped to my room before they changed their minds. It wasn't a win, but it could have been much worse.

CHAPTER THIRTY-THREE

When I shut the door behind me, the solitude was a relief. Some of the evening's tension drained from my shoulders.

Unfamiliar items on my pillow made me alert again. I set the sweating cup on the table and approached cautiously.

The first item was Jake's GoPro. I also found a room key card—which made me exhale a sad laugh—a small bag with the aquarium logo, and two pieces of paper. The larger was a flyer for the photo contest. The other was hotel stationery, with messy boy writing that looked hastily written.

My breath caught in my throat, and my hands shook as I picked it up.

I sank onto the bed to read the note.

K—

You're amazing. Thanks for everything this week.
You were the best fake girlfriend a guy could ask for.
I'm sorry for how things ended. Be brave, be you.

J

P.S. The camera is actually yours. Tyler brought it.
Put it to good use. He'll know how to help.

P.P.S. Don't let a sea creature steal this key, too.

The last line made me sad-laugh again.

I reread the words three times, the chasm reopening in my chest. The note sounded so final, like he didn't expect to see me again. Same as his goodbye outside.

It was fine. It was easier that way.

If only his words didn't show how well he knew me.

I rubbed a palm over my eyes to stop the burning and swallowed hard. I peeked into the bag and found a silver bracelet with two charms—a whale tail and a turtle, because he knew I couldn't choose one. He must have bought it when I thought he was shopping for his sister. The burning in my eyes intensified as I clasped it onto my wrist and made the charms clank.

I picked up the camera. I'd known it had been the same model as mine. That meant Tyler had gone through my closet. I couldn't find the energy to be mad. I clicked through the photos, ones from today I hadn't reviewed yet, that he'd been scrolling through before my parents interrupted. There were also ones from our kayaking trip and the road to Hana.

Looking at the images did what I hoped my pictures would do for others—made me relive the wonder of the inspiring locations, recall the fun moments, be in awe of nature.

Jake's meaning behind *Put it to good use* was obvious, considering it sat next to the contest flyer. Could I even enter? The deadline was in two days, and while some of my photos weren't bad, none of them were edited.

I dug out my phone and scrolled through the pictures on it. I had a few of the two of us, taken by Alana or strangers we'd passed. Jake's dimples and blue eyes beamed at me. I focused on my own face. Other than the pictures from the blowhole on the first day, when I'd wanted to shove him off a cliff and my smile was fake and plastic, I looked happy. Relaxed.

The final one was from the couple at the beach at sunset, when Jake had called me his girlfriend in front of strangers. We were staring at each other as if we didn't notice the beautiful scenery.

My throat tightened again.

Tyler had a computer. Was that what Jake meant, about my brother helping?

No. This was crazy. Why was I considering this?

Without stopping to analyze the decision, I went to Tyler's door and knocked lightly.

"Ty? It's me."

"It's open."

I let myself in and closed the door behind me. My gaze immediately went to the cot, empty of belongings.

Not now.

Tyler was watching me cautiously. "Are you going to yell or hit me or ask for help?"

I leaned against the closed door. "I'm still deciding."

He eyed the camera in my hands. "Want to see what else he left?"

"Huh?"

Tyler typed on his laptop and turned the screen to face me. It showed a folder of more photos, the ones Jake had taken at my direction, as well as some of me that I hadn't known he'd taken.

I swallowed hard, lingering by the door. I bit my lip and flipped the camera over in my hands.

Tyler stood, took the GoPro from me, and grabbed a cable. He'd thought of everything. I watched in silence, waiting, as he transferred the photos to his laptop.

"Want me to do your phone, too?"

"What? Oh. I guess?"

I handed it over and sat on the cot to wait, trying not to imagine where Jake was. Would he find Ethan? Would he be stuck on the street? Would he have money for a hotel?

"These are good, Kenz."

I blinked, focused on my brother, and shrugged. "Some of them."

He rolled his eyes. "Did you want to edit them?"

"Maybe?"

He studied me. "Look, I'm sorry. I should have told you what I was doing. Asked you instead of springing it on you."

"Yeah, you should have."

"I don't know what will happen with you and Jake. I think you guys really liked each other, but after everything . . ."

Yeah.

"Anyway. I know Mom and Dad will work us to death in the office this year, but one thing you can control is these." He nodded to the computer.

I thought of Rob and his story, the old man at the top of the volcano, Jake's encouragement. This was one contest, not the final word on whether I was a good photographer, whether I'd ever be able to make a career of it. Whether I was worthy as a person. Contest results reflected one guy's opinion, nothing more.

The act of entering was a step toward what I wanted. It meant putting myself out there, being brave, being myself. Not shying away because I feared rejection or failure or what others thought.

I'd let one good thing walk out the door today. I wasn't going to do it again.

I set my jaw. "Okay, I'll do it."

Tyler let me take the chair, went to his bed, and put his earbuds in, leaving me to work.

I used my usual strategy—go through one day at a time and pull the best photos into a separate folder. That left me with about twenty. Then I accessed my online editing account, which I hadn't opened in months. But the motions were familiar. I did a basic pass to enhance the contrast and color. I leveled horizons, cropped background objects, and played with zooming in to focus on different things. I applied filters and did more tweaking of colors and clarity, sharpened details.

Time became meaningless, as it always did.

I ended up with four with real potential. I recalled Rob's words, about what drove me, what was in my heart. Which picture reflected my week? What I'd seen, what I'd loved, what I'd learned?

The theme of the contest was Inspiration in the Natural World.

I loaded one image and turned to Tyler.

He pulled out his earbuds.

"What do you think?" I asked.

He was silent a moment, staring at the screen.

Finally he said, "You're an idiot if you give this up."

"Shut up." But I was smiling.

"Now send it in, or I will."

I found the submission info on the contest flyer, used my emergency credit card to pay, and hit submit.

There. It was done.

I was shaky, and also felt a tiny bit like I was ready to conquer the world.

"Can I have my computer back now?" Tyler asked.

I rolled my eyes and moved to the door. "Yes. And, Ty?"

"Have you decided about the yelling?"

"Yeah." I paused and waited until he looked at me. "Thank you."

His mouth twitched. "Whatever."

"And if you, uh, ever want to tell me about your video game, I'd like to know."

He blinked. "Okay. Cool."

I debated asking him for Jake's number. But he'd made his opinion clear on that situation. Besides, I wasn't sure if Jake would want to hear from me. Asking Tyler would set me up for two possible rejections, and I'd taken enough chances for the evening.

When I opened the door, I heard voices from the living room. I didn't want my family to ruin how good I felt about entering the contest, so I snuck back to my room.

If I didn't place in this contest, I could handle it. I'd gained something better—the confidence to keep going and to defend that choice.

The schedule commanded one final day of fun at the beach. But over breakfast, Tyler stood and faced everyone.

"I've decided it's time to talk about you," he said.

I blinked. He was focused on Mom and Dad.

"What do you mean?" my mom asked.

Tyler folded his arms. "The way you kicked Jake out."

"He said he had family here. He was a stranger, and he deceived us."

"He's my friend," Tyler said.

"And he had nowhere to go," I added, hoping Tyler was going where I suspected he was with this. "He didn't stand up for himself, but he was here in Maui to look for a brother he's never met. He had no one, but he was trying to help me yesterday by not arguing."

"That's why I invited him," Tyler said. "To help him find his brother."

"And you couldn't have asked us?"

"Well, yeah, but that wouldn't have been as entertaining. Sorry, sorry, I know it was wrong, both to you guys and to Kenzie. It would have revealed that Kenzie was lying, and I was trying to help her, too."

He looked hopeful like he wasn't sure they'd believe him. *I* didn't believe him.

My parents were frowning.

"I texted him last night, and he didn't respond. What if something happened to him because of you?"

My stomach twisted. Because of *me*.

Mom's eyes widened, and she bit her lip. "Perhaps we were too hasty . . ."

"I suppose he can come back for tonight, if he needs to," Dad added.

Mom nodded. "I certainly don't want to be responsible for a young man having to sleep on the street."

Tyler turned to me. "You should check on him, make sure he's okay."

He held my gaze, as if giving me permission to like his friend, the real one.

"And I can bring him back?" I asked.

My parents looked at each other.

"Yes," Mom said.

My heart surged like a wave before making its inevitable retreat. Assuming he even wanted to come back, which would be incredibly brave of him.

At least I could find him, make sure he was safe. Hopefully he'd be happy to see me, and this wouldn't lead to humiliating rejection and public failure. His final words and his note had said *Thanks, bye,* and I was forcing the issue. But like with the photos, I was going to put myself out there and try.

I could've gotten his number from Tyler, but it would be harder for Jake to ignore me in person, so Gran drove me to the now familiar harbor in Maalaea.

I hoped the boat hadn't left and Jake had gone who-knew-where, to hang out in the airport gift shop for two days or sleep on a random beach while geckos nested in his hair.

"Call me when you're ready," Gran said. "Good luck, Kenzie girl."

I swallowed hard as I walked away from the car and toward the boats, following the slip numbers. Nerves tumbled in my stomach, and every sense felt alert with the promise of possibility and the chance of failure. Maybe I was the only one who thought we had the potential to be real.

I was several slots away when I spotted the boat we'd seen yesterday, the script *West Wind* visible on the back—with its engine chugging as it backed away from a wooden dock.

Two people sat on the deck, and a tanned guy with dark blond hair was entering the boat's cabin.

My heart lurched. They were leaving. I was too late.

"Jake!"

I raced down the jetty sidewalk toward the berth. The boat had finished backing up and was starting to move forward, toward the harbor exit and open sea.

I charged onto the dock, my steps echoing on the boards, once again chasing Jake without success.

The boat was just about to pass by. I gauged the distance. Several more steps from me to the end of the dock, and the boat was a couple of yards from the edge. I might be able to leap the distance.

"Jake," I called again.

But though the people on deck turned toward me, the guy didn't reappear, and the boat kept moving.

A few more steps. I prepared to launch myself.

And skidded to a stop instead. The boat was too far away. I'd never make it.

I halted at the last second, sticking my arms out for balance before I tumbled into the water. Panting, I watched the boat get farther away. Just like the car last night. It felt like a kick to the stomach had taken all the air out of my lungs.

Apparently, I was destined to watch him leave.

Then a familiar voice behind me said, "You were totally thinking about jumping, weren't you?"

CHAPTER THIRTY-FOUR

A thrill shot through me. I whirled.

Jake stood halfway down the dock, hands in his pockets, his mouth curved into a sideways smile. The sight made my chest expand, like light was flooding the chasm inside.

"Jake." I ran over and collided with him, wrapping my arms around his shoulders.

He staggered backward. "Whoa. I don't need to go swimming in the harbor."

Oh. Right. Plus, maybe he didn't want me mauling him in public.

But his arms came around me too, and he steadied us before we toppled over the edge.

I pressed my face into his neck, felt his pulse throbbing and his warm skin. He buried his nose in my hair. Water lapped the dock, boat engines hummed, and the scent of diesel mingled with Jake's familiar coconut. If time froze right here, I would be content.

"What are you doing here?" He pulled far enough away that I could see his eyes. "I'm glad to see you, but this wasn't on the schedule for today."

"You know how I feel about schedules."

"Did you get kicked out, too?" A slight dimple flash relieved my moment of panic at the reminder of what we'd done to him.

I thunked my head against his chest. "I'm so, so sorry about that." I drew back to inspect him. "Are you okay? You don't look like you got eaten by turtles."

"There were no man-eating turtles. And you have nothing to apologize for." He placed his hands on the sides of my face, brushed his thumbs gently across my cheekbones.

My heart skipped. We gazed at each other. What was he thinking? He didn't seem mad. He'd returned my hug. But that was a long way from missing me desperately and not wanting our amazing week to end and declaring he couldn't live without me.

I was getting ahead of myself. I pulled away and rubbed my toe on an uneven board.

"Nice shirt," he said.

I'd worn my jellyfish one. "It's not totally accurate. I went against the flow. Which jellyfish can actually do."

"I want to know everything."

"Well, they contract a ring of muscle that creates—"

Jake's laugh cut off my jellyfish lesson. I'd missed that sound in the last half a day.

"Come on. Let's go somewhere with less possibility of you sending us both into the ocean."

Now that he mentioned it, we were awfully close to the edge of the dock.

"Were you going to jump onto that boat?" he asked again with a smirk.

"I, uh, thought it was you and you were sailing away."

"Ethan," he said.

That made a lot more sense. My face flushed.

He threaded his fingers through mine—that was a good sign, right?—and grabbed his bag from the ground on the jetty. When our arms shifted, my bracelet clinked. He raised our clasped hands in front of us so he could see it, and his eyes crinkled.

We walked along the harbor, going the opposite direction of most people heading toward boats.

"Do your parents know you're here?" he asked. "I hope you didn't get in trouble for me."

"I'm fine. You first. You were the one put out on the street. Are you okay?"

"I found Ethan. Obviously. I stayed on the boat last night. It was nice, with the movement and the water. You would have liked it."

"That sounds amazing. How did it go with him?"

His eyes went slightly unfocused as he stared at the water. "As well as it could have. Definitely weird, but he did know about me, so I didn't totally upend his world. My dad had asked him not to contact us, but he was glad I came to find him. Said he'd wanted to meet me for years, but he knew my dad would hate it, and he didn't know if I'd want to meet him."

We circled the end of the harbor, heading back along the other side on shore. Masts extended toward the sky, where wispy clouds streaked the blue. When we turned, our sides pressed together and our legs bumped. I glanced up to find him looking at me. We half smiled, and my gaze darted away.

"I'm glad everything went okay," I said. "Though I'm sorry you lost all those years you could have had."

"Yeah. His mom moved them to LA right after he was born. I can't help but wonder what it would have been like growing up if I'd known about him. If we'd seen each other some."

"What's he like?" I asked.

"He's cool. You'd like him. Studied marine biology but decided he wanted adventure, so he moved here to work and enjoy the island."

"I do like him already."

"He has other half siblings, younger, from his mom. I'm not technically related to them, but he asked if Audrey and I wanted to visit sometime. It's weird, but I think we can be friends."

"I'm glad it had a happy ending."

"With him, at least. He invited me to come back this summer and stay longer." He paused as we came to the end of the harbor and continued meandering along a sidewalk parallel to the ocean, before continuing. "With my parents, though . . ."

"Have you told them yet? That you met him?"

"I called first thing this morning, so they had time to be mad and get partially over it before I fly home."

"And?"

He sighed. "I tried to remember what you said, to try to understand them."

"Be gentle with them. You have power over them, by knowing this thing they don't want getting out. You can be the better person and not misuse that power."

His face softened. "Sometimes I need someone to remind me to be more compassionate. Thank you for helping."

Warmth spread through me. He'd helped me so much, and I was glad I could return the favor.

"They don't love that I'm here, and I told them it might take some time for me to trust them again, but that I was making this choice for me. It's fine. I didn't expect them to suddenly decide in one week that they'd been wrong for two decades."

I sniffed. "Sounds like my parents."

"Enough about me. What happened with you?"

"I really am sorry they kicked you out."

"Hey. If anyone should be saying sorry, it's me."

"What if we just agree it's Tyler?"

He laughed. "That works, except if he hadn't done what he did, I would never have met you."

"Please don't say I have to thank my brother." I groaned.

"I'll do it for both of us."

We glanced at each other again, darting, with fleeting smiles, and hope bloomed inside me.

"I do think my parents blame you least of everyone," I said. "You're welcome to come back if you need a place to stay tonight. And we have a spot for you at the luau, roasted pig and hula dancing and tropical drinks. Though, I realize that might be supremely awkward and you might not want to."

"I want to."

"Really? Even though it means facing my parents?"

He paused in front of a row of condos and waited until I met his gaze. "You're worth it."

That was brave. If it had been me, I might have opted for the jungle life and eating raw fish, over facing strangers I'd lied to.

His intense expression made me feel like, for him, nothing

else existed in this moment. A buzz shot through me. My attention fell to his lips. His gaze dipped, too, and we swayed toward each other, before the whoosh of a nearby car startled me.

Jake squeezed my hand, and we kept walking. "What about you? Did you guys talk?"

"Didn't have much choice. But yeah." I summarized our conversation and compromise.

He twisted to face me while walking, his eyes bright. "Kenz, that's great. I'm so proud of you."

His joy chased away lingering nerves about how I'd altered my entire life. I ducked my head. "I couldn't have done it without you."

"I may have given you a nudge, but it's all you."

"I also submitted to the contest." I poked his arm. "That flyer on my pillow was very subtle."

His face was soft, his gaze intense, and my stomach fluttered.

"I'm glad," he said. "You deserve to do what makes you happy. What picture did you use?"

I dug out my phone, pulled up the fully edited, final image, and handed it to him.

The picture was of him, standing beneath the waterfall on the road to Hana. His head was tilted back, the expression on his face contemplative. Beyond him, you could see the largest of the three falls and the lush vegetation on shore. The water droplets around him sparkled like diamonds as they caught the light.

He stared at the screen, blinking. "It's perfect. And amazing. *You're* amazing."

My chest expanded, like those droplets of pure light were

bursting inside me. "I wish my parents agreed. They're . . . tolerant. But not thrilled. And I hope it's okay that I used one of you."

"Of course it's okay." His mouth twitched. "It sucks when you can't fully count on family, but that's why it's important, when you do find people who get you, to listen to them."

I squeezed his hand. "You're just trying to get me to listen to you."

"I'll try to get you to listen to anyone who tells you how great you are. But especially me, yeah." He flashed full-on dimples.

The hope in me blossomed further. Maybe, just maybe, my boldness might end the way I wanted—not simply us catching up and saying goodbye, but finding a path forward together.

We came to a small park and passed under a few trees to step onto the beach, then took off our shoes and trudged into the strip of sand. We stopped short of the waves and turned as one to face each other.

"Why'd you come find me?" he asked. "Was it just to invite me to share a pig with you?"

"It is an enormous pig. I can't eat it myself, and I know you enjoy sharing your meat."

We were quiet, listening to the crashing waves, our hands still clasped. I studied him instead of the water, swept by a desire to be closer, to play with his hair and trace his jaw. I searched for the right words.

"Really, though? I wanted to see you, and I didn't know if you wanted to see me. Your note sounded very final. And you drove away last night."

His lips twitched downward. "I'm sorry about that. I was a

little mad. Not at them so much, but they asked if I was the only thing you were lying about, and you said yes."

I sighed. "At the time, I was afraid to make them angrier by telling all the truth at once."

"I get it. And I wanted to stay." His gaze seared me. "To argue, to hide by the pool all night and wait for you. But I was worried I'd make things worse. The last thing I want to do is cause you any problems."

I inhaled, met his gaze steadily. Summoned the boldness. "I told you I like complicated."

"Yeah?" His head dipped toward mine. "Just because we started that way doesn't mean it has to keep being like that. What would you say to uncomplicated? No more pretending to receive texts and video calls from an imaginary person, but getting real ones, from a real boyfriend?"

"Hmm. Depends who this real boyfriend is. Does he like schedules and puzzles and staying inside with a book?"

He shifted closer, his face right above mine. "I know I'm not the Jake of your imagination."

"My imagination was far too boring," I said. "You're much better."

I rose on my toes, sand squishing between them, and pressed my lips against his. His arms immediately came around me, circling my back and holding me close like he never wanted me to get away. I ran my fingers across his stubby ponytail, explored his strong shoulders, inhaled his tropical scent.

If our first kiss had been diving into something thrilling, this was the glowing blush of sunrise, with the promise of more to come.

I sighed. "I wish we didn't have to leave tomorrow."

"Sadly, I have a plane ticket for Jacob Miller."

"I'm going to need to see some ID to prove that."

His grip on me tightened. "I'm hurt that you don't trust your boyfriend."

"I'm just having a hard time believing he's real."

He dipped his head toward mine. "Well, he is. And he's crazy about you."

His lips met mine again, soft and gentle. Then he pulled back and whispered against my lips, "I have a very important question."

"What's that?"

"You didn't lose that key I gave you, did you?"

I smacked him, and he laughed, and I silenced him by kissing him again.

The sun was warm, and the waves crashed beside us, and like when I lingered in a beautiful spot, waiting for the right picture, this was a moment I could get lost in forever, enjoying every second.

Epilogue

Three Months Later

When I walked out of the airport terminal headed for baggage claim, there was a cute guy leaning against a pillar. He was holding a purple lei, and when he approached to hug me, I immediately hugged him back.

"Aloha!" Jake lifted me off my feet and spun me around. "Surprised to see me?"

"Not in the slightest."

He put me down, took my hand, and twirled me once. "Screens don't do you justice."

"So true." I grinned. "I almost didn't recognize you."

"It's been too long." He kissed me long and deep, and we lingered. It felt like coming home.

He took my hand and my suitcase as we left the airport.

"So the gentlemanly stuff wasn't just an act? Helping with bags and serving food and all that?" I smirked at him.

"I am one hundred percent truly a gentleman." His dimples winked at me. "Not to impress your parents or anyone else. Though if it impressed *you,* that's an added bonus."

"Consider me impressed."

The warm tropical air was waiting to greet us.

"Ready for your first official photography job?" he asked.

"I'm not getting paid. It's just room and board."

"It still counts. You'll get to shoot lots of stuff."

"Maybe even your handsome face."

"You can shoot my face anytime."

I leaned over and kissed his cheek.

We had stopped at Rob's gallery one final time on our last day, and I'd asked for advice about pursuing a career in photography. He'd told me he had an idea, had gotten my contact info, and surprised me a few weeks later with the offer of an internship with the nonprofit sponsoring the photography contest—which I hadn't won, but this was better.

I was getting a break from the dreadful office job that sucked out my soul, to spend a month in Maui, sleeping in a tiny room over Rob's sister's garage, and it was totally worth it. I'd tail Rob for a few days, then be on my own, taking pictures of anything and everything across the island, for the conservancy to use for its website, social media, flyers, whatever.

My parents weren't thrilled, but they had let me come, which I hoped meant they were starting to come around.

At least they were coming to accept Jake. His apology at the luau had been sincere, theirs for kicking him out had been halfhearted, but lately they didn't mind when I talked about him. My dad had even said he hoped I enjoyed spending more time with Jake this summer, using the right name and everything.

"How's Ethan?" I asked.

"Great. He saved the boat for a few days. He's happy to be

our guide and let you take all the pictures you want. And . . . are you ready for this?" Jake swung our hands.

I poked him. "Hard to say, since I don't know what it is."

"I may need to wait until you're sitting down. I'm not sure you can handle it."

"I can handle you. That means news is nothing."

"I'll try not to be hurt by that. Ethan has a friend who does scuba certifications . . ."

I stopped. "What, really? No way."

"Yep. But only if you don't get hit by a car first."

He tugged me forward out of the road I'd stopped in.

"I definitely won't be telling my parents about that," I said.

"We might wait for the week Audrey is here. She wants to learn, too."

"I'm excited to meet her."

Jake was also here for a good portion of the summer to spend time with his brother, helping on the boat, studying local plants. His parents were about as happy as mine were.

We planned to explore and take pictures of every inch of the island, see everything we'd missed. And I could spend as long as I wanted, take as many photos as possible. Photos that might help the nonprofit protect the island, might inspire visitors to appreciate the natural beauty of this place and want to preserve it.

"You got the wedding invitation, right?" I asked.

"Properly addressed to Jake Miller in San Diego. I'm mostly looking forward to the pretty maid of honor."

I scrunched my nose at him as we loaded into a beat-up car Jake was sharing with Ethan and his roommate.

He moved as if to let me in but trapped me against the vehicle instead, arms planted on either side of me. We kissed again under the Maui sun before driving off toward what I was sure would be a glorious sunset.

My plans hadn't worked out like intended—big surprise—but life had turned out better.

Acknowledgments

This book wouldn't exist without the help and support of so many people.

Many thanks to my agent, Eva Scalzo, for being an all-around rock star.

Wendy Loggia and Ali Romig, I'm so thrilled that we found each other and get to make books together! Thank you for your enthusiasm and your great insights, and for making my stories better, helping me grow as a writer, and believing in me. Thank you to Ray Shappell and Libby VanderPloeg for another incredible cover. And thanks to the entire team at Delacorte Press, including Cathy Bobak, Tamar Schwartz, and freelancer Bara MacNeill. You made this book happen, and I am grateful for each one of you.

Thank you to my husband, Russ, for your support and encouragement, for listening to me talk and brainstorm for hours, and for going with me on fun travel adventures that always seem to inspire story ideas.

I finished writing this book during a hard time for my family, so it will always remind me of how much I love you all. I'm so grateful to be part of a family like ours. I also apologize for writing families who aren't always supportive and amazing—I promise it's no reflection on you!

I'm very grateful for friends who offered feedback on this book. Jason Joyner, thanks for being a critique partner who not only offers feedback but actively encourages me and wants me to succeed. Kim Kromer, I'm so blessed by your years of support, your eye for proofreading, and most of all that I get to call you my friend. Thanks to Amanda G. Stevens for character help and enthusiasm that keeps me going and for walking the writing path with me. Kim Vandel, thank you for loving fake dating and making sure I did the idea justice. I'm grateful to each of you for being the first fans of this book!

Patrick McAlister, thanks for the insights into Maui, and I hope I didn't mess anything up!

As always, thanks to the Fellowship (Tina Gollings, Josh Hardt, Jason Joyner, J.J. Johnson, Steve Rzasa, Josh Smith, and Liberty Speidel) for being my writing family.

Thank you, readers, for adventuring to Maui with Kenzie and Jake. I hope it inspired you to visit new places, try new things, and most importantly, be the unique you.

Finally, Jesus, my Savior and King, thank You for loving me, saving me, and giving me the wonderful opportunity to write books.

Kenzie Reed's Rules for Creating a Fictional Boyfriend

• Give him a name so common that there will be too many Google results for anyone to narrow down who he is (but make sure your brother doesn't know anyone with that name in real life).

• Claim he doesn't like social media because maintaining a fake profile is too much work.

• Make him live far enough away that he can't be expected to visit, and make sure he lives someplace where your family has no connections.

• Give him parent-approved hobbies and career aspirations; educational pastimes and post-graduate study plans are perfect (the more boring, the better).

• Keep his family small so you don't have to remember too many names.

• Pretend to receive texts and have video chats often enough to make it seem like the long-distance relationship is thriving.

• Guard your phone at all costs so no one (like your brother) can snoop and discover that those texts don't actually exist.

• Don't fall for him for real (oops).

Books, Britain ... Boys?

Turn the page for a preview of
Becky Dean's debut romance!

CHAPTER ONE

Dreams are like knees—you don't realize how fragile they are until something rips them to shreds.

I sank onto the first row of bleachers overlooking Fairview High's athletic field. One hand rubbed the massive brace gripping my leg, which was tight after my cross-campus trek. The other clutched the strange envelope I'd found in my locker but hadn't opened in my rush to arrive.

Arrive, so I could leave before the game started.

Girls in royal blue jerseys and blue-and-white striped socks sat on the grass, stretching. I'd made it in time. Warm-ups, I could handle. Games, however, were more torture than physical therapy, a tactic that could've cracked terror suspects.

If I'd happened to schedule PT during the three playoff games the past two weeks . . . well, it was purely coincidental.

Several teammates waved from the field. One shouted, "We miss you, Britt. Can't wait to have you back."

My heart stutter-stepped as I returned the wave. They'd be

waiting a long, long time. But they only knew about the knee, not the rest of it.

When the soccer ball made its appearance, a shot of pain kicked through my chest.

I yanked my attention to the cream-colored envelope. Handwritten letters across the front spelled out my name: *Brittany J. Hanson.* A round, raised seal on the flap displayed the monogram *PCM,* the C larger in the center. The card inside read:

The honor of your presence is requested
Today, May 20, at fifteen minutes past three
in the afternoon in classroom A-6.
A Unique Opportunity Awaits.

It resembled the announcements we'd received when my sister and brother graduated college, but unlike those, this card didn't say who sent it or the meeting's purpose.

Three-fifteen was . . . I checked the scoreboard clock. Four minutes ago.

Was it worth the trip? I couldn't run, so I'd definitely be late. But it intrigued me.

I shouted "Bye" and hurried across campus as fast as the knee brace allowed.

Unique opportunity. The phrase set my pulse racing. I could use one of those. Didn't even have to be unique—I'd settle for any old opportunity. It had come knocking once this year, but after I let it in, it bolted without the courtesy of a goodbye.

Granted, unique opportunities were rare. I shouldn't get my hopes up. But it was better than the ninety minutes of fingernail-extracting, tooth-yanking misery of a soccer match I couldn't play in.

Plus, someone who used calligraphy might serve snacks like tiny sandwiches or something wrapped in bacon. I never passed up bacon.

A-6 was my English classroom, but why would our teacher, Ms. Carmichael, invite me to anything? Her comments on my essays frequently included the words *uninspired, lack of thought*, and *disappointing*. Was she the mysterious *PCM* who had access to my locker?

When I reached the room, Amberlyn Hartsfield was sitting in the front row. Spence Lopez, a guy from the football team, lounged a few seats away, and another boy slouched in the last row with a book, long hair hiding his face. No one else was present. Also, negative on the bacon snacks.

Fancy invitations for four people? Weird.

Amberlyn grunted, showing my lack of punctuality had not gone unnoticed. "Some things never change."

Her muttered words reached me, which I'm sure she intended.

"Like your constant uptightness?" I dropped into the seat next to Spence, smothering a sigh of relief to be off my feet. "Whatever this is, it hasn't started yet. What's the big deal?"

She straightened a colored notebook and the invitation in the exact center of her desk. The stationery looked natural in her manicured hands. Her mail probably always arrived this way—party invites, credit card offers, and political flyers delivered on heavy cardstock in engraved envelopes.

Her gaze flicked to my leg, and I saw the condescension drain from her face. For a second, she resembled the girl who used to share secrets and red Skittles with me.

Pity-politeness based on failed friendship. Fantastic.

I swallowed a growl. "No spring practice today?" I asked Spence. "Don't you have freshmen to train?"

He shook his head, making the longer hair above his undercut flop. "Girls took over our field for a strange sport called soccer."

I punched his shoulder.

He grinned. "The other guys are watching the game. They were talking about how much the team misses you. Will you be able to play summer league?"

Every time I received a similar question, it felt like a ball to the gut at short range, the air physically forced from my lungs. "Not sure. I might be on my yacht, cruising the Riviera."

He snorted. Our small town south of Santa Barbara, California, contained two types of people—those who owned yachts and those who cleaned them. Spence and I did not own yachts.

Actually, I did know the answer to his question. I just hadn't told anyone. The doctor's diagnosis constantly echoed in my head. Phrases bounced around like out-of-control soccer balls: *blood clotting disorder, blood thinner, no contact sports, change your diet, watch out for sharp objects. Be careful, be careful, be careful.*

But as long as I was the only one who knew, as long as I never spoke the words, I imagined I could contain it. Undo it.

"Any idea what this is about?" He lifted his chin to point to the front of the classroom.

"Nope. I was hoping for snacks." I glanced around, but no bacon had magically appeared.

The guy in the back sprawled in his seat, wearing a Captain America shirt and reading a beat-up paperback with a spaceship on the cover. I recognized him now—Peter Finch, a sullen guy I'd had classes with for years. He looked up and caught me staring. His blank gaze didn't change, but his lip curled.

I thought that expression was reserved for supervillains but apparently not. He aimed his sneer alternately at me and Amberlyn. What was his problem? Captain America was supposed to be nicer than that.

Groaning, I faced front. Whatever this opportunity was, it'd better be good.

"Do you think this is a psychological experiment?" I tapped my non-braced leg against the desk. "To see how long we sit here?"

"No, Ms. Hanson," a proper British voice said from the doorway. "It is not."

My posture straightened at the familiar accent.

Our English teacher, Ms. Carmichael, glided across the room and settled at her desk.

As was usual in her class, she presided. There was no other word for it. In her first year teaching here, she already ruled the school. Her styled, short hair was a pale blond probably called Champagne Bubbles or Old Money. Glasses dangled from a beaded chain around her neck, always accompanied by pearl earrings and flawless makeup that made her appear younger.

"Thank you for coming." She regarded each of us. "As your invitations stated, I have a unique opportunity for you."

Her expression didn't reveal anything. Her cultured voice filled the room, each word enunciated in a crisp British accent.

"I've decided to try something rather exciting. I called you here because I am offering each of you a chance to compete for a prize of one hundred thousand dollars."

A wild laugh escaped my throat.

Spence made a strangled noise.

Amberlyn gasped and sat up straighter.

Our questions tumbled over each other—"Is this for real?" "How is that possible?" "You're joking, right?"

She waited until we fell silent. "Yes, this is real. It's not a joke."

A hundred grand was . . . a lot of money. So much I couldn't comprehend it. And hardly information you dropped so casually. My brain conjured images of stacks of bills, of Scrooge McDuck swimming in a pile of gold coins.

Another image replaced those: the letter from UCLA, saying if I still planned to enroll in the fall, I owed ten thousand dollars by September 1 for registration, housing, and a hundred various fees, many I suspected they had made up.

And that was for this year, to say nothing of the following three, when I wouldn't have partial help. Even if they let me keep this year's money, no more would come. People don't pay for work you can't do.

Since my original Life Plan had been forced into an early retirement, I needed a new one. As my mom and siblings enjoyed pointing out so frequently, most Life Plans required a college education. One I no longer had a way to pay for.

Until now.

This prize would cover those made-up fees and more.

Next to me, Spence leaned forward, his hands gripping the sides of the desk.

Amberlyn capped and uncapped her pen repeatedly.

Were the others dreaming of what they'd do with the money? College, a new car, traveling the world. It seemed too good to be true.

"Where's the money coming from?" I asked. "Is this school-sponsored?"

"The school has approved this trip," Ms. C said. "But it is something of a personal endeavor. I've been blessed with resources and wish to help others."

"I didn't realize teaching paid so well," I muttered to Spence.

"Who said the money came from teaching?" Ms. Carmichael met my gaze.

"Who cares where it comes from," Spence said. "What do we have to do to win?"

Good question.

"Is there an application?" Amberlyn asked. "Do we have to write something?"

"Like a book report or an essay?" I added.

Or something equally likely to eliminate me? I'd had my chance at earning money, and it certainly hadn't involved academics. My odds of winning anything from an English teacher? Whose class discussions I avoided and whose books I found tedious? I might as well leave now.

Ms. Carmichael folded her hands and rested them on the desk. "Ah yes. Now we come to the fun part."

My hopeful heart pounded in my ears. My brain kept repeating that this couldn't be real. The rest of my body ignored the logic. *Don't get excited. You can't win anyway.*

"The contest will be a scavenger hunt," she said.

That sounded promising. Action-oriented, physical, concrete. I might stand a chance.

"Inspired by classic British literature," she continued.

Not so promising. I held my breath.

"To take place in England." She smirked like she knew she'd saved the best for last.

Sweet. I finally breathed. The laugh bubbled out again.

Amberlyn squeaked. Spence met my gaze, his eyes wide and bright. Even Peter grunted behind me.

But . . .

"That's not exactly cheap," I said. "Assuming we need the cash prize, how are we supposed to pay for a trip across the pond?" I tried to mimic her accent on the last three words.

"That will be taken care of."

"You're paying for us to go to England *and* giving one of us cash?" I drummed my fingers on the desk. "What's the catch? Do we have to use this for college or books or something?"

Amberlyn raised her hand even though there were only four of us. "Is this like when the French club went to Paris or the student council to DC?"

"They didn't get cash prizes for those," I said.

"That you know of," Amberlyn replied.

"There is no catch." Ms. C's face remained calm. "You may use the money however you see fit. Consider it an investment in your future."

I tapped the desk. "So how does it work exactly?"

"I'll handle the arrangements, speak with your parents, and ensure you have adequate supervision while overseas. All you have to do is decide if you're willing to be challenged and possibly learn about yourself in the process. Travel tends to have that effect."

Learning about myself didn't sound fun, but I never said no to a challenge. A scavenger hunt in England was a better way to spend my summer than watching from the sidelines as my team played soccer without me. Or wearing a chicken costume on the main drag, holding a sign for the Lord of the Wings restaurant like my siblings had.

"Why us?" Spence asked.

Peter still hadn't spoken, but his posture had straightened and he'd been listening to Ms. C with wide eyes.

"I selected each of you for a specific reason that will be made clear in time." A glint in her eyes, the slightest quirk of her mouth, said Ms. C was enjoying this.

What possible reason could she have for me? English was far from my best subject.

But I could win this, with less contemplation and more action. The familiar pregame energy built inside me—a feeling I'd missed the last few weeks—making my muscles tense, my senses sharper.

Deep breath through the nose, count to ten, release slowly. Better not to imagine how winning could change my life. Wanting things rarely ended well, especially things I didn't have control over. Even things I thought I had control over were ending badly recently.

Indifference was a proven armor.

"When do we leave?" Amberlyn uncapped her pen again and poised it over her notepad. "How long will it take? What can we do to prepare?"

"If you agree, you and your parents will sign a nondisclosure agreement, and I will provide your plane ticket. You'll leave at the end of June and be gone for ten days. Though you'll begin in London, where I will meet you for the start of your journey, the trip will take you throughout the UK. Other details—including the specifics of your tasks—will wait until you arrive."

Amberlyn's grip tightened on her pen, and I could practically hear her teeth grinding. Personally, I figured not being able to prepare favored me.

Plus—London. I'd never been farther from Southern California than the Grand Canyon. If I didn't win, at least I'd be getting a free trip to England. Images of men in red uniforms and tall, black hats paraded through my mind. I couldn't contain a giant grin.

"Why the mystery?" I asked.

"When it is your money involved, you may be as mysterious as you wish." This time she fully smiled, telling me she didn't mind my interrogation.

My mind whipped through questions. Would Mom let me

go? Would I be better off getting a job that guaranteed money? Would I stand a chance against Amberlyn, Peter, and Spence?

Overthinking never accomplished anything. Action was better. Despite my efforts not to get excited, desire ignited inside me. I needed to believe something good could still happen to me.

I nodded once. "Where do I sign?"

About the Author

BECKY DEAN is the author of *Love & Other Great Expectations*. As a child, she wanted to be an author or to study whales. Now she writes books that sometimes include whales. Still a California girl at heart, she currently lives in Texas with her husband, where their walls are covered with photos from their travels. She can frequently be found drinking iced tea, watching science fiction shows, and planning travel adventures for herself and her characters. She's never met a beach she didn't like.

beckydeanwrites.com

Underlined

A Community of Book Nerds & Aspiring Writers!

READ

Get book recommendations, reading lists, YA news

DISCOVER

Take quizzes, watch videos, shop merch, win prizes

CREATE

Write your own stories, enter contests, get inspired

SHARE

Connect with fellow Book Nerds and authors!

GetUnderlined.com • @GetUnderlined

Want a chance to be featured? Use #GetUnderlined on social!